THE SCAM

BY JANET EVANOVICH

The Fox and O'Hare novels
with Lee Goldberg
The Heist
The Chase
The Job
The Scam

The Stephanie Plum novels

One For The Money	Twelve Sharp
Two For The Dough	Lean Mean Thirteen
Three To Get Deadly	Fearless Fourteen
Four To Score	Finger Lickin' Fifteen
High Five	Sizzling Sixteen
Hot Six	Smokin' Seventeen
Seven Up	Explosive Eighteen
Hard Eight	Notorious Nineteen
To The Nines	Takedown Twenty
Ten Big Ones	Top Secret Twenty-One
Eleven On Top	

The Diesel & Tucker series

Wicked Appetite	Wicked Business

Wicked Charms (with Phoef Sutton)

The Between the Numbers novels

Visions of Sugar Plums	Plum Lucky
Plum Lovin'	Plum Spooky

And writing with Charlotte Hughes

Full House	Full Speed
Full Tilt	Full Blast

JANET
EVANOVICH
AND
LEE
GOLDBERG

THE SCAM

headline
review

Published by arrangement with Bantam Books, an imprint of Random House, a division of Penguin Random House LLC, New York.

First published in Great Britain in 2015
by HEADLINE REVIEW
An imprint of HEADLINE PUBLISHING GROUP

1

Cataloguing in Publication Data is available from the British Library

ISBN 978 1 4722 0184 3 (Hardback)
ISBN 978 1 4722 0185 0 (Trade Paperback)

Offset in Minion Pro by Avon DataSet Ltd, Bidford on Avon, Warwickshire

Printed and bound in Great Britain by Clays Ltd, St Ives plc

Headline's policy is to use papers that are natural, renewable and recyclable products and made from wood grown in well-managed forests and other controlled sources. The logging and manufacturing processes are expected to conform to the environmental regulations of the country of origin.

HEADLINE PUBLISHING GROUP
An Hachette UK Company
Carmelite House
50 Victoria Embankment
London EC4Y 0DZ

www.headline.co.uk
www.hachette.co.uk

ACKNOWLEDGMENTS

We'd like to thank Chuck Knief, Kay Chan, Sam Barer, Kathryn O'Keeffe, D. P. Lyle, Winz Tam, Jim Clemente, Doug Stone, and especially Jim Kochel for sharing their specialized knowledge with us.

1

Kate O'Hare bought her Ford Crown Vic at a police auction for abused cop cars. The dented, Bondo-patched four-door beast wasn't the kind of ride that usually appealed to attractive, professional women in their early thirties. Of course, most of those women didn't accessorize their wardrobe with a Glock, an FBI badge, and a small belly scar from a knife fight with an assassin.

Kate liked used cop cars because they were cheap, low-maintenance, and had options that weren't available on a Prius. Options like Kevlar-lined doors that were great for cover in a gun battle, monster V-8 engines that were perfect for high-speed chases, and steel ramming bars on the front grill that came in handy for pushing cars out of her way.

She'd been heading north on the 405 freeway through the

Sepulveda Pass when her boss, Special Agent in Charge Carl Jessup, called. Nicolas Fox, fugitive number seven on the FBI's Ten Most Wanted list, was trying to make his way up to number six.

"I've been thinking that maybe it wasn't such a bright idea for us to help a world-class con man and thief escape from prison," Jessup said in his amiable Kentucky drawl. "And an even worse idea to give him access to the money we secretly plunder from bad guys and use to pay for our covert ops. Both Nick and a million dollars of our money seem to be unaccounted for."

"I'm sure there's an innocent explanation," Kate said.

"There's nothing innocent about Nicolas Fox."

Kate knew that better than anybody. She was the FBI agent who'd chased Nick for five years before she finally put him in prison. Unfortunately, to Kate's horror, Jessup and Deputy Director Fletcher Bolton had Fox back on the street in record time. They had a plan. Fox would work undercover for the FBI. And Kate would partner up with Fox to keep him honest. Together they were tasked with going after major-league criminals who couldn't be caught through legal means. So Nick remained a major-league criminal himself, secretly working for the FBI, and Kate remained a top FBI field agent, secretly working with an international fugitive.

And that's why Kate was currently taking the curves on Sunset like it was the Talladega Superspeedway. She was hoping to catch Nick in his Sunset Strip penthouse. Technically, the penthouse wasn't Nick's. The IRS had seized it from a rapper who'd neglected to pay his taxes, and then the IRS had left it unoccupied pending sale. Nick had posed as the listing agent and quietly moved in. Thanks to rich tax cheats, Nick could always find a swanky place to stay that didn't require him to show a credit card or his face to a desk clerk.

Kate skidded to a stop in front of the fifteen-story building, jumped out of her car, and ran to the locked lobby door. She rang all of the tenants, held her badge up to the security camera, and looked into the lens with as much authority as she could muster.

"FBI! Open up!"

A tenant with a sense of civic duty, and too much trust, kindly buzzed the door open. Kate charged into the lobby only to come face-to-face with an "Out of Order" sign taped to the elevator.

Just her luck. She dashed into the stairwell and sprinted up the stairs. In a training exercise, it had taken her and a dozen other elite military commandos in full assault gear twenty minutes to rush up to the eighty-sixth floor of the Empire State Building. Kate estimated it would take her three minutes to get up to the penthouse in her sensible shoes.

Her cellphone rang between the fifth and sixth floor. Kate touched the Bluetooth device in her ear and answered the call as she climbed.

"O'Hare," she said.

"Where are you?" It was Megan, her younger sister. "Dad's waiting for you to take him to the airport."

"I'm on my way."

Their father, Jake, lived with Megan, her husband, Roger, and their two grade-school-aged kids in a gated community in Calabasas. That was where Kate had been headed when she received the call from Jessup.

"I told you two weeks ago that the kids have a big soccer game today and it's our turn to pass out the sliced oranges at halftime," Megan said. "You *promised* me that you'd take him."

"Relax, Megan. I'll be there."

"Why are you huffing and puffing?"

The stairwell began to rumble with the unmistakable sound of a helicopter closing in overhead. Kate felt a pang in her stomach, and it wasn't from the exertion of climbing twelve stories in two minutes. It was a powerful case of déjà vu and the dread that came with it. Kate had once chased Nick across a rooftop just as his accomplices were lifting off in a helicopter without him. As the chopper flew away, Nick had leapt off the building and grabbed onto a landing skid to make his triumphant escape. Her fear now was that he was going to try to repeat that death-defying performance.

"I've got to go," Kate shouted to her sister, ending the call and taking the remaining flights two steps at a time, past the penthouse and up to the rooftop.

She burst out of the door to see a green helicopter embossed with a U.S. State Department seal idling on the roof. Nicolas Fox was running toward it, his suit jacket flaring like a cape.

To Kate's relief, the helicopter pilot waited for Nick this time. Nick opened the door to the passenger cabin and turned to Kate as she ran up. There was a boyish grin on his face and a sparkle in his brown eyes. It was pretty much a confession that he was up to no good and enjoying it too much.

He was wearing the kind of off-the-rack, basic blue suit that Jos. A. Bank regularly sold two for the price of one. It was very un-Nick-like. He was a stylish six-foot-tall man with a keen and very expensive fashion sense. This suit made him look like an underpaid bureaucrat. She assumed that was the point.

"Perfect timing," he yelled over the sound of the helicopter blades whirring above them. "I'm glad you could make it."

Kate climbed into the chopper and took a seat. "Where are we going?"

"Malibu." Nick secured the door and sat beside her. They slipped on microphone-equipped headsets so they could hear each other over the noise.

Kate wasn't surprised to see Wilma "Willie" Owens in the pilot's seat. Willie was a fifty-something bleached blonde with enhanced boobs that looked like basketballs with nipples. Her typical outfit was a halter top and Daisy Dukes, but today she wore aviator shades, a white shirt with epaulets, and crisp blue slacks. It was an outfit suitable for a licensed pilot, although she wasn't one. She was a Texan with a natural talent for operating any vehicle on land, sea, or air and an unlawful tendency to steal them for joyrides.

"Have you ever flown a helicopter?" Kate asked her.

"Once or twice," Willie said.

"Which is it?"

"That depends, honey. Does this flight count?"

Kate tightened her seatbelt and turned back to Nick. "We aren't going anywhere until you tell me why you're pretending to be a diplomat and what happened to our million dollars."

Nick pressed a button on his headset that cut Willie off from the conversation.

"Most of the money went into buying and repainting this chopper," Nick said. "The rest went to sending a lucky young man on an all-expenses-paid trip to the Caribbean. It was the grand prize in a contest he didn't even know that he'd entered."

"Or that he was the only contestant."

"You catch on quick. He's staying at a very exclusive, very remote island resort that bills itself as 'the true *Gilligan's Island* experience.'"

"No phone, no lights, no motor car, not a single luxury," Kate said, referencing the show's catchy theme song. "You're keeping him off the grid. Who are you hiding him from?"

"His grandfather, Stuart Kelso, the king of 'the grandparent scam.' Are you familiar with it?"

"Yes. A grandparent gets an urgent email, or phone call, from an official with the terrible news that their grandchild has been arrested, robbed, or badly injured while traveling abroad. The fake official tricks the old and easily confused grandparent into wiring tens of thousands of dollars overseas to get the kid out of trouble."

"That's the one. As fate would have it, Stuart Kelso was recently notified by the State Department that his grandson, Ernie, has been arrested in Cuba on a drug-smuggling charge. The bail is five million dollars. Ordinarily he might have not fallen for his own con, but we had inside information about his grandson. And we landed a State Department helo on his front lawn."

Nick grinned, and Kate tried her best *not* to grin. It was genius and well-deserved poetic justice, and it was totally illegal. It felt oh-so-right but also oh-so-wrong ... much like her attraction to Nick. And the worst part was that he'd pulled it off under her nose.

"Why didn't you tell me about this con until now?" she asked, eyes narrowed, blood pressure edging up a notch.

"It was just a lark, something to keep myself amused between jobs. Kelso is small-time compared to our usual targets. I didn't think you'd approve."

"So you sneaked around behind my back."

"Yeah."

"We're supposed to be partners. You just made me look like the village idiot."

"Don't take it so personally," Nick said.

"How else am I supposed to take it? I'm responsible for

you. My career hinges on my ability to control you and your larcenous personality. You're only allowed to break the law when you have permission from the FBI. You can't go around breaking the law on a 'lark.'"

"I like when you get all worked up like this," Nick said. "It puts a sparkle in your eyes."

"If you go down, I go down, too. Rest assured I'll do everything I can to make sure it's not a pleasant experience for you. I'll make sure you're locked up and the key is thrown away."

"So you're in on the con?" Nick asked.

Kate blew out a sigh. "Yes."

"Excellent," Nick said. "Can you play an FBI agent?"

"I'll give it a try," Kate said. "But only if we can pick up my dad and drop him off afterward at LAX."

"No problem," Nick said.

2

Jake O'Hare was waiting for Kate and Nick in his gated community's private park. He was wearing a white golf shirt and tan chinos, his hands in his pockets, casually watching as Willie set the helicopter down on the grass. Jake had spent most of his life in the Army, doing covert ops for the government, but those days were long gone. Now he was in his sixties and most of his battles were fought on the putting green.

"Thanks for the lift," Jake said as he climbed in. He took a seat and put on his headset.

"Where are your suitcases?" Kate asked.

"I don't have any. I'll buy what I need when I get there and leave it behind when I go."

"You're going to Hawaii to visit an old Army buddy. It's a vacation, not a covert op."

"Says the woman taking me to the airport in a phony State Department helicopter," Jake said.

"Good point," Kate said. Her father was the only one, outside of Jessup and Deputy Director Bolton, who knew the truth about her and Nick. "Actually, we have an errand to run before we get to the airport."

"That's what I figured." Jake acknowledged Nick with a friendly nod. "What can I do to help?"

"Do you have any experience getting American captives out of foreign countries?" Nick asked.

"Extensive," Jake said.

Nick smiled. "Then just be yourself."

"I can do that," Jake said.

Thirty years ago, Stuart Kelso was an insurance salesman in Dearborn, Michigan, when he got a call in the middle of the night from a cop in Istanbul. Kelso's pot-smoking teenage son Bernie, who was on a backpacking trip through Europe, had been arrested for drug smuggling. If Kelso didn't send the cops $10,000 in twenty-four hours, they'd throw Bernie in a Turkish prison for five years. Kelso did as he was told and his son was put on a plane back to the United States. It was only later, once Bernie was home safe, that Kelso realized how stupid he'd been to act so quickly. *What if it had all been a con?* It was an epiphany for him . . . and the grandparent scam was born.

Kelso chose to target grandparents because the elderly were less likely to think clearly under pressure, and often had access to fat retirement funds. It was a smart move, because now he was ten times richer, fifty pounds heavier, and lived in Malibu with his third wife, Rilee, an aspiring model, in a Southern Colonial mansion on a bluff overlooking the Pacific.

When the U.S. government chopper landed in his backyard two days ago, he was sure the feds were coming to arrest him. Thankfully, he was wrong. It turned out to be a frantic State Department bureaucrat named Nick Burns arriving with bad news. Kelso's twenty-one-year-old grandson Ernie had been arrested smuggling dope into Havana. The Cubans wanted $5 million to set Ernie free or they'd put him on trial to embarrass the United States. Kelso couldn't believe the cosmic unfairness of it all. History was repeating itself. Burns urged Kelso to make the payoff for the sake of his grandson and the good of his country.

Kelso didn't care about Ernie or Uncle Sam, but he was afraid that the media spotlight might reveal his own crimes. That's why every dollar Kelso had was packed into the four suitcases that were currently standing beside him, waiting to be loaded into the State Department helicopter that was landing in his backyard again.

Burns emerged from the chopper, checking his watch as he approached. He was accompanied by a stocky older guy and a fit young woman in a gray pantsuit with her jacket open to show off the gun on her belt.

"Good morning, Mr. Kelso," Burns said. "Is that all of the money?"

The only cash Kelso had outside the suitcases was the twenty-eight dollars in his wallet. All of his other assets were tied up in debt and ex-wives. It was as if the Cubans *wanted* to clean him out. He could no longer run his business, pay his mortgage, or support his third wife and her posse of yoga instructors, hairdressers, stylists, and personal shoppers. But at least he wouldn't be going to jail.

"It was hell getting it all together," Kelso said. "I still don't see why it had to be in cash."

The stocky guy spoke up. "Let's be honest here, Mr. Kelso. You aren't posting bail. It's a bribe being paid to corrupt cops. Bribing is a cash business. Cash doesn't leave a trail."

Kelso looked at Burns and gestured to Kate's dad. "Who is he?"

"Jake Blake. The bag man who is going to spread the bribes around Havana for you," Burns said. "He's done this kind of thing for us before. For obvious reasons, we can't do it ourselves."

"What's to stop Blake from running off with my money?"

"Me," the woman said, flashing an FBI badge.

Kelso felt his bowels seize up with fear. He'd had nightmares about seeing one of those badges in his face.

"I'm Special Agent Kate Houlihan. I'll be with Blake every step of the way."

"You don't trust me, Houlihan?" Blake asked.

"The problem with mercenaries is that they are mercenary," she said. "Loyalty is not in the job description." She shifted her attention back to Kelso. "I'm also the one who will make sure your grandson gets safely out of Cuba."

"I don't know what that stupid kid was thinking," Kelso said.

"The only reason I'm going to bring him to your door and not to prison is because the State Department doesn't want this episode ever coming to light," Houlihan said. "But if I were you, I'd let him know he just used the only get-out-of-jail-free card he's ever going to get."

"I will," Kelso said.

"We've got to get moving." Burns looked at his watch again. "We need to catch a flight to Guantánamo. They're holding a plane for us at Vandenberg."

Houlihan and Blake each picked up two suitcases and carried them back to the chopper. Kelso watched them go. He'd have to crack the whip on his boiler room full of poverty-wage workers in the Philippines and get them to send out twice as many scam emails as usual. He needed to generate as much cash as he could before the workers realized there was no paycheck coming, stripped the place of anything of value, and walked out on him.

Kelso turned to Burns. "When will I hear from you?"

"You won't. If it all goes well, your grandson will show up at your door. If it doesn't, you'll see him on the news being perp-walked in Havana. Either way, this meeting never happened. The U.S. government was never involved. Are we clear?"

Kelso nodded. "Thanks for your help."

"It's what you pay your taxes for."

Actually, Kelso didn't pay his taxes, because he had no

legitimate income to declare. It was one more reason he'd paid the outrageous bribe to the Cubans.

Burns jogged back to the helicopter and climbed in beside the pilot. The chopper lifted up, veered off over the Pacific, and headed north toward Vandenberg.

As the sound of the chopper receded, Kelso heard a car coming up the driveway. He walked around to the front of the house to see who it was. A black Lincoln MKT with livery plates came to a stop, and a lanky guy in a loose-fitting tank top, board shorts, and sandals hopped out of the backseat with a big smile on his sunburned face. It took Kelso a second to realize it was his grandson Ernie.

"Wow, what an amazing trip," Ernie said. "Thanks for sending the limo, Grandpa. How did you know when I was coming back? Did the contest guys call you?"

The enormity of what this meant hit Kelso like a sucker punch in the gut. He staggered, leaning on the house for support. Ernie rushed over, grabbed him, and held him upright.

"Grandpa, what's wrong? Are you okay?"

The helicopter came back and circled low over the house. For a moment, Kelso couldn't breathe. All he could do was gasp for air and look up into the sky. *How could I have been so stupid?*

3

They couldn't fly the fake State Department helicopter into LAX, so Willie flew to Culver City and landed on top of a parking structure for the DoubleTree hotel. From there Jake took the hotel's airport shuttle to his terminal, and Nick and Kate flew back to the apartment on Sunset. They unloaded the suitcases onto the rooftop, and Willie took off again. This time heading north, on her own.

"Where's she going?" Kate asked.

"To a vacant farm up in Ojai that belongs to the IRS. She'll repaint the chopper and keep it under wraps until we need it again."

"We're keeping it?"

"Why not? We bought it."

Pull out my fingernails, Kate thought. It would be less painful than babysitting Nick Fox.

"Okay, we can hold on to it for a while, but only if Willie gets herself a valid pilot's license," Kate said.

"You need to stop thinking so much like an FBI agent," Nick said.

"I *am* an FBI agent."

"Yes, but you're a criminal when you're with me. The law is for people who have nothing to hide. The purpose of a genuine pilot's license is to identify you, prove you have met all of the legal requirements to fly an aircraft, and hold you responsible for your actions. We don't want anyone to know who we are, or what we've done."

"Okay, I get that, but she's had lessons, right? I mean she didn't just get into the helicopter and take off, did she?"

"She's spent hours with a certified instructor. She's absolutely qualified to fly that aircraft."

Nick picked up two of the suitcases full of cash and headed toward the elevator.

"Don't bother," Kate said, carrying her suitcases toward the stairwell. "It's out of order."

"No, it's not." He pushed the call button. "I wanted to discourage realtors and squatters from encroaching on my privacy. And I thought it would be inspiring to see you all sweaty and breathing heavy."

"I wasn't sweaty and breathing heavy."

"I noticed," Nick said. "If you put those suitcases down and let me have my way with you, I could get you there."

"Good grief. Are you flirting with me?"

"Honey, my intentions are way past flirting."

"Your intentions could get you a knee in the groin."

Nick grinned. "At least your mind's on the right body part."

Kate gave a grunt of feigned disgust and stepped into the open elevator. She was an FBI agent, and sleeping with Nick, a wanted felon, was a line she wasn't willing to cross. She'd already crossed so many lines, helping Nick swindle and steal and stay out of prison, that she often wondered what made keeping Nick at arm's length so important to her.

Nick reached past her and slid a key card into the control panel, and the elevator descended. A moment later the elevator doors opened into the penthouse foyer. The penthouse had floor-to-ceiling windows and a terrific view of the Los Angeles basin. Carl Jessup stood at the window, watching the helicopter fly off. There was a thick file folder under his arm. Nick and Kate walked in and set down their suitcases.

"That looks a lot like a U.S. government helicopter leaving here," Jessup said, turning around to face them.

"Looks can be deceiving," Nick said.

"Well, I wouldn't dare argue with you about that," Jessup said. "You're the expert on that subject."

Jessup had the tanned, weathered face and sinewy body of a man who'd spent his fifty-some years outdoors, working a field or raising cattle, but it came from genes, not experience. He'd been in the FBI since he graduated from college.

"What brings you here, sir?" Kate asked.

"I asked myself the same question a few times as I was going up those stairs," Jessup said. "Damn near had a heart attack."

"The elevator is working now," Kate said. "You won't have any issues with it going down."

Jessup cut his eyes to Nick. "So what have you done with the million dollars you took from us?"

"I turned it into five million in less than a week." Nick gestured to the suitcases. "Not a bad return on our investment."

"The goal of our clandestine operation isn't to make money," Jessup said.

"But it doesn't hurt," Nick said.

Jessup frowned and shifted his gaze to Kate. "Who was the target of this swindle?"

"A con man named Stuart Kelso, a major perpetrator of the grandparent scam," Kate said. "He tricks old people into sending him money to get their grandchildren out of desperate situations. Kelso doesn't deserve our sympathy, sir."

"He won't get any from me, but that's not the issue," Jessup said. "How did you get him to give you five million dollars?"

Nick smiled. "I ran the grandparent scam on him."

"Of course you did," Jessup said. "I'm sure you thought it would be great fun."

"It was," Nick said.

"You aren't supposed to be running cons for fun anymore,"

Jessup said. "You're supposed to be doing it to put very bad people in prison. All you did was take Kelso's money and make a fool out of him. He'll just go back to hustling old people out of their Social Security checks."

"Check your email," Nick said. "You've got an important message from your daughter."

Jessup used his phone to browse his email. "She says that she's in Budapest, her wallet and passport have been stolen, and she needs me to wire her two thousand dollars right away. Where did this email really come from?"

"Kelso's boiler room in Manila, where he's got a dozen Filipinos who send out emails to hundreds of grandparents every month using information gleaned from Facebook," Nick said. "One of my associates hacked into Kelso's computers last night. He sent out emails like the one you got to the U.S. attorney general, all nine justices of the U.S. Supreme Court, and the police chiefs of every major American city. Each email is embedded with digital breadcrumbs that lead directly to Kelso's boiler room. I'll bet you five million dollars that Kelso will be in handcuffs within forty-eight hours."

Jessup nodded, not so much with approval than with grudging respect. "I'd wager that it'll be closer to twenty-four hours."

Kate was relieved. Jessup's comment was the closest thing to his retroactive approval that they were going to get. Probably best not to mention the newly acquired helicopter at this time.

"Since you're in a betting mood, you'll like your next

assignment," Jessup said, handing Kate the file folder under his arm. "We want you to take down Evan Trace."

Evan Trace was the forty-year-old owner of Côte d'Argent, the Las Vegas casino where the generation of celebrities who'd never known a world without *The Simpsons* did their gambling, partying, and general debauchery. He was a dead ringer for Brad Pitt, a resemblance he played to the hilt in a series of stylish commercials for Côte d'Argent. He'd made himself the new, hip face of Vegas.

"Trace's boutique casinos in Las Vegas and Macau are laundromats for terrorists, mobsters, drug lords, street gangs, and despots who want to wash their dirty money," Jessup said. "They turn around and use that clean cash to do all sorts of nasty things, like buy weapons, bribe politicians, and finance terrorist attacks."

"It's simple, really," Nick said. "You walk into a casino with some money, buy a bunch of chips, and gamble for a while. Then you hand over the chips that you have left to someone else, say the owner of a vintage Ferrari you want to buy, and he cashes them in. That's it. There is no record that ties you to the transaction. Your money has been washed."

"Sounds to me like you're speaking from experience," Jessup said.

Kate set the file on the massive coffee table. "I know he is. I've seen the Ferrari."

"Playing baccarat is a much more entertaining way to move

cash than working with crooked bankers, crafty accountants, and shell corporations," Nick said. "And you get free drinks while you're doing it, too."

"I get why you do it," Kate said. "But I don't see what's in it for Trace."

"He gets whatever a player loses gambling and a five percent skim at the cashier's cage when the chips are cashed in," Jessup said. "Plus he makes some very powerful friends."

"It seems so easy," Kate said. "I'm surprised that more casinos aren't doing it."

"That's because we closely watch what goes on here, or at least we try to," Jessup said. "But nobody's watching in Macau."

"Why not?" Kate asked.

"There are thirty-five casinos in Macau, and combined they generate forty billion dollars annually in gambling revenue," Jessup said. "The Chinese government takes forty percent of that in taxes."

"That's *their* skim," Nick said. "Not counting the kickbacks and bribes the casinos pay to local cops and government officials."

"That's a lot of incentive to look the other way," she said.

"And they do," Jessup said. "In Macau, ninety percent of the gambling revenue comes from whales: super-rich gamblers who'll bet millions of dollars in one night. We know from our surveillance that most of the whales that gamble at Côte d'Argent are laundering money for al-Qaeda, ISIS, and other terrorist groups who target Americans. That makes Trace a criminal and a traitor. He has to be stopped. But the U.S. has no jurisdiction in Macau, and the Chinese government won't help."

"Seems like a job for the CIA," Nick said.

"The White House won't let them touch it," Jessup said. "They won't take the risk that U.S. spies might get caught sneaking around in Chinese territory."

"But you don't mind risking us," Nick said.

"You're a fugitive, wanted for crimes in a dozen countries, and she's the FBI agent you seduced into bed and into a scheme to rip off Trace's casino," Jessup said. "That will be an easy story to sell if you get caught."

"Nick hasn't seduced me," Kate said.

"Not for lack of trying," Nick said.

"It will be a tawdry scandal," Jessup said. "But not one that will deeply embarrass the United States."

"It will deeply embarrass me," Kate said.

"So don't get caught," Jessup said.

After Jessup left, Kate read through the file on Trace while Nick emptied the suitcases of cash onto the coffee table and counted the money.

She briefed Nick as she went along.

"Trace got his start in the gambling business running a small Indian casino in the desert outside of Palm Springs," Kate said. "Then, six years ago, he bought an unfinished Vegas condo tower, which had stalled midway through construction because the builder went bankrupt. Trace converted it into a 350-room hotel and casino. When he opened up, he hired beautiful young women and hard-bodied young men to hang around his topless pool as eye candy."

"That beats a high-seas pirate battle outside the hotel or a huge fountain of dancing water," Nick said, stacking the money on one side of the vast coffee table as he counted it. "It's also a lot cheaper."

"He also invites celebrities to stay for free," Kate said. "Especially the ones likely to get into trouble and make tabloid headlines."

"Saving him a fortune on publicity. Either he's a tightwad or he was improvising because he was strapped for cash."

"To lure in customers, he offered winning slot machines, bargain buffets, cheap rooms, and very strong drinks. People came in droves. But what really put him over the top were his TV commercials."

"Never saw one," Nick said.

"They were inescapable."

"I was too busy running from you to watch TV."

"Here's the one everybody knows." Kate powered up Nick's laptop, went to YouTube, and played one of Trace's commercials. Nick watched it over her shoulder.

The commercial was set late at night. The colors were so washed out that the picture was almost black and white. Trace walked down the Vegas Strip in a rumpled Armani tuxedo, his bow tie undone and collar open, and dragged on a cigarette, sucking every last molecule of nicotine out of it. He trudged past the erupting volcano, the Eiffel Tower, the New York skyline, all rendered seedy and crass in the harsh shadows, while he spoke to the camera in a voice made raw from a long night of smoking and drinking.

"*What a f—king joke,*" Trace said.

The obscenity was muted, but it didn't really make a difference. It was obvious what he'd said.

"*You won't find an authentic experience here. Not on this street. Not in these places.*"

Trace turned the corner, off the Strip, and there was Côte d'Argent, a slim black tower, untouched by gaudiness or pretense. He opened the door and looked straight into the camera.

"*Gambling. Partying. No f—king gondolas.*"

The obscenity was lost in the bells and coin clatter of a slot machine paying off. He took one last drag on his cigarette, flicked it into the street, and walked into the casino. The commercial ended.

"That's their slogan," Kate said. " 'No freakin' gondolas.' "

"Catchy," Nick said.

"He put it on T-shirts, hats, and coffee mugs," Kate said. "The first two years that Côte d'Argent was in business, Trace made more money off his branded merchandise than he did from his hotel."

Nick went back to counting stacks of hundred-dollar bills. "If we really want to learn about Evan Trace and the inner workings of his casino, we'll need to take a trip to Vegas. Be a couple of whales."

Kate could see where this was going. "We are not going to gamble with the government's money."

"It's not the government's money. It's cash stolen from Stuart Kelso."

"By the FBI."

"Illegally," he said.

"For the greater good," Kate said, thinking that was kind of lame, but it was the best she could do to justify their actions.

"Fine. We're gambling with this money for the greater good," Nick said. "And for the free drinks."

"Will the buffet be free, too?"

"It'll definitely be comped."

"Let's do it," Kate said.

4

Nick and Kate were on a private jet headed to Las Vegas. It had taken two days to organize, but Nick had needed the extra day to set up their fake identities as Nick Sweet, international entrepreneur, and Kate Porter, his executive assistant. It also gave Jessup time to wipe their real identities from various law enforcement databases and temporarily replace them with their new ones.

Nick wore a gray, impeccably tailored Tom Ford suit with a white shirt and blue silk tie.

Kate wore a skin-tight red Herve Leger bandage dress. It had a plunging neckline, cap sleeves, and a skirt that was so short, there was almost no way Kate could get up from a chair without making everyone her gynecologist. Nick had picked it out for her because she had nothing like it. Kate's closet was mostly full of tank tops and jeans and her FBI windbreaker.

Kate picked an almond from a small bowl of heated nuts. "I don't get it. Nick Sweet and Kate Porter. Why are you a dessert, and I'm a beer?"

Nick looked across the aisle at her. "Would you rather be the dessert?"

Kate ate the almond and thought about it. "No."

"What then?"

"I'd rather be a morning glory muffin."

"Hard to fit that on a passport," Nick said.

Kate nodded. "What exactly is the job of an international entrepreneur?"

"To be charming, mysterious, and extravagantly wealthy," Nick said. "Your job is to take care of all the little things that might distract me from being charming, mysterious, and extravagantly wealthy."

"So you get to have all the fun," she said, "while I do all the busy work."

"I swindle while you investigate. We both do what we do best. I've booked the presidential suite for us at Côte d'Argent to announce our arrival. They'll know a whale is coming and send a limo to pick us up."

"How much is this announcement costing us?"

"Thirty-five thousand a night."

Kate choked on a cashew. "Are you insane?"

"It's only one night, two tops, and it accomplishes some very important things. It establishes that we're among the highest of high rollers and it proves that we're not in law enforcement. No cop could possibly justify this expense to his boss."

"*I'll* have to."

He waved off her concern. "Only if the assignment fails. Until then, enjoy yourself."

Easy for him to say. He wasn't wearing a thong and four-inch heels that were pinching his toes.

"You look great in that dress," he said. "It has me feeling romantic."

"Romantic?"

"Okay, maybe that's not exactly the right word."

"And the right word would be what?"

"Hard to boil it down to one word."

"Give it to me in a couple words then."

"I'd like to rip it off you with my teeth."

"Holy cow."

Nick smiled. "Like I said, you look great in that dress."

Kate squeezed her knees together and crossed her arms over her chest.

Twenty minutes later they landed at Henderson Executive Airport, a few miles southeast of central Las Vegas. A black Bentley Flying Spur from Côte d'Argent was waiting for them on the tarmac along with a chauffeur in a black suit and dark sunglasses.

The chauffeur opened the back door of the Bentley for Nick and Kate, and put the four titanium suitcases full of cash and the two Louis Vuitton bags containing their clothes in the trunk. He headed north on Interstate 15 toward the Strip. They hit the Strip and traveled from Mandalay Bay to the Bellagio, exiting at Flamingo Road, turning west over the freeway. Rising above a sea of budget motels, convenience stores, and fast-food restaurants was a forty-five-story black granite tower shaped like a box cutter blade. "Côte d'Argent" was written in lights along the cutting edge.

The driver pulled up to a private entrance behind the building. It was shielded from public view by an eight-foot-high wall of black marble, lined with a thin layer of water cascading down the surface. A doorman who looked more like a Secret Service agent, down to the sunglasses, earpiece, and probably the gun, opened the back of the Bentley for Nick and Kate, and supervised the unloading of the trunk.

Nick and Kate walked into the VIP lobby. The air conditioner was cranked up high against the desert heat, keeping the elaborate ice sculptures of lions taking down gazelles from melting too quickly.

A slim, beautiful hostess approached them. She was dressed in a black frock jacket, a lace peplum blouse, pencil slacks, and ultra-high heels.

"Welcome to Côte d'Argent," the hostess said, guiding them to the registration desk.

The red-haired woman behind the desk wore the same outfit as the other hostesses. She smiled at them as if she'd been eagerly awaiting Nick and Kate's arrival for months.

"I'm so glad to see you, Mr. Sweet," she said.

"Thank you," Nick said. "This is my associate, Ms. Porter. Please extend to her any courtesies that are offered to me by the hotel."

"It will be my pleasure," the clerk said. "My name is Tara. I will be your personal assistant during your stay."

"I've brought a deposit with me." Nick tipped his head to the door, where the bellman was bringing in the luggage. "It's in those four silver cases. I'd appreciate it if you'd exchange the cash for chips and have them on hand for tonight's game."

"Of course. Would you or Ms. Porter like to be present while the cash is counted?"

"Not necessary. It's five million," he said. "I trust you."

"In that case, I'll call for your personal butler, Mr. Covington, to see you to your suite."

"That won't be necessary, either," Nick said. "We like to find our own way around."

"Very well. Mr. Covington will be on call twenty-four hours a day for you, as well as a maid, a bartender, a personal chef, a doctor, a masseuse, a concert pianist, and anyone else that you might need."

"All the comforts of home," Nick said.

"I hope you enjoy your stay. Let me show you to your private express elevator." Tara stepped out from behind the podium and led them to the elevator. She slid a transparent key card into a slot on the wall and then handed it to Nick.

"Please let me know if there is anything I can do to make your stay more pleasurable. I am entirely at your service." She handed another transparent key to Kate and smiled. "Individually or together."

"Good to know," Nick said.

Nick and Kate stepped into the elevator. The door closed and the elevator rose smoothly, but swiftly, up the forty-five floors to the penthouse.

"When she said 'individually or together' . . . did she mean, you know what?" Kate asked.

Nick grinned. "She implied we could have the ultimate group activity."

"Would it show up on our bill?" Kate asked him.

"Would it matter?"

"Jessup would throw a blood clot."

"I'm sure I could have it removed from the bill," Nick said. "Is this a possibility?"

"No!" Kate said. "Good grief." She grimaced at him. "You would do it, wouldn't you?"

"Only one way to find out."

"*Ick.*"

The elevator opened into a circular marble foyer with a massive crystal chandelier. They crossed the foyer into an expansive living room that opened onto a wraparound terrace with an unobstructed view of the Las Vegas Strip. There was an infinity pool along the edge of the terrace, creating the illusion that the water flowed onto the street forty-five floors below.

The living room walls were paneled in walnut and decorated with abstract art, swirls of paint drippings on canvas in the style of Jackson Pollock. Kate squinted at one of the paintings and saw Pollock's signature.

"Is this the real thing or a forgery?" she asked.

"You'll know if it's in my luggage when we leave."

There were plenty of inviting leather-wrapped couches and easy chairs, a wet bar, a sixty-five-inch flat-screen TV, a stacked-stone fireplace, and a Steinway grand piano.

"Well, this explains the on-call concert pianist," Kate said.

"I was wondering about that myself," Nick said. "There are his and hers bedrooms and boardrooms on either end of the penthouse."

"Boardrooms?"

"You never know when you might want to hold a meeting with your personal staff."

Kate checked out a bedroom. It was the size of her entire apartment. There was a couch, two easy chairs, a fireplace, a flat-screen TV, and a massive king-size bed covered with fluffy pillows and a thick comforter. The marble-tiled bathroom had a steam shower built for two, a whirlpool tub, and a massage table.

"Decadent," Kate said.

"Yeah," Nick said. "I especially like the furry pillows. I'm guessing Mongolian lamb. Or maybe a rabbit on steroids."

Kate peeked into the private boardroom. There was a long conference table for eight, another flat-screen TV, and another bar.

"I feel a sudden desire to have a meeting," Kate said.

"Yeah, I've got some sudden desires, too," Nick said. "They have to do with the dress you're wearing and how fast I could get you out of it."

Kate looked down at herself. "It's not that easy. I'm stuffed into this like a bratwurst."

"I like a challenge," Nick said.

"Not this one. It would come with pain. Possibly a broken bone."

"I'm not really into pain," Nick said. "Especially if it's mine."

"You need to focus," Kate said. "This is all about the mission."

"There's all kinds of missions," Nick said.

But first it was all about the buffet. Kate loved buffets. And the one at Côte d'Argent was spectacular. She brought two plates with mountains of food on them back to her booth, where Nick sat with an iced tea and a small Caesar salad.

"I don't know what we're doing here," Nick said. "We have a private chef."

"It's not the same as a buffet," she said, digging meat from a crab leg with a tiny fork. "This is all-you-can-eat. And you can make last-minute choices. And there's all this *stuff.*"

"Quantity and quality are not the same things."

"I grew up on Army bases, eating in canteens where food was basic. And now that I'm on my own I mostly eat out of a fast-food container. Getting access to a buffet, even a bad one, is like someone handing me a free pass to heaven."

Nick smiled wide. "You're equating a buffet to heaven?"

"Okay, so maybe not heaven. Maybe to Disneyland."

Nick watched her clean off both plates. "Where do you put it all?"

"I have a very fast metabolism," she said, dabbing her lips with a napkin. "Did I spill anything on myself?"

He looked her over. "Not a drop or a crumb."

"Then we'd better get to the casino before my good luck fades."

They left the buffet and crossed the casino toward the high-limit room. It was separated from the rest of the casino by partially drawn red curtains.

"Tonight we're playing blackjack," Nick said. "We'll take a table for ourselves. There are five seats. I'll play three hands at once and you'll play two."

"I'm not sure that's such a good idea. I could lose twice as much twice as fast."

"Win or lose, it doesn't matter. What we're trying to do is attract attention as whales with money to burn."

The walls of the salon were covered with hand-stitched leather and framed with dark wood. There were eight gaming tables and only seven men gambling. Four of them were at the same table, playing pai gow poker, the other three were playing baccarat. A few women sat drinking at the bar, where backlit multicolored bottles of liquor were arranged by hue on glass shelves.

Nick and Kate were greeted by a round-bodied, round-faced man wearing a three-piece suit. The way he waddled up to them reminded Kate of the Penguin, from *Batman*.

"Good evening to you both. I am Niles Goodwell, manager of player relations." Goodwell took a slight bow and whispered to Nick. "Your credit is good here, sir, up to five million."

"What's your table limit for blackjack?" Nick asked.

"Two hundred and fifty thousand."

"What are your chip denominations over ten thousand?"

"We have twenty-five-thousand, fifty-thousand, and one-hundred-thousand-dollar chips."

"We'd like a table to ourselves. We'll each start with one million to get warmed up," Nick said. "Half in twenty-five-thousand chips and half in fifty-thousand chips."

"Make yourselves comfortable." Goodwell gestured to a blackjack table where a young woman stood, smiling warmly at them. "I'll be right back with your chips."

They went to the table. Kate sat to the dealer's left, what blackjack players called "first base," and Nick took the seat to the right, known as "third base." A waitress came by to offer them drinks. Nick ordered a martini. Kate settled for a Coke. Goodwell brought them their chips on a gold platter.

"Good luck," he said, stepping away, but lingering close enough to keep his eye on the action.

Nick smiled at the dealer. "Let's have some fun."

5

If Nick had chosen craps, Kate would have been lost, but she figured she could handle blackjack. The goal, for both the player and the dealer, was to get as close as possible to twenty-one without going over. Simple, right?

Nick placed fifty thousand dollars on each of the three betting circles on his side of the table. Kate did the same on her two spots and broke into an immediate sweat. There was *a lot* of money on the table. Money for which she was more or less accountable.

The dealer smiled and patted the table. "Good luck."

She dealt the cards from a six-deck shoe. There were two cards dealt face up for each of their five playing positions. The dealer showed a four.

Kate had a sixteen on one of her hands and a seventeen on the other. She decided to stand.

Nick had a nineteen, an eighteen, and a twenty.

The dealer flipped her hole card. It was a six. The dealer dealt herself another card. It was a ten, giving her a total of twenty. The dealer winced politely, and swept up their chips.

Poof. Their two hundred fifty grand was gone.

It wasn't Kate's own money, but she couldn't help thinking of all the things that she could have bought with it. A house in Las Vegas. Or a Lamborghini Gallardo. Or fifty-four thousand In-N-Out double-double cheeseburgers. Instead they had bought two mighty expensive drinks.

"With the way things are going we could be done early and need a couples massage," Nick said to Kate. "Do you remember the conversation we had in the elevator?"

"Vividly."

"And?"

"And I think I'll stick with the game for a while longer."

After a half hour of play, Nick and Kate were up $1.5 million, and Kate was into the game, riding on a steady drip of adrenaline and her competitive nature. She put $250,000 down on each of her spots, and at the bar behind them, Goodwell picked up the receiver on a red telephone and made a call.

One floor below the casino, at the end of a long hallway, behind a door marked "Customer Relations," a wall-mounted telephone rang. Evan Trace stepped out of the shadows and answered it. His face was meticulously unshaven and the sleeves on his handmade monogrammed white shirt were neatly folded up to the elbows.

"This is Trace."

"We've got a couple whales up here," Goodwell said. "Nick Sweet and Kate Porter. They've taken a blackjack table and are betting two hundred and fifty thousand a hand. They're up one and a half million at the moment and they don't show any signs of slowing down."

"What do we know about them?"

"They came into town from L.A. on a private jet, walked in the door with five million dollars in cash, and booked the presidential suite for the night," Goodwell said. "That's it."

"I want to meet them."

"I thought you would," Goodwell said.

"Invite them to my private dining room for a drink when either they've tapped out or we have."

Trace hung up the phone. He wasn't concerned about the couple winning, even if it added up to tens of millions of dollars. He was a firm believer that his profits came from the winners, not the losers. The winners always came back for more, giving up what they'd won and then some. He knew that from personal experience, which brought him back to the task at hand.

He turned to the center of the windowless room. The only furniture was a stainless steel workbench and the chair behind it. They were placed under the room's single light fixture, a naked bulb that hung on a wire from the ceiling. A sandy-haired man in his late twenties sat in the chair. He was good-looking enough to be a model, or at least he had been before the beating. His eyes were swollen nearly shut, his lips were split, and his nose was bleeding.

Trace stepped up to the table and looked down at the terrified man. "You made a mistake, Stan."

"I know that," Stan said, his voice wavering, and glanced fearfully to his right, where another man stood in the shadows. "Mr. Garver can stop hitting me now."

Garver was also in his shirtsleeves and was wiping Stan's blood off his huge, meaty hands with a towel. His face looked like a head of cauliflower, the result of the beatings he'd taken prizefighting in his youth. He also had thick calluses on his walnut-sized knuckles, the result of the beatings he'd inflicted in the forty-odd years he'd spent in customer relations.

"I run an honest casino," Trace said. "Sure, we give the players free booze to make them careless, but we never cheat them. We expect the players to treat us with that same respect. You didn't do that, Stan. You cheated."

"I've had a run of bad luck and I'm deep in debt," Stan said. "I couldn't wait for my luck to turn. So I nudged it along. It won't happen again."

Garver spoke up. His voice sounded like each word was serrated and scratched his throat on the way out. "Show Mr. Trace your hands."

Stan placed his shaky hands on the table. He had long, slender fingers and manicured nails. Trace examined them and nodded with appreciation. Garver slipped back into the shadows.

"They're very nice. You take very good care of them, Stan, and that's smart. Your fingers are the tools of your trade."

Garver returned to the table. He'd picked up a wooden mallet somewhere. It was chipped from age and heavy use.

"No, no, no." Stan started to lift his hands from the table but Garver shook his head, warning him against it, so he stopped. He left his hands where they were but looked imploringly at Trace. "Please don't."

"I'm doing you a favor. Twenty years ago, I was the guy in that chair. Garver broke my hands with that mallet. It changed my whole outlook on life," Trace said. "Now I own a casino and he works for me. I owe it all to that night."

Trace held his hand out to Garver, who gave him the mallet, and then pinned Stan's wrists to the table with his massive hands.

"You don't have to do this," Stan said, pleading. "I promise you that I will never cheat again."

"I know you won't," Trace said, raising the mallet over his head. "Think positive. Maybe I'll end up working for you someday."

Nick and Kate played blackjack for three more hours. At one point, they were up by $3 million. But by the time it was over, they'd lost all of their winnings and were out of pocket another $2 million.

Kate's adrenaline drip had slowed to barely a trickle, and she was thinking more about cheese puffs than blackjack.

"Do you think the buffet is still open?" Kate asked.

"You're hungry?" Nick asked.

"Ravenous," she said. "I could eat two million dollars' worth of crab legs and tiny key lime pies."

"I like this side of you."

Goodwell approached the blackjack table. "Pardon me. If you're done for the night, Mr. Trace would like to invite you to his private dining room for drinks."

Nick glanced at Kate, then back at Goodwell. "If he'll throw in a couple of steaks, we'll be there."

"How do you like your steaks prepared?" Goodwell asked.

Trace's private dining room was behind an unmarked door near the high-limit parlor of the casino. Goodwell opened the door for Nick and Kate and waved them through. They stepped into an atrium that was filled with tropical plants and flowers. A sleek Plexiglas-bottomed bridge arched over a koi pond and into the wood-paneled dining room decorated with contemporary artwork. Kate looked down at the pond as they walked over the bridge, taking note of the silver-green fish. They were about five inches long and had red bellies. Piranha, she thought. More appropriate to the setting than koi.

Trace was waiting to greet them on the other side of the

bridge. He wore a midnight blue silk tux jacket, a white dress shirt, skinny jeans, and black crocodile loafers.

"I'm so glad to meet you. I'm Evan Trace."

"We appreciate the invitation," Nick said. "It was an unexpected treat."

"I could say the same about the two of you," Trace said, smiling at Kate, his attention momentarily caught by the red dress. "It's not often that people we don't know walk in off the street, book our best suite, and gamble millions of dollars."

"Surely you don't know everyone with money," Kate said.

"Everyone but you," Trace said.

A table near the atrium was set for three, and a bottle of red wine had been decanted.

Trace pulled out a chair for Kate. "I've taken the liberty of choosing a bottle of wine from my private reserve. I hope that's okay."

"I'm sure it's lovely," Kate said.

Lovely, she thought. She had actually said *lovely.* Good Godfrey, she sounded like a lady.

She was facing the dining room and looking across the table at the artwork on the walls. All large abstract paintings and a familiar painting of seven dogs sitting around a table playing poker. She'd seen the picture a thousand times before. It wasn't something she'd expect to see in Trace's private dining room.

"I like that you've included the painting of the dogs playing poker," Kate said. "It adds some whimsy to your collection."

"A print of that painting was on the wall in the motel room I rented when I first came to Vegas. But what you see there is the original oil painting, created in 1903 for a cigar advertisement. I bought it to always remind me of how I got started."

"How did you end up in the casino business?" Nick asked.

"I like to say it was a sign from God," Trace said. "I'd gone bust as a gambler in Vegas, so I headed for Palm Springs to be a tennis instructor. I was driving across the desert when my Chevette broke down. It was a thousand degrees outside. I had to walk miles to the nearest gas station, which was this wooden shack in the middle of nowhere run by this grizzled old Indian. I staggered in, sunburned and thirsty, and the old coot welcomed me to the sovereign Chuckwalla Indian nation, total tribal population: one. I had a revelation then and there."

"You saw a vision of a casino," Nick said.

"That's right, my sign from God. My burning bush. Once I proved that the old coot's obscure tribe was real, that his barren patch of desert was truly their ancestral land, and that he was the one Indian left, raising the money to build a casino there was no problem."

The butler brought their steaks to the table and, while they ate, Trace talked about running the Indian casino, selling out his shares once it was a huge success, and using his profits to build Côte d'Argent.

"That's quite a story," Nick said.

"What's yours?" Trace asked.

"I'm an international entrepreneur," Nick said.

"I see. And what type of entrepreneurial endeavors do you favor?"

"You could say I'm a professional gambler, only not at cards," Nick said. "I invest in business ventures of various sorts around the world and hope that they work out. Fortunately for me, they usually do."

"What sort of ventures?"

"Moneymaking ones that involve considerable risk," Nick said. "The risk is almost as important to me as the profit potential."

"You're being vague," Trace said.

"Yes," Nick said. "I am."

Trace shifted his attention to Kate. "And you? What do you do, Ms. Porter?"

"While Nick's busy looking for the next big thing, he forgets to take care of the last big thing and everything else that's going on in his life. That's my job. I manage the details."

"I get bored easily," Nick said.

"As do I," Trace said, his eyes drawn to Kate's cleavage.

Trace redirected his focus and cut what was left of his steak into tiny, bloody squares. "I hope, at least, we've managed to keep you entertained so far at Côte d'Argent." Trace tossed the squares of meat into the koi pond, and the water churned like it was boiling. The piranha swarmed on the meat in a feeding frenzy.

"I always thought the idea of a koi pond was to provide peace and tranquillity," Nick said as he watched the seething water.

"Koi just swim around getting old and fat. I don't get any serenity from that," Trace said. "Piranha are the only small fish with any energy, any joie de vivre. I could watch them do this for hours. The hard part is finding someone willing to clean the pond."

"That would be an authentic experience," Nick said.

Trace gave up a tight smile. "I'll be sure to put that in my next commercial."

Kate's cellphone vibrated in her clutch purse. She'd received a text message. Only Nick, Jessup, and her father had the number to her phone. It couldn't be good news.

"Forgive me, gentlemen," Kate said, standing up. "It's been a real pleasure meeting you, Evan, but I think I've had too much excitement for one night. If you don't mind, I'm going to leave you two and head back to my room."

Both men got to their feet.

"I should go as well," Nick said. "You've been a wonderful host, Evan. But we're leaving in the morning and I want a chance to enjoy the view from our terrace pool."

"You're going to love it," Trace said. "I hope we'll see you both at Côte d'Argent again soon."

Nick smiled. "You can bet on it."

6

"**Y**ou're not going to like what I have to tell you," Goodwell said to Trace when they were alone. "We got some good shots of Sweet and Porter on the security cameras in the high-roller room and ran them through the biometric facial recognition system. We came up with nothing. If they've gambled before, it hasn't been in Las Vegas."

"What about their fingerprints?"

"We lifted perfect prints off their cocktail glasses and I had my contact at the Las Vegas Police Department run them through AFIS. Nothing came up. Sweet has an American passport and lives in New York in a Park Avenue apartment owned by an offshore shell company that exists in name only. They produce no products or offer any services, at least as far as we can tell at the moment."

So Nick Sweet probably made his money illegally. That much Trace knew before Goodwell's report, and it didn't bother him. What did bother him was that it was hard to exploit a man's weaknesses and desires without knowing what they were. Trace believed the key to successfully recruiting high rollers was to get them to see that exploitation as exceptionally attentive customer service.

"What about Kate Porter?"

"She's also a U.S. citizen. Sweet's shell company owns her home in Park Slope. She graduated with an MBA from Stanford and worked for a couple of major accounting firms before he hired her. The details on her are suspiciously thin, too. They clearly don't want anybody to know who they are or what they are doing, and they have the resources to make that happen. That concerns me."

"I don't see why. It means they have plenty of money to spend. Comp his suite and give him your card. I want to be sure he does all of his future gambling with us."

Trace didn't care where Nick's money came from as long as he continued losing it at Côte d'Argent. If that laissez-faire attitude turned out to be a mistake, and Nick ever became a serious problem, it would be Thanksgiving Day for the piranha.

Nick and Kate walked across the casino and stopped just short of their elevator.

"You could have stayed with Trace," Kate said. "I left because I got a text message and thought it might be important."

"Alone time with Trace isn't high on my list of preferred activities," Nick said. "That guy is scary."

"The piranha got to you?"

"The way he thinks got to me. He's a con man and a sociopath. Did you see the hostess take our glasses when we left the blackjack table? She wore gloves and held the glasses by the rim. I don't think she was worried about catching Ebola. She didn't want to smudge our fingerprints."

"Don't worry, Jessup has our back. The prints won't bring up your shameful criminal record or my triumphant accomplishments in law enforcement."

"And the text message?" Nick asked.

"It's from my dad," Kate said. *"SOS Bludd's Money."*

"Any idea what it means?"

"None, but I'm a little freaked by it. I've never received an SOS from him before. I just texted him back but it's not getting delivered."

"Try calling."

Kate tapped in Jake's name on her speed dial. No answer.

She tried Jake's friend in Hawaii, Harlan Appleton.

"Appleton residence. Lieutenant Gregg Steadman, Kahuku Police Department, speaking."

Kate felt a twinge of panic. A cop was in Harlan's home, answering the phone. That probably meant the home was a crime scene. More bad news.

"This is FBI Special Agent Kate O'Hare," Kate said. "A couple days ago, my father flew out to visit Harlan. They're old Army buddies. Now I'm having trouble contacting my father."

"Do you know if he arrived before or after the explosion?"

"Explosion?"

"Harlan's food truck blew up while it was parked at the old sugar mill. He's in the Kahuku Medical Center, recovering from the injuries. Nothing serious. He's got some broken bones, and he's a little burned around the edges."

"What are you doing in his house?"

"A few hours ago someone shot the place up with a machine gun. The windows are shattered, and they must have pumped a thousand rounds into the walls. Doesn't look like anyone was in the house when it happened."

Kate thanked the lieutenant, ended the call, and took a beat to compose herself. Her military and FBI training told her to stay calm, to think logically. But this was her father, and she was having difficulty breathing.

Nick watched Kate struggle with emotion. He wrapped his arms around her and held her close against him, waiting patiently while she gained control.

"Are you okay?" he asked.

She nodded. "Yeah, I had a moment, but I'm fine now." She stepped away. "Cash in our chips, and I'll send the bellman up for our bags. We're leaving now."

"Where are we going?"

"I'm going to Hawaii," Kate said. "You're going to have to

stay behind. We can't be seen there together. I've already identified myself to the police as an FBI agent, and I may need the resources of the local field office to help find my dad."

"No way am I staying behind. He's your father and my friend. We're all family. Besides, how many regimes has he helped overthrow in his career? He might be plotting a revolution. Hawaii could declare its independence if we don't do something."

The private jet carrying Nick and Kate landed at Van Nuys Airport at midnight. Nick was met by a chauffeured Rolls-Royce and motored away into the darkness for parts unknown. Kate drove to her apartment in Tarzana, packed a bag, booked a seat on an 8 A.M. flight out of LAX to Honolulu, and stole a few hours of sleep. At 6 A.M. she called Jessup on her way to the airport. "I need to take a couple personal days. I'm having trouble contacting my father in Hawaii. I'm worried something is wrong."

"I'll alert the TSA you're traveling and notify our field office in Honolulu. If there is anything else I can do, just let me know. All I ask is that you please take care of yourself, limit the property damage, and try to avoid killing anyone."

"I'll do my best," Kate said.

Her plane landed in Honolulu a little before noon. Kate rented a Jeep Wrangler and headed for the North Shore, following the directions to the Kahuku police station on her phone's map app.

The freeway snaked up through the mountains, lush with palms and pines, then descended on the other side, passing through vast pineapple fields that led to the sleepy beach town of Haleiwa, the heart of the North Shore.

Haleiwa had a pleasant laid-back, hippie vibe. Oceanfront homes ran along the coastline, buffered from the two-lane highway by groves of banyan trees. There were a few parking lots for public access to the sand and the rocky shoreline. The beaches were stunning, and the waves were huge. On the south side of the highway there were some bungalows, an occasional small restaurant or shop, and beyond that, the thick forest leading back up to the jagged green mountain range.

Kate continued to follow the Kamehameha Highway for a few more miles, and finally came to an old sugar mill. The blackened wreckage of what must have been some sort of vehicle was parked in the lot. She assumed this was Harlan's food truck.

The Kahuku police station was just up the road from the sugar mill—so close that the cops could have arrived at the crime scene faster on foot than in their cars. It was a significant fact to Kate. If the explosion *wasn't* an accident, someone had either big cojones or the cops in his pocket. Neither prospect thrilled her.

Kate parked beside the lone police car, got out, and walked into the station. She flashed her FBI badge to the desk clerk, a bored Hawaiian woman doing paperwork, and asked to see Lieutenant Gregg Steadman. The clerk nodded in the direction of the door behind her. Kate walked through the door into a cramped squad room that looked like a storage unit for surplus office furniture, old files, and obsolete computer equipment. Sitting in the middle of it all, behind a gray metal desk, was a slim, slightly rumpled guy in his thirties.

"Lieutenant Steadman? I'm Special Agent Kate O'Hare." She offered him her hand.

He stood up, shook her hand, and cleared some files off the seat beside his desk. "It's Gregg, and you don't need to play the FBI card. I'm going to help you all I can, and since you're in law enforcement, I'm going to be more candid with you than I would be with a civilian."

"I appreciate that. All I'm interested in is finding my dad and making sure he's safe."

"I don't know where he is, but I doubt he's safe. Harlan Appleton operates a food truck in the old sugar mill parking lot. He makes some tasty barbecue and gets a long line at lunchtime. This doesn't please the locals running the shrimp trucks. I don't have proof, but I suspect Harlan's food truck was blown up because he refused to pay protection money to Lono Alika's gang. Now Harlan's in the hospital, and the next thing I know I'm getting a call that Lono's chromed Ford F-150, the Hawaiian Bentley, has also been blown sky-high. Lono loved that truck. Might be why Lono's gang shot up Harlan's place. If your dad was staying there it's a miracle he got away. They pretty much demolished the house with gunfire."

"So why aren't you sweating Lono and searching for my father?"

"Both Harlan and Lono say their trucks exploded by

accident. Harlan isn't filing charges over the damage to his house, and there's no evidence your father is doing anything but enjoying his vacation."

"You know that's not true," she said.

"Look, Lono Alika owns the North Shore. He's not just running a protection racket. He's the Yakuza's major drug distributor on Oahu and one of the biggest meth producers in Hawaii. I'm sure you're familiar with Yakuza."

"They're members of a Japanese transnational organized crime syndicate. I know of them, but I haven't had any personal contact."

"I've been trying to make a case against Alika for years," Steadman said, "but even the locals are terrified of him. Some of the cops, too. You don't blow up that man's truck unless you have a death wish. Not only will he kill you but he'll do it in the most agonizing, horrible way."

Kate was pretty sure she knew who blew up Alika's truck. It was justice, Jake-style. Jake was fiercely loyal to his friends and had taken on brutal dictators, revolutionary generals, and international terrorists in his career. He wouldn't let some island mobster intimidate him.

"Does the name 'Bludd' mean anything to you? Or 'Bludd's Money'?"

He shook his head. "No. Why?"

"It was a message my dad sent me before he disappeared. I can't figure it out." Kate stood. "Thanks for filling me in. I appreciate you taking the time."

7

Harlan Appleton lived at the end of a dirt road in a one-story eight-hundred-square-foot home that backed up against the dense forest. His home was a typical Hawaiian camp house, built in the early 1900s for the sugar mill workers. It had a tin roof, a long porch, double-hung windows, and thin walls made only of tongue-and-groove redwood planks. The bullets had destroyed all of the windows and punched holes through the wooden walls. Harlan's bullet-riddled Jeep was slumped in the mud like a dead animal, the tires shredded by gunfire.

Kate drove up to find Harlan standing outside in a tank top, baggy shorts, and a single flip-flop. His other foot was encased in a hard cast that ended just above his knee. His broken arm was in a sling and his other arm was resting around a woman's shoulders. She was in her early forties, wore nursing scrubs, and had an arm around Harlan's waist, more to provide comfort than physical support.

Harlan turned as Kate got out of her Jeep. It took him a second to recognize her, but when he did, he broke into a smile.

"My God, Kate, is that you?" With his good arm, he pulled Kate into a hug. "You've grown so much."

"So have you," Kate said, giving his gut a playful pat.

"That's old age, good living, and plenty of BBQ," Harlan said. "This is my friend Cassie Walner, a nurse at the hospital. This is Kate, Jake's kid. I haven't seen her since I taught her how to throw grenades."

"How old were you then?" Cassie asked Kate.

"Twelve," Kate said.

"*Twelve?*" Cassie said.

"Yeah, she was a good four years past the age when every girl should know her way around a live grenade," Harlan said. "But I remedied that. I didn't let Jake forget it, either." Harlan's smile and good cheer faded. "She's an FBI agent now. I'm guessing you've come to find your dad. Am I right?"

Kate nodded grimly and gestured to the house. "I heard about the friends you've made on the island."

"Yeah, I knew Lono Alika was the Hawaiian Godfather, but I didn't think he was stupid enough to mess with me."

"Would you have paid Alika the protection money if you'd known?" Kate asked.

"No, but I wouldn't have let Jake get caught up in my troubles. I'm real sorry about that, Kate."

"Don't be," she said. "He's the one who blew up that truck, isn't he? He probably had a lot of fun."

Harlan nodded. "I know he's out there in the brush somewhere, and I've been trying to figure out how I can help him, but I'm not real mobile, what with the broken foot and fractured leg bone."

"You can help by keeping a low profile right now, and let me work at finding him. Does 'Bludd's Money' mean anything to either one of you?"

They both shook their heads.

"Are you missing anything from the house?" Kate asked.

"No," Harlan said. "But I did notice that the first-aid kit, shovel, and tire iron are missing from the back of my Jeep."

Kate looked at the lush tropical forest and the mountains of the Koolau Range beyond. This might be Alika's island, but her father would have the advantage in the wild. He was trained in jungle warfare and loved a good booby trap.

Even with all that, Kate knew that eventually Jake would get caught if she didn't rescue him first. She was sure that he knew it, too. That was why he'd sent her the SOS text.

"Harlan," Kate said. "I could use a little firepower."

"Good news. My gun safe is still picture-perfect."

Ten minutes later, Kate got back into her Jeep with a Remington 870 twelve-gauge short-barreled shotgun, sixty rounds of 00 buckshot for killing, twenty rounds of number 6 for close-up defense, and twenty rounds of rifled slugs. Jungle fighting was close-quarters combat, and at that range, a shotgun blast beat a rifle or handgun any day. She hoped she wouldn't have to use any of it.

Kate's phone rang, with the caller ID "Nick McGarrett."

"I'm guessing you're here on Oahu," Kate said, answering her phone.

"I am and I've got good news," Nick said. "I know where Jake is hiding out. Meet me in the ruins of the Waialee reform school. It's between Haleiwa and Kahuku on the south side of the Kamehameha Highway."

Vines wrapped around the concrete ruins of the former Waialee Industrial School for Boys, dragging the building into the moist, green darkness of the forest as if the trees wanted to eat it. The roof had caved in long ago, and now the rotted, splintered remains lay across a smashed grand piano, mattress springs, and dozens of empty beer bottles.

Nick stood by the piano and was wearing sunglasses, a floral Hilo Hattie aloha shirt, Faded Glory cargo shorts, white tennis shoes, and a large straw hat. There was an Oahu guidebook sticking out of one of his cargo pockets and an Oahu map in another. He was just another mainland tourist, identical to thousands of others crawling all over the island. No one would ever notice him.

Kate made her way toward him. "You picked a lovely place to meet."

"It was close to you and no one is likely to spot us here," he said. "Besides, I'm a sucker for creepy, abandoned buildings. Any news on your dad?"

"The local mob, run by a guy named Lono Alika, blew up a food truck owned by Dad's friend Harlan to convince him to pay for protection. So Dad blew up Alika's truck for not being very nice to his friend. Then Alika came gunning for Dad, who escaped into the forest."

"Sounds like Jake." Nick pulled the map out of his pocket and spread it open on the piano. It was labeled *Oahu Movie & TV Locations*. "I found out about *Bludd's Money*. It was a cheesy, direct-to-video action movie. The big finale was shot in the forest here, doubling for Vietnam. Turns out hundreds of movies and TV shows have been shot here and have left bits of their sets behind. They're like ancient ruins for film buffs, who've erected signs identifying them. *Bludd* left the fake fuselage of a downed aircraft up there. I think that's where Jake was when he sent you that text."

"How did you figure it out?"

"I Googled *Bludd's Money*, saw that it was a movie, and watched it on Netflix on my flight out here. When I landed, I bought this locations map."

"You should have been a detective instead of a crook."

"It's not as much fun or as lucrative."

Kate folded up the map and stuck it in her own pocket. "I've got to go. I need to reach him before nightfall."

"If you don't come out of that forest within twenty-four hours, I'm coming to get you."

Kate squelched a grimace. It was nice to know he cared enough to risk his own safety, but it was frightening to think of Nick bumbling through the forest. Especially since her dad probably had it booby-trapped.

Virgil Cleet ran a helicopter tour business out of Honolulu, about an hour's drive from Waialee. And Virgil owed Kate a favor from back in the day when they were both Special Forces. So Virgil was happy to give Kate a lift to the *Bludd's Money* location, which was deep in the forest along the slopes of the Koolau Range.

Before hooking up with Virgil, Kate had stopped at an Army surplus store in downtown Honolulu and bought insect repellant, a dozen protein bars, a slim-profile backpack, cowhide-leather rappelling gloves, night vision goggles, a compass, two canteens, a combat knife, a rifle lanyard, four tubes of camouflage face paint, and 120 feet of 44 mm–thick braided polyester fast rope with an aircraft connection ring on one end.

"What are you planning on doing with all of this?" the clerk asked, packing everything in a box for her.

"Survive the zombie apocalypse."

The clerk smiled and nodded as if they shared a secret understanding.

Kate took the box to her Jeep, and stuffed everything but the rope, the knife, and the gloves into the daypack, and then drove around until she found a gas station.

She locked herself inside the gas station restroom with the duffel bag that she'd brought from L.A., sprayed her entire body with the insect repellant, and then put on a long-sleeved brown T-shirt, camouflage cargo pants, and low-quarter hiking shoes. She holstered her Glock on her hip, put the gloves and the knife in her pockets, and got back in her Jeep.

The heliport was on the west bank of the Ke'ehi Lagoon, just south of the Honolulu International Airport. Kate walked in wearing the backpack with the shotgun over her shoulder and carrying seventy-five pounds of coiled fast rope in her hands.

She was met at the door by Virgil, an African American in his forties who was tall enough to play professional basketball and muscular enough to be a linebacker. His hair was cut so short it looked like a shadow on his head.

Virgil gave her a quick once-over. "Looks like you're ready to party. Do you need help?"

"Thanks," she said. "But I can handle this on my own."

"I'll give you a radio. If you change your mind, all you have to do is call and I'll be there, guns blazing." He took the coil of rope from her. "When do you want to go?"

"Now. I'm racing the sun."

Virgil nodded and led her out to the helipad, where a retired MH-6 Little Bird light utility military gunship was waiting, minus the guns. "This isn't what I use for the tourists. It's my personal ride."

Kate loved it. It was the helicopter equivalent of a Crown Vic.

Kate climbed in, and Virgil powered up the chopper. A few minutes later, they were in the air over Honolulu and heading toward the North Shore. Kate applied green, brown, and black camouflage paint to her face and neck in diagonal streaks. This was the only kind of makeup she really knew how to use and was truly comfortable wearing.

The Koolau mountains were steep, craggy, and lush, with dense jungle along the slopes. There was no place to land close to the remains of the *Bludd's Money* set. She'd have to drop in by rope.

Kate couldn't see Alika's men in the jungle, but she did see their off-road vehicles strategically parked in clearings and trailheads to the north, east, and south of the area where the fake *Bludd's Money* airplane fuselage was located. It was clear to her they were trying to corner Jake against the steep ridge to the west.

"We're in position," Virgil said. "If there's anybody down there they're gonna be watching you drop."

"I'll be in the treetops before they have a chance to pick me off."

The chopper was hovering a hundred feet over the canopy of trees. Kate put on her gloves, tightened the straps of her back-pack and the lanyard of her shotgun, attached one end of the fast rope to the fixed connection ring, and dropped the other end out the open cabin door of the chopper. The heavy rope ran straight down into the forest of tall bamboo, huge palms, wild guava, banyan trees, and Norfolk pines.

She strung the rope behind her back and around one leg, putting her right hand on the rope above her head and her left hand on the rope below her waist.

"Ready," Kate said.

"Good luck," Virgil said.

Kate jumped out of the helicopter and slid rapidly down the rope, through the thick layer of leaves and branches to the muddy ground below. It took her less than thirty seconds, and gave her an adrenaline rush.

She let go of the rope and immediately crouched down low, listening and waiting. The chopper rose, the rope dangling beneath it, and veered away toward the mountains.

Kate checked her compass and her GPS app to confirm her position. She was roughly fifty yards southwest of the abandoned *Bludd's Money* set. There was a trail, but rather than take it, Kate moved slowly on a parallel course through the brush, keeping her eyes open for trip wires and anything that didn't seem to fit the natural pattern of forest floor. She didn't want to get nailed by one of her father's booby traps.

She moved slowly until she reached a school-bus-sized section of a passenger jet cabin. It was completely wrapped with vines, and a plastic sign was nailed to the fuselage and engraved with the words *"Bludd's Money* 2009."

There was movement in the trees. Kate dropped flat in the mud amid a thick patch of philodendrons. Three Hawaiians emerged from another trail. Two of the men were large enough to be sumo wrestlers and carried machetes casually at their sides. One was wearing flip-flops, the other neon-bright yellow Nikes. The third man had the lean build and stoned demeanor of a surfer. He held an M16 rifle tightly in both of his hands.

The guy in flip-flops squinted at the sign and read it aloud, sounding the words out phonetically, then turned to the two other men. "You ever see this movie, brah?"

"Three times." The surfer pointed his M16 into the fuselage and peered inside for any signs of life. "It could only have been better if Steven Seagal was in it. Steven Seagal is a badass. He's like Alika only he's not fat."

The guy in the Nikes gave a bark of laughter. "I'm telling Alika you said he was fat."

They moved on with Flip-Flops at point, flanked by his two buddies. He'd gone only a couple steps when his right foot plunged into a hole that had been hidden under a blanket of leaves. He pitched over with a shriek of pain, his trapped ankle breaking with a snap.

Small punji-stake pit, Kate thought. One of Dad's favorite booby traps.

Neon Nikes quickly moved away from the trail, breaking a trip wire at his ankles. He instinctively looked down at his feet to see what he'd walked into, heard something move in the jungle, and then straightened up to see whatever was coming at him. It was a coconut tied to a vine like a tetherball. The coconut slammed into his shoulder with bone-breaking force and knocked Neon Nikes to the ground.

The surfer raised his M16, let out a furious banshee roar, and sprayed the dense foliage ahead of him with bullets until he'd emptied his clip. He was reaching into his pocket for a fresh clip when a long branch whipped out of nowhere and swatted him out of his sandals.

Jake sprang out of the mud beside the trail and snatched the fallen M16 and ammo clip, jammed the clip into the rifle, and aimed it at the three men on the ground.

"You have thirty seconds to get out of here," Jake said. "Or I start shooting."

The surfer and Neon Nikes each took Flip-Flops by an arm, and the three Hawaiians staggered away. Once they were out of sight, Jake lowered the M16 and grinned at Kate, who was still lying flat amid the philodendrons.

"What did you think of that?" he asked.

Kate stood up and smiled at her father. "You're having way too much fun, Dad."

"That's what vacations are for."

"Why did you send me such a cryptic message?"

"I didn't mean to. My battery was near death, and there was barely a signal here. I figured I had just enough juice for two or three words. I was right. As soon as I hit send, the phone died. To tell you the truth, I was sure the message didn't go out, so it was a nice surprise when you showed up."

"Why did you go off into the jungle?"

"Alika didn't see the ironic justice of *an eye for an eye,* or in this case *a truck for a truck.* The F-150 was still smoking when he sent his goons out to get me."

"How did he know it was you?"

"We'd had a chitchat prior to the explosion."

"Nice."

"Turns out he has anger issues," Jake said. "Hidden inside all that tattooed fat is an insecure, angry man."

Kate did a grimace. "You could have gone to the police."

"I didn't know if I could trust the police. I knew I could trust the jungle. Problem was I had no exit strategy. Alika has too much of the island covered. So what's *your* exit strategy?"

"We wait until sunrise, hike to a clearing about five miles southeast of here, and then I'll call in a chopper for an extraction."

"It's weak on shock and awe, but it sounds like a fine plan to me." He put his arm around her and sighed with contentment. "I don't know how people can come here and surf when they could be doing this."

Kate grinned. "Neither do I."

8

Nick Fox blew into the office of the Hawaii Film Commission just as Allan Mingus, the only employee still on duty, was about to lock up and call it a day. Nick was in mid-conversation on his cellphone and held up a finger to Mingus, instructing him to wait.

"Tom Cruise is too short and too old. This is a movie about a young, virile action hero." Nick spoke rapidly in a foreign accent of his own creation that he hoped could pass for Swedish, not that many people would know a Swedish accent if they heard one. He'd colored his hair blond and wore sunglasses, a soul patch under his lip, and a pair of phony diamond studs in his ears. "Get me a Hemsworth. Chris, Liam, Luke, Mario, or Zippy. I don't care which one. Nobody can tell them apart anyway."

Nick ended his call and faced Mingus, a stout man in his fifties in the obligatory aloha shirt. They stood in the center of the office, which looked like a small travel agency. The walls were decorated with posters of tropical Hawaiian beaches and movies like *From Here to Eternity* and *Raiders of the Lost Ark* that were shot on the islands.

"Show me what you've got," Nick said.

"I'm sorry, but I was just closing for the day," Mingus said.

"Not anymore. I'm looking for Vietnam, South America, and Florida in one place and I need it quick."

"Who are you?"

"I am Krister Blomkvistbjurman-Malm, of course. Don't you recognize me? Writer, director, and cinematographer of *Sherm de Sherm den Hurf.*"

"I am not familiar with that movie."

"It won the Oscar for best foreign picture," Nick said. "How can you call yourself a film office when you know *nothing* about film?"

"Oh, yes, now I remember it," Mingus said, his cheeks flushing with embarrassment. "Great movie. I just forgot the original Russian title."

"It's Swedish."

"Right," Mingus said, his flush deepening. "I'm afraid you'll have to come back tomorrow."

"That's too late. Tomorrow night I go to Australia to see what they have to offer. So tonight you'll show me photos and tomorrow you'll take me on a helicopter and ground tour of the locations I've selected or you're out of the running."

"That's not the way it goes," Mingus said. "We need more advance notice and a lot more details before we go scouting. For one thing, we have to see a script—"

Nick interrupted him. "Nobody sees a script. It's the latest installment in a major billion-dollar movie franchise. Anyone who wants to read the screenplay must come to the studio, surrender their cellphones, and lock themselves in my office."

"Okay, but before we can get started, we need some basic information," Mingus said. "We need to know the production company and studio, where the financing is coming from, whether the project is union or nonunion, whether—"

Nick interrupted him. "Say that again."

"What?"

"What you said before, only this time with coiled rage and greater authority." Nick pointed at him and said, "Go!"

Mingus stared at him for a moment, not sure what to make of the request, so he just soldiered on. "What I'm saying is that I need to make sure that you and your movie are legit. Anybody can just walk in here and claim—"

"Wonderful," Nick said, cutting him off again. "I believed it. Where did you get your training as an actor?"

"I don't have any, but before I got this job, I did some small parts. I was one of the airline passengers in the *Lost* pilot. I didn't have any lines, but I was in the background of every scene."

"Those roles are crucial. They are even harder than speaking parts."

"They are?"

"Of course. They give a film its inherent reality. You have that and natural gravitas, too."

"I do?"

"Inherent reality and natural gravitas are just what I am looking for in the actor who plays Indy's boss."

"Did you say 'Indy'?" Mingus's gaze flicked to the *Raiders of the Lost Ark* poster on the wall. "As in 'Indiana Jones'?"

Nick winced, as if realizing he'd let something slip. "No, I most emphatically did not. Forget I said that. All you need to know is that it's a key speaking part, and I need to cast a local rather than fly someone in. You'd be doing me a big favor if you'd take the role. It's a two-day job, tops. Would you do it for me?"

"I'd be glad to," Mingus said, breaking out in a huge grin.

"Then it's done, assuming we shoot here, of course," Nick said. "What can you show me tomorrow?"

"We have some spectacular locations, among the best on earth," Mingus said. "Let me go grab the binders."

Kate and Jake awoke at dawn and worked their way slowly to the southeast, keeping low and staying off the trails. It took them three hours to slog through the heavy vegetation and reach their destination, which was marked by a pair of iron gates under a massive stone arch with the words "Cretaceous Zoo" carved across the top.

Jake knocked on the arch. It was a molded fiberglass veneer nailed to plywood. "What is this place?"

"The old set for a movie about a zoo filled with genetically re-created dinosaurs and cavemen. The dinosaurs escape and eat all of the guests," Kate said. "The cavemen team up with a retired New York cop, a busty medical student, and a novelist to battle the monsters."

"You saw it?"

"I think it's probably the best work Gunter Jorgenson has ever done. In the finale the survivors fight their way through hordes of raptors to get to the brontosaurus paddock. That's the field where the helicopters landed to get the heroes off the island before the nukes were dropped. If it worked for them, it could work for us."

Kate took the lead, her shotgun at the ready, and sprinted under the arch, then hugged the tree line along the trail that led inside. Jake followed, wielding the M16 he'd acquired the day before. They moved from tree to tree, one person at a time, covering each other as they went.

The *Cretaceous Zoo* Welcome Center loomed at the end of the trail in front of them. It was a two-story Polynesian-style building with a domed glass atrium. The plants in the atrium had grown and broken through the glass. There were several Jeeps that had been crushed by rampaging dinosaurs scattered around the Welcome Center.

Kate and Jake used the Jeeps as cover, going from one to another, as they approached the Welcome Center and then worked their way behind the building, sticking close to the walls. They peeked around the edge of the building to see what lay beyond it.

They faced the zoo itself. To their left was the caveman habitat, a neighborhood of stone-and-log cabins covered in layers of graffiti and arranged in a half circle facing a statue of two raging T. rexes tearing apart a struggling pterodactyl. To their right was a fake hillside, riddled with caves and overgrown with plants. At the far end, directly across from the Welcome Center, was another arch that lead to the next section of the zoo.

"The brontosaurus corral and the clearing are on the other side of that arch," Kate said.

"We'll be out in the open between here and those T. rex statues," Jake said. "Then in the open again to the clearing."

"You go first and I'll cover you." Kate drew her Glock and held it out to Jake. "But I'll need your M16 to do the job right."

They swapped weapons. She gave him her extra clips for the Glock and he stuck them in his pocket. She removed the shotgun from over her shoulder, and moved into position with the M16. She pressed her cheek against the stock, looked down the weld line through the sight, and targeted the statues. She put her finger on the trigger.

"Ready," Kate said.

"That's my girl," he said.

Jake held the Glock at his side and dashed out into the open, zigzagging as he went. He was halfway to the fighting dinosaurs when gunfire rang out and bullets cut divots into the dirt around him. Two shooters with M16s were firing down at him from the hillside caves.

Kate opened fire on the hill, driving the startled shooters back into their caves. She pivoted and sprayed the caveman cabins, too, pinning down two other shooters who were about to let loose a barrage of their own. Her suppression fire gave Jake the crucial seconds he needed to dive for cover amid the legs of the fighting T. rexes. Kate had caught them by surprise, but it wore off quickly.

The instant Jake landed, bullets chipped away at the dinosaurs' legs from both the cabins and the caves, showering him with bits of wood and plaster. Alika's men also let loose on Kate. She ducked back as bullets slammed into the wall beside her.

There were at least two men in the cabins and two in the hillside caves, all armed with M16s. Jake was pinned down. He had a Glock and very little cover. Kate's clip was empty, which left her with the twelve-gauge short-barreled shotgun, a perfect weapon for close-quarters fighting but lousy for situations like this. She'd have to get much closer to her enemy for the shotgun to be effective. The question was whether Jake could hold out long enough for Kate to sneak up on the cabins and start taking the shooters out, one by one.

Her other option was to call Virgil on the radio. Tell him to come in the chopper right away, and bring all the firepower he could muster.

Kate was about to make a decision when she heard the unmistakable sound of a helicopter approaching. She looked up apprehensively, and a white helicopter flew in low over the Welcome Center. As it passed, she could clearly see the Hawaii state seal on the side of the aircraft.

9

"This is where they shot *Cretaceous Zoo*," Alan Mingus told Nick as they flew over the statues of the two battling T. rexes in the center of the park. "Those are caveman houses. You can remodel the buildings or tear them all down. It makes no difference to us."

Nick had a director's viewfinder hanging on a lanyard around his neck. He used it to peer out the window at the set below, and glimpsed what he thought was someone hunkered down among the fighting dinosaurs. He couldn't be sure, and even if it was someone, it didn't mean it was Kate or her father.

"I wish you'd tear the sets down," said Larry Kealoha, the uniformed park ranger who sat across from them. "People love to party up here. Over the years, we've probably had to rescue a dozen drunken fools who've fallen into the raptor pit and broken their legs."

"I would never use another director's sets," Nick said. "The vision of this film must be completely my own. I would be morally and artistically bankrupt to do otherwise. It would be like asking the women in my films to shave their underarm hair."

"Is that a thing in Swedish films?" Kealoha asked.

"It is in mine," Nick said.

The pilot landed the chopper in the center of a field with enormous cages on one end and bleachers on another.

"What was this?" Nick asked.

"The brontosaurus corral," Mingus said. "In the movie, the dinosaurs were in those big cages, and their trainers rode them around this field like horses, doing tricks, while the audience watched from the bleachers."

Nick hopped out, dashed a few yards away from the helicopter, then held the viewfinder up to his eye with one hand and scanned the statues. He could definitely see someone standing with his back against the leg of a T. rex. The man turned to look at Nick. It was Jake, covered in mud and holding a gun. Nick panned the viewfinder up over to the cabins and saw a Hawaiian peek out of a doorway holding an M16. Nick figured Kate was here somewhere, either taking cover herself or moving in for the kill.

Mingus and Kealoha came up beside Nick.

"What do you think of the location?" Mingus asked.

Nick dropped the viewfinder, letting it fall against his chest. "Very nice. Lots of possibilities here. Let's take a closer look."

He tramped purposefully toward the statues, followed by Mingus and Kealoha.

Kate didn't know who the three men were, but they'd arrived in a government helicopter and she doubted Alika's men would dare open fire in front of state officials. The blowback for Alika from the authorities would be too severe. Kate was willing to stake her life on that assumption.

She slung the shotgun over her shoulder by its strap, stepped out from behind the wall into the open, and strode casually toward her father. Jake saw her coming and peeked out from behind one of the T. rex legs to sneak a look at the caves. The gunmen were hiding in the dark recesses of the caves and cabins, wrestling with the decision of whether or not to shoot.

Kate reached her dad just as the three men from the chopper were crossing under the arch from the brontosaurus paddock. That's when she realized that the blond one with the ridiculous soul patch was Nick.

Mingus and Kealoha were surprised to see the couple who'd walked out of the zoo to meet them. The old man was shirtless, covered in mud, and holding a gun at his side. The younger woman's face was painted in streaks like some sort of jungle savage, and she had a shotgun slung over her shoulder.

"My God," Mingus said to Kealoha. "Who are those people?"

"Crazy tourists," Kealoha said. "Maybe a couple of survivalists. We get all kinds out here."

"Sven!" Nick said. "Gita!"

Mingus looked at Nick in astonishment. "You *know* these people?"

"They are two of my actors. They have lived in the jungle for days, immersing themselves in the roles that they will play," Nick said, loud enough for Jake and Kate to hear as they approached. "This is the commitment you must have to be in my movies."

"You didn't mention anything to me about having actors in the jungle," Mingus said.

"We *became* the jungle," Kate corrected him in an accent as unrecognizable as Nick's.

"I'm certain that it will add enormous depth to your roles," Nick said, then turned back to Mingus. "Sven and Gita are huge stars in Sweden, and their total dedication is the reason they are so popular. You could learn something from them. I want you to become the jungle, too."

The color drained from Mingus's face. "Is that really necessary?"

"It is if you want to achieve greatness as an actor. Think about it, because I love this location. This is where I'll make my movie."

"Excellent," Mingus said, his enthusiasm tempered by the terrifying prospect of having to become the jungle himself.

Nick faced Kate and Jake. "You two must come back to Honolulu with me and tell me all about your experiences."

He put one arm around Jake and another around Kate, and led them back toward the chopper. Mingus and Kealoha lagged behind so they could confer in private.

"Out of curiosity," Nick whispered. "How many shooters are there?"

"At least four," Jake said. "With M16s."

"Poor guys," Nick said. "They never stood a chance."

Nick took Kate and Jake back to his two-bedroom suite at the historic Royal Hawaiian Hotel, on Waikiki Beach, so they could shower and change into clean clothes.

Jake was happy to see a white polo shirt, khaki slacks, and a pair of leather loafers, all in his size, laid out on the bed. He was *ecstatic* to find the correct Dr. Scholl's inserts in the shoes, because his feet were killing him.

A luncheon buffet of fresh fruit, kalua pork, and an assortment of desserts that included lilikoi cheesecake and haupia cream pie was laid out on the dining table. The doors to the lanai were open, letting in a gentle breeze and offering a spectacular panoramic view of Diamond Head, Waikiki Beach, and the shimmering Pacific.

"Feeling better?" Nick asked Jake.

"I was feeling great before." Jake took a plate and nodded in approval. "But this isn't bad."

"We'll have lunch, relax on the lanai for a bit, and then you and I will head back to Los Angeles by private jet. Kate will settle up with the local authorities and take a commercial flight home."

"I'm not going anywhere until I take down Lono Alika," Jake said. "He destroyed Harlan's food truck and shot up his house. I can't let him get away with that."

"I met a local cop who I think is a good man," Kate said. "I'll have a talk with him and the agents in the FBI field office. They'll make sure Alika knows that it would be a big mistake to give Harlan any trouble."

Jake shook his head. "That's not good enough."

"I think it's possible that we can take down Alika and Evan Trace at the same time," Nick said. "Since we left Vegas, I've been noodling with an idea for a con to destroy Trace's money laundering operation, but it wasn't coming together. It was missing the key piece, the fulcrum, you might say."

"Fulcrum," Jake said. "Like a seesaw?"

"Like a tipping point," Nick said. "We're going to insinuate ourselves into the money laundering operation at Trace's casino in Macau by becoming junket operators."

"I have no idea what that means," Kate said.

"Most of the major money laundering in Macau is done through junket operators. They are middlemen who bring high rollers to the casinos to gamble in private VIP rooms. The gamblers book their travel, rent their hotel rooms, and buy their chips through the junket operators, who are actually the ones on the hook with the casino for everything."

"So, technically, the players aren't actually gambling in Macau with their own money," Kate said. "They are playing with the junket's money."

"That's how the money gets laundered," Nick said. "The cash the players use to buy their 'vacations' in Macau is dirty. But the money they get when they cash in their chips is clean."

"How do the junkets make money on the deal?" Jake asked.

"By imposing a surcharge on all of their services and by requiring the gamblers to wager a certain amount of money over the course of their VIP play. The junket takes forty percent of whatever the house brings in at the tables. The casino takes the other sixty percent."

"That's crazy," Jake said. "Why doesn't the casino get· rid of the middleman and deal directly with the high rollers themselves?"

"Risk avoidance. A lot of these high rollers come from countries like China, where it's virtually impossible for the casinos to collect on gambling debts. But the casinos can collect from the junket operator, who assumes all of the financial and legal risks," Nick said. "It's the junket operator, not the casino, who has the relationship with the players. If anybody ever asks, the casino can say they don't have any idea who the gamblers are in those VIP rooms or how much money they're winning or losing."

"So how do we take down Trace by running a junket?" Kate asked.

"We're going to bring a Canadian mobster and a Somali

warlord to Trace's casino in Macau to launder their dirty cash," Nick said. "Only the two bad guys will be our friends playing parts, and the money they'll be washing will be ours. We go in, we gamble, we leave."

"Which will establish our credibility as junket operators if anybody asks Côte d'Argent about us," Kate said.

Jake smiled. "Someone like Lono Alika."

"Now you're catching on," Nick said. "We're going to invite Alika on a gambling junket to launder his money with us. We'll go back to Macau with him and our two fake bad guys, wash his cash and ours, and everybody leaves happy."

"You seem to be missing the part where we put the criminals in jail," Kate said. "So far we're just washing our money and making the bad guys richer."

"We're going to have to bait the trap for Alika first," Nick said. "He isn't going to go all in on the laundering scheme the first time around. He'll gamble only a little of what he has and see how it goes. Once he discovers how well the washing machine works, he'll come rushing back to us to launder all of the cash that he's been hoarding. Only this time, I'm going to run away with his money, leaving him broke and Trace holding the bag."

"That's a dangerous play," Jake said. "I like that you're ruining Alika, but he and his Yakuza backers will be in a bloody rage. They'll go after you and Trace."

"I'm counting on it," Nick said. "That's what makes Alika the key element of this con. We need to scare the crap out of Trace.

We want him to absolutely believe that his life is in serious danger."

"It *will* be," Jake said. "The Yakuza take revenge to extremes."

"It won't come to that," Nick said. "Before there is any real threat, Kate is going to reveal herself to Trace as an undercover FBI agent."

"What will my story be?" Kate asked.

"That you've spent two long years infiltrating Nick Sweet's criminal operation to bring him down, but now that he's in the wind, you're screwed and looking for a way to turn a disaster into a win," Nick said. "So you'll offer Trace protection from the Yakuza, the Canadian mob, and the Somali warlords if he agrees to rat out all of the terrorists, despots, and crooks that he's ever helped. Or you could keep him in business as an FBI front and gather invaluable intelligence. Either way, Trace will jump at the offer."

Kate smiled at her dad. "He's good."

"Not as good as you," Jake said. "Because you caught him."

"Hey," Nick said. "Whose side are you on?"

"Kate's," Jake said. "Always."

Nick nodded. "As it should be."

"I think your scam is great," Jake said, "but in the meantime, I'm not convinced that Harlan will be safe from Alika. So there's something I'd like to do before we go."

"I'm not going to let you blow up anything else," Kate said. "Or kill anybody."

"Don't worry," Jake said. "All I have in mind is some friendly persuasion."

Kate raised an eyebrow. "Because that worked so well last time?"

Jake grinned. "I think we're developing a relationship."

Da Grinds & Da Shave Ice was a dive restaurant with a red-dirt parking lot on the Kamehameha Highway near Kahuku. It was a wooden shack with a corrugated metal roof that extended out over a sagging porch and a few picnic tables. Food was served through a takeout window that had a hand-painted, flaking menu board beside it.

The restaurant was owned by Lono Alika, who was often the only patron besides the occasional ignorant tourists who didn't know any better and never would because they were always politely served and not harassed in any way. But the locals saw it for what it was—Alika's front office, a place you didn't go unless you were summoned, which inevitably meant pain and suffering, or if you sought his help, which also inevitably meant pain and suffering. Everyone on the North Shore knew him but few wanted *him* to know *them*.

Alika sat at his picnic table, eating a plate lunch, when Jake took a seat across from the 350-pound, six-foot-tall, bald-headed Hawaiian. The huge man, who always wore a tank top and board shorts to show off the Polynesian tattoos that covered his arms and legs, looked up from his two scoops of white rice, macaroni salad, teriyaki chicken, and short ribs and regarded Jake with a slow, sleepy gaze.

"Eh, watchu want, buggah?" Alika said, speaking in Hawaiian pidgin English, the local dialect.

"I want you to apologize to my friend Harlan Appleton and buy him a new food truck."

"Last time you say dat I have my men chase you into da woods, you old fut."

"And I put three of your men in the hospital."

Alika showed his teeth like a dog, and started to rise from his seat. "I'm gonna give you da dirty lickin's and put you in da ground."

"I wouldn't if I were you." Jake calmly wagged a finger at him in warning. "Do you really think I'd be here without backup? You're in the crosshairs of a sniper right now." Jake pointed his finger at Alika's chest.

Alika looked down and saw a red laser dot over his heart, then looked up into the dense thicket of trees that was alongside the restaurant and that ran up the slope to the mountains beyond. He sat back down, but his face was tomato red with rage.

"How I know dat's not just some fool wit' a laser pointer in da trees?"

"You don't. So go ahead and make your move, though you're so fat and slow, I could probably save my friend a bullet and kill you myself before you cleared the bench."

Alika snorted. "Oh, yeah? How you do dat, old man?"

Jake tipped his head toward Alika's plate lunch. "I'd shove that fork in your neck and watch you choke to death on your own blood."

Jake was relaxed when he spoke, and his general posture conveyed complete confidence in his safety. It clearly unnerved Alika, who swiped his fork off the table.

"Say what you wanna say," Alika said. "Tink hard cuz dey be your last words."

"First off, Harlan had nothing to do with what happened to your pickup truck. I did that on my own. Secondly, my friend doesn't owe you anything. He's already paid his dues on the battlefield so *mokes* like you can enjoy your freedom. So you're going to show him some respect and back off."

"We have dis talk before. If he fool nuff to go back in business, he pays me or he gets real buss'up. Dat's how it is."

"Harlan has a lot of friends on this island from his days in the military," Jake said. "Whatever happens to him, happens to you. That's how it is. That's how it was with your truck."

Alika looked down at the laser targeting dot on his chest then back at Jake. "I wanna show you something. Come wit' me."

"Only if we stay in the open."

"Chillax," Alika said, rising slowly, the dot moving along with him as he walked off the porch to the red-dirt parking lot. "I want you to meet somebody."

Alika stopped and pointed at the ground. Jake looked down and saw a man buried up to his neck in red dirt, his face sunburned and crawling with ants. The man opened one pleading eye for a moment, then quickly closed it again before an ant could crawl in.

"Dis Kimo," Alika said. "His job was to take care of my truck. Now he got a new job. He fertilizer."

Kimo whimpered.

"It wasn't his fault," Jake said. "Dig him out."

"I will, maybe tonight, maybe tomorrow," Alika said. "Point is, I evah see you again, dat brah be you, only you stay buried till the ants get fat an' I see yo' skull."

Jake drove up the highway for fifty yards, and then pulled over to the shoulder to pick up Kate, who was dressed in camo and carried a rifle case. She climbed in and Jake drove off.

"Thanks for covering me," he said.

"Any time."

"I think Alika will lay off Harlan for the time being. But I'm worried about that guy in the dirt."

"Don't be. Alika won't kill the guy now that he's shown him off to you. It's too risky. You could call the cops. But to be on the safe side, I'll ask Steadman to swing by."

"Were you tempted to shoot Alika while you had him in your sights?"

"Hell, yes," she said.

"What stopped you?"

"The rifle wasn't loaded," she said.

10

Nick and Jake left Honolulu later that afternoon. Kate stayed behind and met with the local FBI agent in charge. She asked him to let Alika know that it would be very bad for his business if any further harm came to Harlan Appleton. The agent said he'd be glad to do it. Next she drove to Kahuku and visited Lieutenant Gregg Steadman at the Kahuku police station to make the same request and to inform him that Jake was safely off the island.

Steadman agreed to have a word with Alika, too, and was confident that Harlan wouldn't be harassed any further, at least not until he opened another food truck in the sugar mill parking lot. Kate was counting on Alika being out of the picture by the time Harlan was ready to open for business again.

The next morning Kate caught the first flight to Las Vegas.

She arrived late in the afternoon and took a taxi straight to the Treasure Island casino to see Billy Dee Snipes, a retired Somali pirate. Billy Dee now lived in a condo complex in Summerlin for "active seniors," and liked to spend his afternoons playing the nickel slots. In the past he had occasionally worked with Kate's father on some black-ops missions in the South China Sea. More recently Billy Dee had worked with Kate and Nick on a con in Portugal.

Kate found Billy Dee sitting at a Blazing Sevens slot machine near the buffet, drinking a cocktail with one hand and tapping the "spin" button with the other. He looked like a scarecrow in a blue tracksuit, propped on a stool to keep birds away from the machines.

Although Billy Dee appeared to be mortally ill or suffering from starvation, Kate had been assured by her father that the pirate had always had zero percent body fat.

Kate sat down at the slot machine next to Billy Dee. "I hope you haven't fed that machine all of the money you made from us."

Billy Dee turned and smiled at her. "I believe my savings are safe at my current rate of play."

"How would you feel about switching your game to baccarat for a while?"

"Well, baccarat is all luck and no skill, like slots, and the house edge is small, but they don't let you play baccarat for a nickel a hand. I'd burn through my retirement money way too fast. So, I think I'll stick to this."

In fact, he hadn't stopped playing for a second while he spoke with her. He constantly tapped the spin button as if it were a necessary part of his breathing.

"How would you feel about playing high-stakes baccarat in Macau with our money? We don't care if you win or lose and we'll pay you a hundred thousand dollars to do it."

"What's the catch?" he asked.

"You'd have to travel to Hong Kong from Mogadishu and pretend to be a ruthless Somali pirate."

"I *am* a ruthless Somali pirate," he said.

She gestured to his feet. "You're wearing sneakers with Velcro straps."

"You need comfortable footwear to be ruthless."

"You'll be playing the part of a Somali pirate who is gambling with the millions of dollars that you've made hijacking oil tankers and cargo ships in the Strait of Malacca," Kate said. "But what you'll really be doing is helping us bring down a casino money laundering operation. If it goes wrong, you don't need to worry about getting arrested. You'll need to worry about getting out of Macau alive."

"That used to be the charm of Macau. You *always* had to worry about getting killed. For five hundred years, it was a Portuguese trading port for smugglers, slavers, and pirates. I sold a lot of stolen ships and cargoes there. But then the Portuguese handed Macau over to the Chinese and they turned it into this." Billy Dee waved his hand around to indicate the casino around them. "Treasure Island. The world is becoming too clean and safe. Soon there won't be any place left where hookers, assassins, and thieves roam the streets and will slit your throat for the coins in your pocket."

"Most people don't have a problem with that change."

"Most people aren't ruthless Somali pirates. We like a little danger in our lives, and since I have absolutely none now, I'd be glad to gamble with your money and my life. When do I leave for Mogadishu?"

"In a couple days," she said. "We still have arrangements to make, identities to create, and documents to forge. Speaking of which, I've got to go back to the airport and catch a flight to Los Angeles tonight."

"How about having a bite with me before you go? My treat." He took his Treasure Island Players Club card out of the slot machine and held it up. "I get a club discount at the buffet and it opens for dinner in five minutes."

Kate checked her watch. "It's only four thirty."

"So you're not going to join me?"

"Of course I will," Kate said. "It's never too early for an all-you-can-eat buffet."

A few blocks from Treasure Island, Evan Trace sat at his million-dollar desk in his office suite atop the Côte d'Argent tower. His desk was essentially an iPad the size of a dining room table, and he was typing furiously on his virtual keyboard and making lots of mistakes. He'd been a lousy typist even before his hands were smashed with a mallet.

Elsewhere on the desktop, hundreds of security camera images from throughout the casino played in thumbnails like a checkerboard tablecloth with animated squares. If he wanted to, he could touch and expand any of the video squares to full screen or shuffle them around like mahjong tiles. But he wasn't interested in that right now. All of his attention was focused on the email he was writing to TMZ, the notorious gossip website and TV show.

He'd logged onto the TMZ site as Emilia Guttierez, a nonexistent Côte d'Argent maid, a character he'd created as a seemingly legitimate front for the anonymous tips that he regularly sent to the media. To make Emilia more credible, just in case anyone decided to snoop, he'd put her on the Côte d'Argent payroll, rented an apartment for her, and had credit cards and various utility company accounts opened in her name.

Trace was tipping off TMZ that a world-famous young singer, a twenty-year-old man who'd once been a Disney star, had just registered in the hotel under the pseudonym *Bolt Stryker* and had two cross-dressers in his room. He attached a photo to Emilia's email of the disguised singer slipping into the hotel through the VIP entrance and another photo of him letting the two "ladies" into his room. Trace added one more line.

He's with them right now!!! You can't ever say where you got this information or hint that it was someone on the cleaning staff. After the last tip I sent you, Trace went ballistic and threatened to fire every single employee.

Trace was sure that the news would go viral on a global scale and would generate a million dollars' worth of free publicity for Côte d'Argent. Of course, he'd booked the room for the singer, he'd arranged for the cross-dressing hookers, and promised him absolute secrecy. But Trace didn't have any qualms about breaking that promise, or lying to the singer about it later when the news broke. The lurid publicity, and with it the constant association of Côte d'Argent with celebrity and scandal, was worth a lot more to Trace than the singer's future business. He clicked the SEND button just as Niles Goodwell, his manager of player relations, waddled in like an enormous penguin.

"I hope I'm not disturbing you," Goodwell said.

"Not at all. I was just catching up on my email."

"I got a call from Nick Sweet, the guy who blew a couple million at one of our blackjack tables last week," Goodwell said. "He's wired fifteen million dollars from a bank account in St. Kitts to our casino in Macau to establish a credit line."

It was amazing to Trace what he could accomplish with his personal touch. High rollers like Sweet were always flattered to get attention from the man in charge, and it took the sting out of their gambling losses. It had obviously sealed the deal this time.

"Make sure he gets the royal treatment," Trace said. "Offer to fly him to Macau on our jet as our guest. Comp his suite and have one of our chauffeur-driven Rolls-Royce Phantoms available for his personal use at all times during his stay. Whatever he desires, he gets, especially if it's kinky and disgraceful. That way we've got leverage to use against him in the future. We want him to continue losing his money with us until we have it all."

"There's just one wrinkle, sir," Goodwell said. "Sweet doesn't want the credit for his own play. He'd like to establish an account with us as a junket operator so he can bring in some high rollers. He's asking for a VIP suite with a baccarat table and all of the amenities."

"We'll still treat him well, but don't offer to fly him in. He'll have to get himself and his guests to Macau and pay top dollar for his rooms," Trace said. "But at least now we know what his short visit here was all about. He wanted to show us his credentials."

"We don't know anything about him," Goodwell said. "All he showed us was his money."

"That's all that matters," Trace said. "Especially now."

Trace was on the brink of a bold expansion in Macau. In addition to his existing property in old Macau, he wanted to build a much larger resort. Monde d'Argent would sit on the Cotai Strip, two square miles of reclaimed land that joined the former islands of Taipa and Coloane into one.

The Cotai Strip was already home to the Venetian Macao, the largest hotel casino complex on earth, and a half dozen other mega-casinos that were either finished or in the midst of being built. If his company was going to survive, Trace believed that he had to be on the Cotai Strip, too. He desperately needed the revenue that came from high-roller play to fund the construction. But there was a problem.

"There's new leadership in China and they're cracking down on high-level corruption on the mainland," Trace told Goodwell. "It's a publicity stunt, and it'll go away in a few months, but until then, the richest people in China are afraid to draw attention to themselves by gambling in Macau. This couldn't have come at a worse time for me. We've broken ground on Monde d'Argent and everybody is fighting over the handful of high rollers that are left."

"I understand that, sir," Goodwell said. "But I don't trust Sweet and Porter. I'm worried that they are working on some kind of a big score."

"I'm certain they are, but I can't let them take their fifteen million dollars and their future business across the street to one of the other casinos," Trace said. "So we'll welcome Sweet and we'll keep our eyes on him. Just make sure that he knows the ground rules. We run the table and the chips need to be rolled three times."

That meant that Nick's whales would have to gamble their chips at least three times, greatly increasing their chances of losing their initial stake and any winnings they got along the way.

"Our dealer in the room will stay on top of it," Goodwell said. "We'll watch every chip and guarantee that the games are honest."

"When is this junket supposed to come in?"

"Next Wednesday."

That was a week away. "What do we know about his guests?"

"Nothing, sir," Goodwell said. "Do you really want to know about them?"

It was a sensible question to ask. It was often better not to know who was in the room, especially if the players were coming to Côte d'Argent Macau to launder their money. The junkets gave Trace plausible deniability if the money was used to finance the bombing of a U.S. embassy somewhere and the Justice Department ever started asking him questions. But Trace's curiosity was stronger than his caution.

"Get whatever information you can," Trace said. "But make sure your inquiries don't leave a trail of any kind back to us."

"Will do," Goodwell said and walked out.

Trace tapped a virtual button that activated the speakerphone on his digital desktop and called Garver, his enforcer and body-guard. Garver answered his phone after one ring.

"Yeah?" Garver replied. He was the only man who worked for Trace who didn't feel the slightest need to grovel to him.

"Pack your mallet," Trace said. "We're going to Macau."

11

Thanks to the success of *The Lego Movie,* there was a mad scramble among Hollywood producers to make films based on children's toys. So perhaps it was inevitable that Mr. Potato Head would inspire a new animated feature. But few people, besides savvy studio accountants, could have foreseen that it would be an all-potato adaptation of Charles Dickens's *Great Expectations.* The novel was in the public domain, meaning that it was free to use, saving the producers the money, time, and creativity required to come up with an original story suitable for talking potatoes. The studio accountants were thrilled.

The movie's cast recorded their parts individually in a studio located in a small office building on Hollywood Way in Burbank. The studio had originally been a dentist's office and still smelled like mint mouthwash. Not because the scent had tenaciously lingered through the remodeling, but because the voice actors were constantly sucking on breath mints and throat lozenges.

One of those actors was Boyd Capwell, a fortyish man with great teeth, a strong chin, and perfect hair who behaved as if he was always playing to an audience or a camera, even when they existed only in his mind. Boyd was in a soundproof booth the size of a closet. He was facing the window into the control room, where the director and the sound editor were watching him.

He'd been cast as the voice of Magwitch, the escaped convict that young Pip encounters one fateful, foggy night in a church-yard cemetery at the beginning of Dickens's tale. Magwitch was described by Dickens as a fearful man in leg irons, wearing wet, filthy clothes and a dirty rag tied around his head, who'd limped and shivered, glared and growled. So Boyd was limping and shivering within the cramped confines of the booth as he recorded his lines into the microphone. He wore tattered clothes and a dirty rag on his head, and addressed a potato in his hand as if it were young Pip. It was a pose intentionally reminiscent of Hamlet.

"You'll bring me a file to cut these chains and food to fill my stomach, you little devil, and you won't say a word to anyone." Boyd spoke with a heavy Irish accent while he glared and growled. "Or else my friend who is hiding in the marshes will cut you into fries and shred you into hash browns for us to eat."

"Cut," the director said into his microphone. His name was Milt Freiberger, and he was a twenty-year veteran of Saturday morning cartoons who was making his first feature film. He took off his tortoiseshell glasses, rubbed his eyes, and ran his hands through his thick, curly hair before speaking quietly and patiently. "Boyd, what are you doing?"

"Acting."

"Yes, I know that. But this isn't the same performance you gave in the audition."

"That's because all I knew then was that I was auditioning for an animated version of *Great Expectations*," Boyd said. "I wasn't aware that the characters would be potatoes."

"What difference does it make?" Milt asked.

"It goes to the essence of the characters. I have to embody that. I've spent the last two weeks eating nothing but potatoes to fill myself with the taste, smell, and texture of the noble tuber."

"I see," Milt said. "Why are you using an Irish accent?"

"Because I did my research. Clearly, Magwitch is an Irish lumper, the prevalent variety of potato at the time. But here's where it gets interesting. Twenty years after this story ends, the Irish lumper crops were decimated by a horrible disease, causing the great potato famine of 1845, so my accent is also dramatic foreshadowing."

"But in the Charles Dickens novel, Magwitch wasn't Irish."

"He wasn't a potato, either."

"Go back to the cockney accent you used in the audition. And please, stick to the lines as written, too. You're supposed to say to Pip that your friend will 'cut out your heart and your liver, roast them and eat them.' You changed it to something about French fries and hash browns."

"Because Pip is a potato," Boyd said, shaking the potato in his hand for emphasis. "He doesn't have a heart or a liver."

"He's got arms and legs and he talks," Milt said. "So he has a heart and liver."

"That makes no biological or botanical sense."

"Mr. Potato Head is a plastic toy potato that you can snap different facial features onto, like noses, eyes, ears, and mouths, to create new characters," Milt said. "It's not an actual potato. None of these characters are. Think of them as people who happen to resemble potatoes."

Perhaps Boyd might have argued the point, or even given in to the director's wishes, but then he saw Nick walk into the studio. Boyd didn't know anything, really, about Nick or his partner, Kate, or Intertect, the mysterious private security company they claimed to work for. All that Boyd knew, and all that really mattered to him, was that whenever they showed up, it meant he'd have a chance to earn $100,000 by playing a character in an elaborate con to capture a criminal. The colorful roles they gave him were played on the stage of life, where a bad performance could get him killed. The danger made the roles even more thrilling.

"I quit," Boyd said.

"You can't quit," Milt said.

"Take it up with my agent," Boyd said, pointing to Nick. "He just walked in."

Milt turned to Nick. "He has a contract. If he walks, I'll ruin him in this business."

"If you had that kind of pull," Nick said, "you wouldn't be directing a cartoon version of *Great Expectations* with talking potatoes."

"*The Lego Movie* made half a billion dollars worldwide, and Legos aren't even characters. They're plastic bricks. Mr. Potato Head is a beloved global personality, an icon. We could top what Lego did."

"If you do, then you won't care that Boyd walked, will you?" Nick said. "You'll be too busy basking in your success."

Boyd emerged from the booth. "If you want success to happen, Milt, you can't pretend the potatoes aren't potatoes. You have to embrace your inner potato."

"I don't have an inner potato," Milt said.

"Then you are the wrong man to be directing this movie," Boyd said and dropped his potato in Milt's lap.

Nick and Boyd walked outside to the parking lot where Nick's Porsche 911 was parked next to Boyd's Cadillac CTS.

"So how much were you making as a potato?" Nick asked.

"It's not about the money, it's about living. I am an actor. I need to act, the same way that I need to breathe, or eat or sleep. I saw playing a potato as a creative challenge. I've played an apple in a Fruit of the Loom commercial, and even a pancake once, but I've never had a chance to be a vegetable, and certainly not with classy material like this," Boyd said. "It's *Great*

Expectations, a Charles Dickens masterpiece. There will never be a better vegetable part. How could I say no?"

"And, yet, you're walking away."

"I can't work with directors who don't have passion for what they're doing. But you certainly do. What role do you have for me?"

"A powerful, vicious, and amoral Canadian mobster who is going to Macau to play high-stakes baccarat," Nick said. "You like the game, but what you're really there to do is launder your money through the casino. You're mixing business with pleasure."

"I'll be Tony Soprano meets Snidely Whiplash."

"The bad guy with the handlebar mustache that Dudley Do-Right, the Canadian Mountie, was always battling in the cartoons?"

"He's a perfect touchstone for my character," Boyd said. "I particularly like the mustache."

"Just don't wear the top hat and black cape," Nick said. "Keep it subtle."

Nick and Kate spent the first part of the week establishing identities for Boyd and Billy Dee.

Kate used her FBI access to create criminal backgrounds for "Shane Blackmore," Boyd's nonexistent Canadian mobster, in all of the key law enforcement databases worldwide. She also sensationalized the criminal files that already existed for Lou

Ould-Abdallah, Billy Dee Snipes's real name, so he'd appear to be an active, brutal power player in high-seas piracy. When the con was over, she'd erase all of her creative writing.

Nick got in touch with his tech wizard in Hong Kong. They planted fake articles and references about Shane Blackmore and Lou Ould-Abdallah on the Internet, and forged the necessary passports, credit cards, and driver's licenses that would be needed.

Once Nick and Kate were done, Boyd flew to Vancouver, British Columbia, on his U.S. passport. In Canada, he switched to Shane Blackmore's Canadian passport and flew to Hong Kong. This established a trail that led back to Canada in case anyone checked into his identity.

Billy Dee flew from Las Vegas to Mogadishu, by way of London, Istanbul, and Djibouti. He spent a night in Mogadishu, and then used his Somali passport to take a flight to Kenya, a two-hour flight to Ethiopia, and finally a ten-hour flight to Hong Kong. It was a belabored way to get from Las Vegas to Hong Kong but, as with Boyd, it was necessary to establish his cover.

Nick and Kate didn't have to worry about leaving a trail. They focused instead on making the right impression. So Nick chartered a private jet for their trip. He met Kate at the Van Nuys Airport early in the morning on their departure day.

"The last time we went to China together, it was in the trunk of a '69 Dodge Charger in the cargo hold of a passenger jet," Nick said. "This time, I thought we should go in style."

Kate climbed the stairs to the G650, said hello to the flight attendant and the pilots, and settled into one of the eight cushy leather club chairs. The crew compartment and galley were in front of her. A credenza with a wine cooler and flat-screen TV were behind her. A couch and the restroom were also behind her.

"This is really extravagant," Kate said. "Couldn't you have chartered something smaller and cheaper?"

"Sure, but we would have had to stop somewhere on the way for refueling," he said. "This baby will take us straight to Hong Kong without stopping and makes a bold statement."

"What does a bold statement cost?"

"Two hundred and fifty thousand dollars."

Kate squelched a grimace. "Jessup is going to pop a hemorrhoid."

They were an hour into the flight, Kate was halfway through her third bowl of heated nuts, and Nick reached for his messenger bag. "I'm going to teach you how to play baccarat," he said. "I packed three decks of cards and a big bag of M&M's for the trip."

"What are the M&M's for?"

"Gambling chips. I wanted them to have some value to you." He handed Kate the bag of candy. "Separate these by color. Yellow M&M's will be a hundred thousand, red will be fifty thousand, blue will be twenty-five thousand, and brown will be five thousand."

"What about the orange and green M&M's?"

"Those are for you to snack on so you won't be tempted to devour your chips."

"My kind of game. I'm liking it already."

"Baccarat is a lot like betting on a sporting event," Nick said, shuffling the cards. "There are two teams, the dealer and the player. You're going to place a bet on who you think will be dealt the cards that come closest to adding up to nine."

"What's the strategy?"

"There is none," Nick said. "It's pure luck. Unlike blackjack or poker, you don't get to make any choices. You're dealt your cards and that's that."

"You mean you just sit there and do nothing?"

"Yep," he said.

"There's no bluffing?"

"Nope," he said.

"So why is baccarat the game that James Bond always plays against the bad guys to prove how clever he is?"

"Because that's not what he's doing. He's showing them that he's willing to take huge risks and that he has unwavering confidence in his own good luck."

"And that he looks great in a tuxedo," Kate added.

"That's the part that takes true finesse. Here's how the game works. To start, you and the dealer are each dealt two cards, facedown." He dealt out the cards to Kate and himself. "An ace counts as one, the ten and face cards count as zero. You subtract ten from any combination of cards that adds up to more than nine. For example, an eight and a three would add up to one. Two tens would equal zero. The player looks at her cards first."

Kate turned over her cards. She had a nine and a three. "So am I stuck with this lousy two?"

"Nope. If the player draws two cards that total zero to five, she automatically gets a third card. You never get more than three cards."

He dealt her a four, giving her a total of six.

"That's better," she said. "How does it work for the dealer?"

"That's more complicated." Nick turned over his cards, revealing a queen and a three. "The dealer isn't allowed another card unless the player has drawn three cards, and it depends on what that third card was. The rules vary from casino to casino, but usually the dealer must stand if he has a seven, eight, or nine and must draw a card if he has a zero, one, or two. If the dealer has a three, like I do, he'll draw if the player's third card is any number but eight."

"Why eight?"

"I have absolutely no idea. But none of it really matters since you're already finished with your part of the game. You just have to go along with it, knowing that the rules are designed to give the house a statistical advantage." Nick drew a card, a five, giving him a total of eight to win the game.

Kate tossed her cards back to Nick. "I'll bet with the house every time."

"If you do that, the house takes a five percent commission on each bet you win."

They played for a couple hours, and Kate eventually started to lose more often than she won. She was down to her last $200,000 in blue and brown M&M's, when she scooped them up and ate them.

"I guess this means we're done," Nick said.

"I'd rather watch grass grow."

"It was kind of sexy the way you ate all those M&M's. I like an aggressive, take-charge woman."

"You should see me in combat gear."

12

In the late 1990s, the few farmers that occupied the small, hilly islands of Chek Lap Kok and Lam Chau, twenty-one miles southwest of Hong Kong, were told to pack up and move. Their tiny villages were razed, the hillsides were shaved off, and everything was dumped into the water between the two islands to create one completely flat piece of land for a new international airport. From the sky, the unnaturally level and squared-off island that was Hong Kong International Airport looked to Kate like a gray rug floating on the sea.

Nick and Kate landed in the late afternoon. They were fast-tracked through customs and walked a short distance to the heliport, where a white Peninsula Hotel helicopter was waiting for them. A young Chinese valet in an all-white mandarin-collared uniform, pillbox hat, and gloves cheerfully relieved them of their suitcases and escorted them to the chopper. They climbed in, the valet stowed their bags and secured their door, and they were off, soaring over the hills, the ports, and the bridges toward the city center.

Within moments, Hong Kong Island loomed up in front of them with its spectacular skyline of densely packed skyscrapers. The island consisted of a narrow strip of land between Victoria Peak and a harbor that was a freeway filled with ferries, jetfoils, yachts, ocean liners, and Chinese junks. The Kowloon Peninsula was just across the harbor. Here the skyscrapers had more shoulder room, but still rose up from a closely packed warren of buildings on overcrowded streets.

The Peninsula Hotel, built in 1928, was on the Kowloon waterfront, facing the harbor. The helicopter landed on top of the hotel's thirty-story tower, a relatively recent addition to the original building, which was an elegant and fiercely beloved relic of Hong Kong's British colonial era. The flight from the airport had taken only seven minutes.

Nick and Kate exited the helicopter and walked into the China Clipper lounge on the thirtieth floor. A crisply dressed female clerk greeted them and presented Nick and Kate with their key cards. She assured them that their bags would be delivered to their rooms while they dined. Nick thanked her, and he and Kate took the elevator two floors down to Felix, the hotel's renowned restaurant and bar.

They emerged from the elevator into a wildly overdesigned restaurant that looked like a SPECTRE villain's secret lair from a 1960s-era Bond movie. It was a big, bold, two-story-tall space, gleaming with bronze, zinc, and undulating aluminum sheathing. There were dramatically lit walls, pillars, and two oval structures that, if this *were* SPECTRE headquarters, would have been stylized silos for nuclear missiles instead of fancy bars. The real grabber in the room was the commanding view of the Hong Kong skyline from the wall-to-wall floor-to-ceiling windows that would have pleased any supervillain bent on world domination. But instead of finding Dr. Evil sitting in the center of it all, stroking his hairless cat, Kate spotted Boyd Capwell at a table, twirling his handlebar mustache.

Boyd's hair was colored jet black to match his well-oiled mustache. He'd mimicked Tony Soprano's fashion sense, wearing a navy blue short-sleeved bowling shirt, with cream panels and two embroidered martini glasses on the left chest, a pair of khaki slacks, and leather loafers with no socks.

"Welcome to Hong Kong," Boyd said, gesturing to three empty chairs with seatbacks decorated with black-and-white drawings of longtime, and mostly deceased, Peninsula employees. "Have a seat."

"You look like you're on Snidely Whiplash's bowling team," Kate said.

"Thank you," Boyd said. "Now Snidely is flesh and blood and embodied in Shane Blackmore, a man to be feared. But because I'm dressed in a relaxed, lighthearted manner, I'll catch people completely off guard with my seething menace." Boyd sat back, smiled, and twirled one end of his mustache.

Kate could feel an eye twitch coming on. "The mustache-twirling bad guy was already a cliché when they were doing silent movies."

"In other words, it's a powerful symbol embedded deep in our collective psyche. By twirling my mustache, I'll provoke primal fear in my adversaries," Boyd said. "That's why this mustache is perfect. Nick gave me the idea."

Kate turned to Nick. "You didn't."

"I did. I may grow one myself. It would hint at *my* inner menace," Nick said.

"I had a goatee once," Billy Dee Snipes said, walking up behind Nick and Kate. "But it was like drawing a circle with a Sharpie around my mouth and saying 'Look at my crooked, yellow teeth.' So I shaved it off."

Billy Dee wore another silk tracksuit similar to the one he'd had on in Las Vegas. The only change he'd made to his wardrobe was the addition of a *koofiyad,* a Somali skullcap embroidered with an elaborate design of interlocking triangles.

"Have you seen the bathrooms in here?" Billy Dee asked Nick. "You pee facing a wall of glass that looks out over Kowloon."

"It's a display of aggression, dominance, profanity, freedom, and exhibitionism all rolled into one," Boyd said. "Urination as performance art and political statement."

"I think it's just a great place to pee. It's the first time I've ever enjoyed having prostate trouble," Billy Dee said. "I've gone twice already and I'm looking forward to going again in ten minutes."

The waiter appeared at the table and passed out iPad menus. Kate scrolled through the selections and examined pictures of dishes such as soy-marinated pigeon and French duck liver with caramelized strawberries. What she really craved was an In-N-Out burger or a bucket of KFC. What she ordered instead was a Kobe steak and fries, and a double-chocolate brownie with espresso ice cream and custard sauce for dessert.

"Your job tomorrow is easy, gentlemen," Nick said over dessert. "Gamble six million dollars each and have a fabulous time."

"I can do that," Billy Dee said.

Boyd added cream to his coffee. "That's easy for you to say. You have the benefit of actually being a Somali pirate, while I must draw on a lifetime of acting experience to deliver a rich and nuanced performance as a Canadian mobster."

"It's okay to win," Nick continued. "But if you're losing, pace yourself. Try to walk away with at least five million if you can. You're here to launder your money, so up to a ten percent loss is acceptable as a washing fee, and I suppose that another five percent loss could be written off to having too much fun."

"I'm going to play baccarat like it's nickel slots," Billy Dee said.

"I've seen you play the slots," Kate said. "You never stop hitting the spin button."

"Come to think of it," Nick said, "if we lose it all, it's only going to make Trace more eager for us to come back, so don't sweat the money."

Kate looked at Nick. "You have a lot to learn about encouraging fiscal restraint."

"Because I don't have any," he said.

"I've noticed," she said.

Nick received a text message just as everyone was finishing dessert.

"Gentlemen, it's been a pleasure, as usual," Nick said. "A small business matter that Kate and I need to attend to has come up. Feel free to continue enjoying yourselves, but remember, we have a big day tomorrow."

Kate left the dining room with Nick and paused at the elevator. "What's up?"

"There's someone in Kowloon that I want you to meet," Nick said. "Sorry about it being so last-minute, but we don't get to Hong Kong very often and we're only here for the night."

They took the elevator to the lobby, and Kate thought the hotel's entryway, filled with neoclassical columns, gilded ceilings, and a string quartet, was reminiscent of an elegant bygone era. That feeling passed the moment she stepped outside and saw the scores of tourists posing along the Victoria Harbor waterfront with their smart phones attached to telescoping selfie sticks, trying to get the perfect shot of themselves against the Hong Kong skyline.

The sidewalks were teeming with people, more than she'd ever seen before on any city street. The roads were clogged with European luxury cars, tour buses, and countless identical red-and-white Toyota taxis.

They stepped into the flow of people and let it carry them up Canton Road, which was lined with flagship stores for such luxury brands as Louis Vuitton, Hermès, Prada, Harry Winston, and Gucci. The stores were packed with customers, desperate for their chance to spend top dollar on the priciest Western goods. Outside the high-end store doors, and at every street corner, there were relentless hucksters whispering offers of "cheap Gucci, cheap Rolex," and handing out cards with directions to back-alley shops that sold bootlegs of everything.

"Who are we meeting?" Kate asked.

"My tech wizard, Lucie," Nick said.

Kate stopped in the middle of the sidewalk and stared at him. "When you made your deal with the FBI, you said you would never do anything that could potentially expose the people you've worked with before."

"You're right, I did. And I won't share her with the FBI. But you're more than the FBI to me. If the day should come where a con goes wrong, you might need Lucie's help to disappear. I would rather see you retire to a beach in Thailand than waste away in some federal prison."

"Wow."

"Yeah, it took me by surprise, too," Nick said.

"Probably we don't want to talk about it."

"For sure. Absolutely. Still, if you're really grateful . . ."

"I don't think so."

A little old man and a young woman bumped into them and said something in rushed Chinese. Nick bowed, gave his apologies to the man, and tugged Kate forward onto a side street, where the sidewalks weren't quite as mobbed. Garish neon signs for restaurants, shops, and massage parlors hung out over the road, cluttering the air above her head and clamoring for her attention in blazing yellow, orange, and red Chinese letters. The signs cast enough light for the tourists to easily read their pocket maps and for some locals to look natural wearing sunglasses at night. Music blared out of electronics stores. Frustrated drivers leaned on their car horns. The humid air was thick, almost chewable, with the smell of cooking oil, fish, perfume, and bus exhaust. The atmosphere was electric, chaotic, and overwhelming.

Nick stopped in front of a glass door set in an elegant, marbled façade that looked out of place amid the garishness of the street. Kate looked up and saw that it was the ground floor entrance to a glass-and-marble-sheathed tower that was about as wide as three parking spaces and rose thirty stories into the night sky. Nick punched a code into the security keypad and the door unlocked.

They rode an elevator up to the twentieth floor. When the door opened, Kate saw two apartment doors that were about a foot apart from each other, and maybe four feet in front of them.

"This is the smallest apartment corridor I've ever seen," she said.

"Real estate is tight in Hong Kong."

"Literally," Kate said.

Nick knocked on the door on the left. It was immediately opened by a young, very thin Chinese woman in her early twenties. She was dressed in a sharp black business suit and white blouse and smiled when she saw Nick. She said something to him affectionately in Chinese, Nick replied back to her in Chinese, and then the young woman turned to Kate.

"It's so nice to finally meet you." She spoke perfect English with a slight British accent. "I'm Lucie Wan. Please come in."

Lucie stepped aside and they walked into a small living area with an amazing view. To their left was a large picture window with a cushioned sill that looked out at the towers along Victoria Harbor. To their right was a single bed, the covers neatly tucked into tight military corners. Directly across from them, not even ten feet away, were two pocket doors, one partially open to reveal a two-burner stove, a mini-refrigerator, and a small sink. Kate assumed that behind the other door was a bathroom, probably about the same size of an airplane lavatory.

"What do you think of my place?" Lucie asked Nick.

"It's terrific," Nick said and kissed her on the cheek. "Congratulations."

"Thank you," Lucie said, beaming with pride. "When this building opened, over two thousand prospective buyers showed up but I was one of only sixty people who scored a place."

"You were lucky," he said.

"Screw luck," she said. "I hacked into the developer's computer and put myself at the top of the list."

Lucie turned to a tiny desk that held her laptop computer and two hard drives.

"The identity for Shane Blackmore is all set if Trace's people start snooping. He's listed in Canadian government databases—birth records, tax rolls, DMV, et cetera," Lucie said. "I've also planted news stories that mention him in the *Toronto Star* and *The Vancouver Sun* archives. Lou Ould-Abdallah's identity was much easier to create, since he really is a Somali pirate."

"Excellent work," Nick said. "As usual."

"Do you create all of Nick's false identities, forged passports, and phony credit cards?" Kate asked.

"I create the identities and accounts in the necessary databases, but I don't do the physical forgeries," Lucie said. "I subcontract that out."

"There's no better place than Hong Kong to get a high-quality knockoff," Nick said, "whether it's a bootleg Hermès bag or a false passport."

"He's right," Lucie said. "This dress is fake Prada. Nick doesn't pay me enough to get the real thing."

"I've paid you enough to get this apartment," he said.

"But now I'm broke," she said. "I may have to go back to picking pockets."

"That's how Lucie and I met," Nick said. "She picked my pocket on the street in Lan Kwai Fong, cloned my identity, and emptied out my bank account within the hour. She was only fifteen."

"It also only took Nick an hour to find me," Lucie said. "I was living in a homemade shelter under an overpass in the Central District and tapping into phone lines with a stolen laptop. Instead of having me thrown in jail, he sent me to boarding school."

"She obviously had a natural gift for larceny and technology," Nick said. "All she was missing to succeed was a real education. Now she works in computer services for an international bank."

"That's my menial day job," Lucie said. "The legitimate front for my real profession, which is keeping Nicolas Fox out of jail. Of course, that's been a lot easier since you stopped chasing him."

Kate felt her throat go dry. "You know who I am?"

"Of course I do, FBI Special Agent Kate O'Hare. It would be hard to create all of those false identities for you if I didn't know your real one."

It was late when Kate and Nick left Lucie and returned to their hotel. Kate staggered into her eighteenth-floor suite, not noticing the amazing view or the lacquered tea blossoms etched on the wall, or the high-tech tablet that controlled everything in the room, or the low-tech nail dryer built into the dresser. She was exhausted and all she saw was the bed. She stripped down to a T-shirt and panties, slipped between the perfectly ironed sheets, and thought about what a different world China was from her own, and how much she missed the comfort of having a loaded Glock under her pillow.

The next morning, before taking the elevator up to the Peninsula helipad, Nick handed out tiny flesh-colored earbud radio transmitters/receivers to Kate, Boyd, and Billy Dee.

"We'll wear these at all times so we can be in constant, simultaneous contact. They're practically invisible."

Nick was wearing a trim-fit gray Armani silk and wool sport coat, white Hermès slim dress shirt, and Dsquared2 jeans. Kate was in a sleeveless Givenchy black satin top with a very deep V-neck that pretty much guaranteed every man she faced would be distracted by her cleavage. That was the intention. Anything that might distract a possible adversary, even for a split second, was an advantage that she might need. Her knee-length skirt with a ruffled tiered overlay was loose enough to allow her plenty of flexibility for a spin kick, which is what she looked for in a dress. Her silver-studded Yves Saint Laurent calfskin ballerina flats were equally practical, being fancy shoes with pointed toes, while still maintaining the capability to haul ass, if the need should arise.

The team slipped the earbuds into their ears and took the elevator up to the China Clipper lounge. They passed quickly through and outside to the helipad, where a white-suited, white-gloved valet stowed their luggage and ushered them into the waiting helicopter for their fifteen-minute ride to Macau.

Billy Dee looked back wistfully at the hotel as the helicopter rose and carried them out over the harbor.

"I'm going to miss that bathroom," he said.

The helicopter soared westward across the Pearl River Delta. Kate's first glimpse of Macau was the Grand Lisboa hotel and casino, a fifty-three-story tower of gold-tinted glass shaped like the feathered headdress of a showgirl.

Macau encompassed a three-mile peninsula as well as the former islands of Taipa and Coloane, which were now joined together by the Cotai Strip. Three two-mile-long bridges linked the city to Taipa, one of which was arched to resemble the back of a sleeping dragon, its tail on the island and its head resting in front of the Grand Lisboa.

They landed on the helipad atop the Macau Ferry Terminal, breezed through the VIP customs checkpoint, and were met outside by a Rolls-Royce Phantom sent by Côte d'Argent. Nick got up front with the chauffeur and Kate sat in the back, sandwiched between Boyd and Billy Dee for the ten-minute drive to the casino along Avenida da Amizade.

"Macau is over five centuries old," Nick said, playing tour guide to his junket guests and their eavesdropping driver. "It was built to resemble Lisbon by homesick Portuguese traders. The Vegas casino moguls came much later, and they also wanted to feel at home."

A twenty-story replica of Evan Trace's Côte d'Argent tower appeared to their right. Directly across the street was Steve

Wynn's small-scale copy of his namesake Las Vegas resort. Both properties faced the harbor and Taipa, where the medieval castle-like spires of the Galaxy Macau on the Cotai Strip peeked out beyond the top of Small Taipa Hill.

"That's real interesting, Nick. Is there a Tim Hortons around?" Boyd asked, referring to the ubiquitous Canadian coffee chain. He spoke with a slight lilt in his voice, his attempt at a Canadian accent now that he was in character as Shane Blackmore.

"I don't think so," Nick said.

"Then it isn't going to feel like home to me," Boyd said. "If Canadians had settled this place, there'd be a Tim Hortons on every corner, a loon on every dollar, and the Grand Lisboa would be shaped like a golden maple leaf instead of Daffy Duck's ass."

"Is that what it's supposed to be?" Billy Dee said, craning his neck to look up at it.

"You know Daffy Duck in Somalia?" Boyd asked as they arrived at Côte d'Argent.

"No," Billy Dee shifted his gaze to Boyd and his eyes turned cold, "but I know an ass when I see one."

Boyd smiled broadly and wagged a finger at Billy Dee. "That was good, Sheik," he said. "I think I'm gonna like you."

The driver pulled up to the Côte d'Argent VIP entrance, and the four of them stepped out of the Rolls-Royce and into the lobby. It was identical to the one in Las Vegas, right down to the ice sculptures and chilly temperature. The slender, long-legged Macanese hostess who approached them wore high heels and a body-hugging black silk *qipao,* a sleeveless one-piece dress with a severe Mandarin collar and a subtle pattern of Chinese symbols.

"I'm Natasha Ling, vice president of guest relations, and I'd like to welcome you to Côte d'Argent," she said, taking a slight bow in front of them. "I will be seeing to your needs throughout your stay."

"That's great news," Boyd said. "What are those drawings on your dress?"

"Chinese lucky charms," she said.

"Do I rub you to get good luck?" Boyd asked.

"You'll find these same charms incorporated into the décor throughout the property," Natasha said. "So good luck surrounds you in Côte d'Argent. Rubbing the staff isn't necessary."

"But it couldn't hurt," Boyd said, twirling his mustache. "Especially the pretty ones."

Kate caught Nick's eye and pretended to gag.

Natasha smiled politely and passed out transparent plastic key cards in paper sleeves with room numbers on them. "These are the keys to your harbor-view suites and the express elevators. They also allow you into your private gaming suite on the eighth floor."

"I thought we'd be higher up," Boyd said. "The penthouse, maybe."

"It's a privilege to be on the eighth floor," Nick said. "Eight is a lucky number that has great power in Chinese culture. It equals prosperity."

"I hope that means for us," Boyd said. "And not the casino."

"We won't find out standing here," Billy Dee said impatiently. "Let's get to the table and play some cards."

"This way, please." Natasha led them through a set of double doors and out into the casino.

The casino floor was filled with hundreds of baccarat tables. Mobs of Chinese men and women crowded around them, cheering and yelling. The gamblers who couldn't find seats were standing, reaching across over the heads of the seated players to place bets. Kate slowed her pace beside one of the tables to peek at a game.

The player who'd been dealt two cards lifted them up very slowly, peeling them up by the edges, as if they were stickers glued to the table. The technique mangled the cards in the process, but the dealer didn't seem to mind, sweeping them into a trash slot at the end of the hand.

"Letting players destroy the cards like that would never fly in Vegas," Billy Dee said.

"The players aren't as superstitious there," Natasha said. "Many players here believe the way they reveal the cards has the power to change the numerical value."

"It didn't work for that guy," Boyd said.

"He may not be a powerful person," Natasha said. "I believe truly powerful men make their own luck."

They continued on across the casino floor toward a bank of elevators, and up to the eighth floor.

13

Dumah was a big and broad-chested descendent of an Indonesian tribe that, as recently as a hundred years ago, had been feared throughout the South China Sea as headhunters and slave traders. Back then, he would have been a warrior, and his traditional dress would have been a necklace of wild boar teeth and tusks, a battle vest of woven rattan and water buffalo bone, and a rigid two-foot-long penis sheath with a sharp pointed end.

Instead, as a security operative for Côte d'Argent, he wore a gray Dolce & Gabbana suit, a Patek Philippe gold watch, a radio transmitter in his ear, and nothing sheathing his penis but bikini briefs. His forefathers would have been deeply ashamed to see him like this.

Nevertheless, Dumah was still a warrior, of sorts. He'd never lopped off a head or traded a slave, but he'd made his living throughout Asia on his muscles, menace, and willingness to commit acts of extreme violence to protect whomever hired him. He'd worked for corporate executives, government officials, Triad mobsters, and, for a short time, a U.S. investment banker who'd embezzled a half billion dollars and fled to a tiny Indonesian island, safe from extradition.

That last job hadn't ended well. It started to go bad the instant a spoiled American heiress and her servants showed up in a bullet-riddled yacht, leading the Bugis pirates who'd attacked them right to the island. The pirates took all the Americans hostage, but they let Dumah go unharmed. He'd bounced around Asia for a few months after that, before ending up as a security guard at Côte d'Argent. It was pure fate that he happened to be standing in the casino when Natasha Ling walked by with her latest group of junket guests.

Dumah recognized two members of the group immediately. It was the heiress and her servant. Only that's not who they were today, and that probably wasn't who they were before. Either way, they deserved agony.

He didn't have a spear to fling at them, or a knife to cut their throats. What he had was a radio. He pressed the button in his pocket, activating the microphone, so that he could speak to his supervisor.

"I need to see Mr. Trace," Dumah said. "It's urgent."

· · ·

The only difference between Trace's private dining room in Côte d'Argent Macau and the one in Las Vegas were the paintings on the wall. In Macau, he displayed masterpieces by Qi Baishi, Chen Yifei, and Ai Weiwei to impress his Asian guests. He also had a print of the seven dogs playing poker to amuse himself. The dining room had the same atrium and koi pond, though the only koi that were ever in the pond were ones that he fed to the piranhas.

Trace sat at his table beside the pond, browsing the *South China Morning Post* and eating a breakfast of steamed dim sum, Portuguese egg custard tarts, fresh fruit, and hot milk tea. He sported a carefully groomed three-day beard and was dressed casually in a blue-striped mandarin-collared, knot-buttoned dress shirt that was untucked over faded black jeans. He thought it was a look that straddled East and West but that fit with his devil-may-care image.

Natasha Ling came in, smiling at him as she crossed the Plexiglas bridge that arched over the pond and into the dining room.

"Mr. Sweet and Miss Porter have arrived with their guests," Natasha said, taking a seat at the table. "They are up in the eighth-floor suite and are already gambling."

He set the newspaper aside. "What do we know about their guests?"

"Lou Ould-Abdallah is from Mogadishu. He is a Somali warlord who has hijacked everything from oil tankers to yachts moving through the Strait of Malacca and the Gulf of Aden. Sometimes he sets the crews free and sells the boats and cargo, and other times he holds the crew and vessels for ransom. He's been known to behead his captives when negotiations aren't going to his satisfaction."

"My kind of guy." Trace took a sip of his milk tea. "How much did his last ransom bring him?"

"One hundred million dollars," Natasha said.

Trace whistled appreciatively. "Nice haul. So he's sitting on a pile of cash in the desert and looking to spend it on something besides another camel. What's the other high roller's story?"

"Shane Blackmore is a Canadian mobster. He started in the trucking business, smuggling stolen goods between the U.S. and Canada, then branched out into narcotics distribution and sex trafficking," she said. "He controls the drug and sex trade from Vancouver to Toronto."

"Vancouver and Toronto is about all there is between Vancouver and Toronto."

"That's why he's anxious to expand," she said. "He's got enough money stashed to buy his way into a business, legitimate or otherwise, somewhere else. He just needs to get his cash out of Canada to do it."

"I'm glad to be of service," Trace said. "We could make a lot of money from these two. How did Sweet hook up with them?"

"I don't know yet." Natasha reached for one of the egg tarts on Trace's plate, and he slapped her hand.

She slapped his face, hard enough to draw blood from the corner of his mouth.

Trace licked the blood away and smiled. "That's nice, but it's more fun somehow when you're wearing leather and stiletto heels."

She picked up the egg tart and took a bite out of it before speaking. "I can change my clothes if you'd like."

He was considering the pros and cons of that offer when Garver walked in. Garver moved with a lumbering, slightly hunched gait that looked as if he was fighting the urge to knuckle-walk like a gorilla. He was accompanied by one of Côte d'Argent's security men, a big Indonesian who kept a respectful step or two behind Garver. Trace had seen the Indonesian around the casino but had never actually met him.

"There's something you've got to hear," Garver said. "It's about Sweet and Porter." Garver gave the Indonesian a nod. "Tell him, Dumah."

"I met them two years ago, while I was a bodyguard for Derek Griffin," Dumah said. If a grizzly bear could talk, Trace thought, he would sound like this guy.

"The investment banker who ran off with a half billion dollars of his clients' money? You were working for a celebrity. Why didn't I know that?" Trace looked at Garver. "Do you remember seeing Griffin on Dumah's résumé?"

"I don't read résumés," Garver said. "I read scars."

"I haven't told anyone about that job, Mr. Trace," Dumah

said. "The story I'm about to tell you is the reason why. Griffin was hiding out on an island, safe from extradition, when that woman arrived on a yacht. She said that she'd been attacked by Bugis pirates. The man she was with today was there, too, only he was her servant back then. That night, the pirates invaded the island, took the Americans hostage, and let me go."

"No wonder you don't use Griffin as a reference," Trace said. "I hope you show me more loyalty than you showed him."

"It's true, I didn't protect him. I saved myself instead. But I think by telling you about those two, and revealing my personal shame, that I am demonstrating my loyalty," Dumah said. "I could have just waited for the right moment, slit their throats, and restored my dignity without anyone but me knowing that it had ever been lost."

"Fair point," Trace said. "Go on."

"Two days after I left the island, Griffin was arrested in Palm Springs, California. It made no sense. How did he get there? What happened to the woman and her servant? There was never any news about them. It was as if they never existed."

"I can see why you'd be angry at the pirates," Natasha said. "But why do you want to kill Sweet and Porter?"

"Because they are responsible for my shame," Dumah said. "They either led the pirates to the island through their stupidity, or they brought them there intentionally. I knew something wasn't right about those two the moment they came ashore. I warned Griffin that they were trouble, but he wouldn't listen to me. He just wanted to get the woman into bed."

"Did he succeed?" Trace asked.

Dumah shook his head, no. "Now he's in prison and those two are here, but as entirely different people. They're frauds. Whatever they've told you is a lie. They're here to take something."

Or *someone*, Trace thought. Was it him? Or was it the Canadian mobster and the Somali warlord that they were entertaining upstairs? Or were they after something else entirely?

Trace stood up. "I think it's time we had a candid conversation with Sweet."

"Okay," Garver said. "I'll go get my lie detector."

"You do that," Trace said. "Dumah, come with me."

Another hand was about to be dealt in the eighth-floor VIP gambling suite, a luxury two-bedroom, harbor-view apartment with a baccarat table, a sitting area, and a well-stocked bar. Boyd put $1 million in chips on the betting line. Nick gambled $250,000 on Boyd's hand, and Billy Dee wagered $100,000 with the dealer.

"Thanks for the vote of confidence," Boyd said to Billy Dee.

"I've seen your luck," Billy Dee said. "I'm here to win, not make friends."

They were an hour into play, and Nick and Billy Dee were up about $200,000, but Boyd was already down over a million dollars. This was Boyd's swing for the fences to get it all back in one hand.

Kate sat on a stool at the bar, watching the game and absentmindedly plucking items from the platters of dim sum and Portuguese pastries on the counter. At the rate Boyd was going, she was worried that he'd be tapped out in the next half hour and that she'd eat everything on the bar.

The dealer was a pretty, young Macanese woman named Luisa, who was all smiles and girly enthusiasm on the surface, but in complete command of her table. She dealt the cards with swift efficiency. Luisa was ordered to do that by the casino. The faster the men played, the more they'd bet and the more likely it was that they'd lose.

Standing beside Luisa was a grim-faced Macanese man named Tony who made notations on an iPad and watched the chips.

Boyd flipped over his cards to reveal a pair of twos. He swallowed half of the Bloody Mary that was in front of him.

"Hit me again, honey," Boyd said, though he had no choice but to take another card. "Make it a five."

Luisa gave him a card. Boyd winked at her. She smiled coyly back at him and he flipped the card over. It was a seven. That gave him a measly one.

"Bad luck," Nick said.

"The game isn't over yet," Boyd said and twirled his mustache.

The dim sum was sitting like a rock in Kate's gut. She could face down a two-hundred-pound man attacking with a knife and not break a sweat, but she was terrified at the thought of explaining the loss of a million dollars to her boss. Even without the threat of reprisal, Kate had a hard time justifying this kind of gambling. She was thrifty and law-abiding by nature, and that didn't change just because she zipped herself into a sexpot dress.

Luisa flipped over her cards, dealt herself one more, and came up with a hand that added up to ten, which in baccarat is equivalent to zero. She'd lost the game. Boyd had taken it with a one. It took a beat for it to sink in to Kate. Saved by the luck of the draw, she thought, letting out a *whoosh* of air.

Boyd whooped, pumping his fist in the air. "*That's* how you play the game. Watch and learn, boys."

Evan Trace strolled casually into the suite.

Nick looked over at him. "Well, this is a nice surprise."

"For both of us," Trace said, flashing his warmest smile. "I'm glad our trips here coincided. Now I can personally welcome you and your friends to Côte d'Argent Macau."

Nick stood up and turned to the others. "Gentlemen, I'd like to introduce you to—"

"*No freakin' gondolas!*" Boyd said, shouldering past Nick and thrusting his hand out to Trace. "Gambling straight up, that's how I like it, too. Just deal the cards and screw the show. I'm Shane Blackmore."

Trace shook his hand. "I'll tell you a little secret, Mr. Blackmore. Back when I was a gambler myself, my favorite casinos were the ones off the Strip, the dark rooms so thick with cigarette smoke that you could barely see the cards in your hands, but you could still smell the sweat, beer, and puke in the air."

"You just described my living room," Boyd said. "And my office."

"That does not surprise me," Billy Dee said to Boyd, then offered his hand to Trace. "I'm Lou Ould-Abdallah, but you may call me Lou. I'm glad you settled on a compromise between a casino that reeks of urine and one that's shaken every twenty minutes by the eruption of a fake volcano. This suite is perfect. I couldn't ask for anything more except, perhaps, a change in my luck."

"I can't do anything about your luck, Lou," Trace said, shaking Billy Dee's hand, "but if you do think of something else you'd like, perhaps a masseuse to loosen your muscles after sitting at the table all day, just ask Natasha or one of our other staff members. We will see to your needs immediately."

"I've got some," Boyd said with a mischievous grin. "I'd like a large Tim Hortons Caramel Latte Supreme and a dozen Honey Dip Timbits when you get a chance."

"We'll see what we can do," Trace said and slipped his arm around Nick's shoulder, like they were old chums. "Nick, do you have a few minutes? I'd like to steal you away for a quick chat."

"Of course." Nick turned and winked at Kate as he walked away with Trace. "Keep my seat warm, honey. Win me a quarter million while you're at it."

Billy Dee and Boyd returned to their seats at the table.

"There probably isn't a Tim Hortons within ten thousand miles of here." Boyd grinned at Billy Dee and bet $100,000 on the next hand.

"You like to needle people just to see how far you can push," Billy Dee said, betting $100,000 with Boyd this time. "I've known men like you before, may they rest in peace."

The dealer looked up at Kate.

"Will you be joining us?" Luisa asked.

"Maybe later," Kate said, moving to the bar while she eavesdropped on Nick and Trace through her earbud.

Nick and Trace walked out of the suite, closed the door, and went to the elevator directly across the hall. Trace pressed the elevator call button.

"What would you like to talk about?" Nick asked.

"You, Nick. I'd like to get to know you better now that we're doing business together."

"There isn't much to tell. I'm just an international entrepreneur who takes advantage of new opportunities as they come along."

The elevator doors opened, and there was a Côte d'Argent security man waiting for them inside.

Dumah, Nick thought. *Crap.*

14

"Remember me?" Dumah asked Nick as Nick stepped into the elevator.

"Of course I remember you," Nick said, thinking how to choose his words so Kate would get a grip on this new development. "Congratulations, Dumah. It's good to see you've found a job worthy of your skills."

Dumah caught him with a brutal sucker punch just below the rib cage and Nick folded, unable to breathe. Dumah grabbed him by the arm and propped him up.

"You understand now that we need to have a serious discussion?" Trace asked Nick.

Nick nodded, making an effort to relax, to give his lungs a chance to expand.

"Good," Trace said. "You're going to allow Dumah to assist you across the floor to my office."

Nick nodded again.

Kate heard everything that was happening in the elevator through her earbud. So did Billy Dee and Boyd. They looked over at her with concern, and she smiled at them from behind the bar.

"Go ahead and play without me, gentlemen," she said. "I think I need some air. I'll be right back."

Kate palmed a corkscrew from the bar and walked into the foyer. Natasha Ling was at the door, quietly standing, waiting to be of service.

"I'm just stepping out for some air," Kate said to Natasha.

"I'm so sorry, but you're not permitted to leave the suite at the present time," Natasha said, blocking Kate's path. "I suggest you go back to the bar and enjoy the game. Maybe have an egg tart. They're quite delicious."

"I suppose I could." Kate looked over her shoulder to make sure they were both out of view of the baccarat table before stepping close to Natasha and head-butting her. "But I won't."

The hostess staggered back, stunned by the blow. Kate shifted the corkscrew to her left hand and decked Natasha with a solid right hook, bouncing her head off the door and knocking her out cold. Kate caught Natasha before she reached the floor, dragged the woman into the adjoining bedroom, closed the door, and continued on her way to rescue Nick.

. . .

Nick had recovered by the time the elevator reached the ground floor, but he stayed doubled over, gasping for air, forcing Dumah to support him. He needed a moment to organize his thoughts, to stall for time.

Dumah half-carried, half-dragged Nick out of the elevator and across the noisy casino floor to the VIP salon.

"The VIP salon seems like a nice place to talk," Nick said. "We can have a few drinks, maybe play some cards after I catch my breath."

"I'd like a little more privacy," Trace said. "I'm sure you understand."

He did. He also knew that Kate was listening and he wanted to let her know where he was, and the seriousness of their situation, without being too obvious about it.

They led Nick through the salon, past the bar, to the door leading to Trace's private dining room. There was a security man standing guard at the door. As they approached, the guard took a transparent key card out of his pocket and passed it over a sensor on the wall, and the door unlocked.

"I'm either having déjà vu or the internal bleeding has deprived my brain of oxygen," Nick said. "Isn't your private dining room in the same place in Las Vegas?"

"It's exactly the same building, only with half as many floors," Trace said. "Ironically, it was twice as expensive to build, if you factor in all the bribes I had to pay Chinese officials."

138

Nick wasn't in the mood to appreciate irony. He was trying to think of how he was going to talk his way out of this.

The guard held the door for the three men as they passed, then closed it behind them. They walked into the sunny atrium, over the bridge, and into the open dining room. There was a man waiting for them who looked like he'd used his face to pound in fence posts. He was holding a mallet.

Not a good sign, Nick thought. This guy wasn't wearing a chef coat so you could assume he wasn't going to use the mallet to pound the heck out of a veal cutlet.

Dumah pushed Nick into a chair at the pond's edge and secured Nick's wrists to the arms of the chair with zip ties.

"You already know Dumah, from your experience in Dajmaboutu," Trace said. "This other gentleman is Mr. Garver, our senior customer relations technician. You really don't want to know him."

"At least not until I can put some plastic sheeting on the floor," Garver said, hefting his mallet, enjoying the weight. "This is nice carpet."

"Look, this has gone way too far already," Nick said. "Untie me, pour me a drink, and let's have a civilized conversation about whatever has got you riled up. You don't want to do something you're going to regret."

Trace smiled and leaned close to Nick. "I don't have regrets. Only losers have those. Tell me about the scam you're running. Every detail. Don't leave anything out."

"I'm not scamming anyone," Nick said. "I'm getting into the junket business."

"Wrong answer."

Garver tipped Nick's chair so that the back of the chair was flat to the floor and extended over the pond filled with piranha.

Kate didn't wait for the elevator. She took the stairs down to the casino, listening on the earbud as Nick pointed her to the VIP salon and Trace's private dining room.

She reached the ground floor and opened the door to the casino. A security guard stood in the doorway, his wide body blocking her path. He looked like a Macanese weightlifter stuffed into a Dolce & Gabbana suit that was a size too small.

"Going somewhere?" he asked.

Kate jammed the corkscrew into his crotch, puncturing the fabric of his pants and pressing the sharp point against his shriveling scrotum. His entire body went rigid.

"Unless you want to become a eunuch, you'll step very slowly inside here with me," she said, backing up into the stairwell. He did as he was told, but the instant the door closed behind him, he head-butted her.

Kate fell back, dazed and angry that she'd been surprised by the same move she'd used on Natasha. He swatted the corkscrew away from her and then backhanded her across the face.

Kate retaliated with a brutal kick to the inside of the guard's left knee, buckling him. He toppled to one side, grabbing Kate's other leg while going down and taking her to the floor with him.

Kate pulled his other leg out from under him as they fell, flipped him over on his back, and drove her elbow into his solar plexus with her full body weight. It was an elbow drop. A *WWE SmackDown* move that took the wind out of him. A follow-up punch in the face put him down for the count.

She searched through his jacket pockets and found a five-inch telescoping steel baton. It was a nice trade up from the corkscrew. Kate got to her feet, held the baton down between her arm and her side to shield it from view, and walked out into the casino.

Nick was balanced on the tipped-over chair with the back of his head hanging an inch above the water.

Trace tossed a piece of dim sum into the pond and the water roiled with piranha, fighting over the morsel.

"All it takes is one piranha brushing against your cheek, smelling your flesh, and they'll all swarm on you," Trace said to Nick. "They'll eat your face right off your skull and then start chewing their way into your brain. That could happen any second now."

"I'd like to prevent that from happening," Nick said.

"Then tell me what you and Kate did to Derek Griffin."

"We wanted his half a billion dollars," Nick said in a rush. "We found out where he was hiding and decided the best way to get his money was to kidnap him. Make him pay a ransom to free himself."

Trace tossed another piece of dim sum just under Nick's head, and Nick could actually hear teeth gnashing, as the piranha chewed on one another in their mad lust to get a share of the steamed dumpling. He wondered if Kate, Boyd, and Billy Dee could hear it, too.

Kate could hear it. She didn't know exactly *what* she was hearing, but she knew it couldn't be good. She crossed through the crowded VIP salon toward the guard who was posted at the door to Trace's dining room. As she neared him, she whipped the baton open in her hand. It expanded to two feet of solid tempered steel with a satisfying metallic snap.

The guard reached for his gun. Kate whacked his arm, then his knee, and, as he fell, she brought the baton down across his back, finishing the job.

Kate dropped the baton and took the guard's holstered gun, trading up her weapon once again. If this trend continued, the next guard she disarmed would have a rocket launcher.

She rummaged through the guard's pockets, got his key card, and swept it over the sensor by the door.

"Did Griffin pay?" Trace asked Nick.

"Not the half billion, but we got ten million dollars out of him. We split that with the pirates and set him adrift in international waters," Nick said. "That's it."

Trace sighed in a show of disappointment. "You're still holding back. You haven't explained how Griffin ended up in Palm Springs two days later."

Trace tossed an egg custard tart into the water above Nick's head. The tart broke apart when it hit the water and the piranha went insane. The water boiled with them. The razor-toothed fish were jumping all around Nick's head. One of the monsters was bound to land on his face soon.

"We told some bounty hunters where they could find him," Nick said. "I've got no idea how he ended up in Palm Springs after that."

"Why would you give him to bounty hunters?"

"To protect ourselves," Nick said. "Griffin couldn't come after us if he was broke and in a prison cell."

"So you're just two lowlife swindlers trying to make a buck any way you can."

"Of course we are," Kate said.

Trace, Garver, and Dumah had been so caught up in the piranha frenzy happening around Nick's head that they hadn't heard Kate come in. Now there she was, standing on the bridge, aiming a gun at Trace. She had a strong and natural firing stance. She was firmly in control of herself. Trace saw beads of sweat on her chest, flecks of blood on her knuckles, and stony determination in her gaze. In that moment, she was the sexiest and most dangerous woman Trace had ever seen.

"Who else would have friends like Ould-Abdallah and Blackmore?" Kate said as she walked toward Trace, keeping her gun leveled at him as she did. "Who else would set up a junket to launder money through a casino in Macau? I don't know what kind of people you thought we were supposed to be. Missionaries, perhaps?"

Trace didn't move as she approached. "I see your point."

"Do you? You're making money on this deal and so are we. So what difference does it make what we did in the past? Are you in this business to make money or not?"

She stepped right up to him and pressed the gun barrel against his forehead. Trace looked her in the eye for a long moment. He thought about what she'd said and about the violence that she must have inflicted just to get to this room. He totally understood why Griffin risked everything to get her into bed.

"I guess I lost my head," he finally said.

"Not yet, but you almost did. The only reason your brains aren't all over the wall is because I don't want to jeopardize the money that we're making upstairs." Kate lowered the gun, handed it to Trace, and then looked past him to Dumah. "Don't just stand there, you dumb ape, get Nick out of that chair."

Trace gave Dumah and Garver a nod and the two men lifted the chair upright. Dumah cut the zip ties, freeing Nick's wrists.

"I'm disappointed in you, Evan," Nick said. "I thought you were a smart man. You could have made a lot of money with us. But after tonight, we're taking our business to the Grand Lisboa. Now if you'll excuse us, we've got a game running upstairs."

Nick put his arm around Kate, and they walked over the

bridge just as a bunch of security guards came rushing through the door from the VIP salon. Trace ordered the guards to stand down with a simple wave of his hand. The bewildered guards moved aside and let Nick and Kate pass.

"That was an amazing performance," Nick said once they were clear of the VIP salon and strolling casually through the casino toward the elevator.

"I was going to say the same thing to you," Kate said.

"I had the easy part," Nick said. "I just told them the truth with a lie or two thrown in. You had to intimidate them into folding."

"That's not so hard when you're holding a gun," she said.

"It wasn't the gun that sealed the deal," he said. "It was how you got there and what it revealed about you. I wouldn't want to get on your bad side."

"You have been on my bad side," she said.

Nick broke into a grin. "That's right, and it was a lot of fun. I kind of miss it. And by the way, did you notice you gave Trace a stiffie?"

"That wasn't me," Kate said. "He had it when I came in."

15

Trace sent everyone away except Garver and Dumah.

"I'm surprised that you let Sweet and Porter just walk out of here," Dumah said. "They're playing you."

"I'm a reasonable man and they made a convincing argument," Trace said. "Griffin was fair game, a swindler who got swindled. There's nothing wrong with what Nick and Kate did to him. In fact, I admire how they did it. It shows that they're smart and daring. The fact is, those two have done nothing to me but make me richer."

"It's just a part of their plan," Dumah said.

"I really like that part. But now it could be over because I let my curiosity override my good judgment," Trace said. "I have to find a way to apologize and win back their business."

"You don't want to do that," Dumah said. "They're liars and crooks."

"My best customers are liars and crooks. I can live with that. But do you know what I can't live with?" Trace stepped up to Dumah. "Underlings who question my decisions."

"I'm sorry, Mr. Trace." Dumah lowered his head. "I'm just trying to serve you better than I did Griffin."

"No, you want to avenge your honor," Trace said. "So listen to me very closely. If anything bad happens to Nick and Kate while they are in Macau, I will hold you personally responsible. If Nick stubs his toe and breaks it getting out of bed, it's on you. If Kate gets bitten by a mosquito and has an allergic reaction, it's on you. And the consequences for you will be extreme and disfiguring. Do I make myself clear?"

"Yes, sir," Dumah said.

"You can go now," Trace said.

Dumah nodded and walked out.

Trace watched him go. He would never admit it to Dumah, but he had taken the bodyguard's warning to heart. He wasn't going to act on it the way Dumah, or even Nick and Kate, would expect him to act. He was going to follow Nick and Kate's example instead. He'd swindle the swindlers.

Garver joined Trace at his side and gestured to the chair with a swing of his mallet.

"This wasn't a mistake," Garver said. "Now you know who they really are."

"And they know me," Trace said.

"That's a good thing," Garver said.

It certainly was. Because the next time one of them was in that chair, and Trace believed it was likely that one of them would be, they'd know that they deserved their suffering and that he had every right to thoroughly enjoy it.

Kate went back to her room to change her blood-splattered clothes, making a mental note to do more sucker punches to the throat and hand out fewer broken noses. She discarded the clothes, showered in steaming hot water, and dressed in an indigo cap-sleeved cashmere pullover and white slacks that were like a second skin thanks to a large percentage of spandex. She swiped on some lip gloss and mascara, pulled her hair into a ponytail, and returned to the VIP suite.

The woman who opened the door to the suite introduced herself as Birgita.

"Natasha has fallen ill," Birgita said. "It hit her very suddenly, but she'll be fine tomorrow. May I offer you a cocktail?"

Kate declined and went into the living room, where the game was still in progress. Billy Dee and Boyd were still seated at the baccarat table. They'd each bet $150,000 against the dealer. Nick had joined them.

"You're missing out," Boyd said to Kate. "Birgita makes an amazing lemon-drop martini."

He held up his empty glass to Birgita, who took it with her to the bar. "Another one, Mr. Blackmore?"

"Absolutely," Boyd said. "With lots of sugar on the rim."

"That's a manly drink," Billy Dee said. "Maybe you'd like some whipped cream on it, too? And a little umbrella stuck into it."

Boyd turned to Birgita. "Make sure the martini is shaken, not stirred."

"Now it's manly," Kate said.

The four of them shared a smile. It was an acknowledgment that they were glad to be together again, alive and well.

They could have stayed at Côte d'Argent for dinner, but Billy Dee was eager to explore Macau and see what remained of the dangerous port city he once knew. Kate, Nick, and Boyd were glad to join him after being cooped up in the suite all day. They'd gone from the chopper to the car to the hotel without really stepping outside. They were in Macau, but they could have been anywhere.

They left the casino and followed the tiled sidewalks along Avenida de Almeida Ribeiro toward Senado Square, the heart of the old city. The sidewalk was a uniquely Portuguese mosaic of black and white stones, known as *calçada portuguesa,* that had been painstakingly laid by hand to depict the fish, boats, and sunshine that had been vital to Macau's economy before the casinos came along.

The tiles in Senado Square had a wave pattern that became dizzying, almost animated, when it was revealed in glimpses beneath the feet of the hundreds of Chinese tourists and

Macanese locals in the wide plaza. Kate kept her eyes up, taking in the pastel-colored neoclassical buildings around her, each one filled with history and one with a crowded McDonald's.

Billy Dee shook his head with disgust as they passed the McDonald's. "There used to be a terrific whorehouse in there."

"This is better," Boyd said. "They have a dollar menu."

"They had a dollar menu at the whorehouse," Billy Dee said.

"Do we have a destination?" Kate asked.

"Lorca's Hideaway," Billy Dee said. "Hopefully it hasn't been taken over by a Gap. Back in the day, it was run by a one-eyed fisherman and opium addict. Fabulous Macanese food upstairs and the best opium den in the city in the basement."

"It would be a shame to visit Macau and not sample the opium," Boyd said. "It would be like going to New York and not having a hot dog."

There were several narrow roads spiraling off from the square. Billy Dee started to go up one of them, then abruptly doubled back, choosing to go on a different one. The road that he picked was crammed with people and weaved up through a tangle of side streets and dead-end alleys, toward the ruins of St. Paul's Cathedral. Both sides of the road were lined with *pastelarias,* open store fronts that sold cookies, candies, and sheets of meat jerky that were stacked like reams of paper. The competition between the *pastelarias* was fierce. Shopkeepers cut samples from the jerky with scissors and used tongs to thrust pieces of meat out at the passersby. Other shopkeepers held out baskets and platters of cookie pieces. It created a bottleneck. People bunched up as they stopped to grab samples or avoid colliding into someone.

When Billy Dee doubled back Kate caught three men in her peripheral vision who doubled back with them. She couldn't see their faces, but she had a fix on their clothes and their size. The men were doing their best to stay close but were hugging the walls to avoid being caught behind in the bottleneck or, worse, being shoved up against their quarry.

Kate sampled the thick boar fillet from one *pastelaria,* the top beef filet with black pepper from another, then zigzagged across the street for a taste of spicy pork with abalone sauce. Along the way she managed to steal a pair of greasy scissors from a shopkeeper's apron pocket.

"Where is Lorca's?" Kate asked Billy Dee.

"On Travessa da Fortuna," he said. "It's a side street that's coming up."

"You keep going," Kate said. "I'll catch up with you."

Nick kept his gaze focused in front of him as he navigated through the crowd. "You're worried about the three guys following us."

"When did you spot them?" she asked.

"When Billy Dee changed his mind about which street to take," Nick said.

She wasn't surprised that he'd noticed the tail when she did. He'd been a con man and a fugitive for years, so looking over his shoulder for the police or someone that he'd swindled had become instinctive.

"I picked up a pair of scissors, if you'd like them," Nick said.

That didn't surprise her, either. He was a gifted pickpocket. "Already got my own, thanks."

"I've also got tongs and an entire sheet of pork neck jerky wrapped in paper."

"Now you're just showing off."

They turned right onto Travessa da Fortuna, a tight, dark alley that dead-ended at a retaining wall with a mossy concrete staircase cut into it that went up the hillside. The only light in the alley was cast by the windows of a small restaurant in a lopsided old stone building that seemed to be leaning against the retaining wall for support.

Billy Dee, Boyd, and Nick went on ahead toward the restaurant, but Kate slipped into a dark alcove, pulled out her scissors, and waited. On the stoop beside her, there was a smoking stick of incense in a small bucket of ashes. The bucket was on a decorative platter with a lemon, dried flower petals, and several small cups of tea. It was a shrine, left for good luck by whoever lived or worked behind the closed door. Kate put the scissors in her back pocket and picked up the bucket of ashes. She said a small silent prayer, asking forgiveness from whoever or whatever was in the bucket. And as the three figures passed the alcove, she heaved the ashes on them. She leapt out while they were blinded and coughing, smacked one across the face with the bucket, hit another in the groin, then whirled around, taking out the third with a spin kick. She whipped the scissors out of her pocket and jammed them against the throat of the guy she'd hit with the bucket. His head was covered with ash, but she recognized him. It was Dumah.

"Did Trace send you, or is this personal?" Kate said.

"No, you've got it all wrong," Dumah said, coughing on the ash.

"You boys weren't just out for an evening stroll." Kate looked over at the other two men, who were getting slowly to their feet. One was the man she'd fought in the Côte d'Argent stairwell, the other was the guy who'd been guarding the door to Trace's dining room. They all had good reason to want her dead. "Were you looking for an opportunity to kill me or just give me a good beating?"

"We're here to protect you," Dumah said. "Mr. Trace has put us in charge of your safety. If anything happens to you in Macau, we'll be held accountable."

"So do us a favor and stay out of dark alleys while you're here," the stairwell guy said, slightly pitched forward, his hand cupping his privates.

This was the second time she'd assaulted him today. She almost felt sorry for him.

"And please watch what you eat," the other guard said. "Make sure the egg tarts are fresh and avoid oysters."

"You're in trouble even if we get food poisoning?" Kate asked.

"We don't want to find out," Dumah said.

Kate saw the fear in his eyes and didn't think it was from the scissors at his throat. "Have you ever considered a different line of work?"

"Not until today," he said.

The dining room décor and the menu at Lorca's hadn't changed since Billy Dee's day, but everything else was different. The one-eyed opium addict who'd established Lorca's had died, and the restaurant was now run by his grandson Ernesto, who'd honed his culinary skills in the finest kitchens in Lisbon and Hong Kong. The opium den downstairs had been turned into a coffeehouse and performance space used mostly for poetry readings. The customers appeared to be clean-cut and middle-class. The only pirates, con men, and thieves in the room, as far as Kate could tell, were the four of them.

They ate pork-stuffed squid, grilled sardines, deep-fried salted cod balls, and *minchi,* a bowl of minced meat, onions, cheese, soy sauce, and a fried egg. Kate thought the food was incredible. It was a tasty fusion of Portuguese and Chinese flavors, unlike anything she'd had before. Billy Dee remained sour faced throughout the meal.

"What's wrong with you?" Boyd asked him.

"Macau has lost its charm," Billy Dee said. "All of the danger is gone."

"I almost got killed today," Nick said. "Doesn't that count?"

"It's not the same. The only person attacking anyone in dark alleys with knives these days is Kate, and she lets them live."

Billy Dee tipped his head toward the front window, where they could see Dumah and the two other security men milling around outside, smoking cigarettes.

"Technically it was a pair of scissors," Kate said. "And I let them go because they're protecting us."

"From what?" Billy Dee said. "A painful reading from a desperate poet? Seeing Macau today is like looking at a toothless lion. It's sad and pathetic."

"Your disappointment with Macau aside, this trip has been a smashing success," Nick said. "I toast you all."

He raised a glass of 2011 Douros Muxagat Tinto, a fine Portuguese wine, to them and took a sip.

"But isn't the show over?" Boyd said. "You told Trace that you're finished, that you're taking your business to the Grand Lisboa."

"So that's it," Billy Dee said. "We're done. It would be extremely suspicious if you went back to him after what he did to you."

"You're absolutely right," Nick said. "That's why it's the best possible thing that could have happened for the success of our scam. Now we don't have to entice Trace into our scheme. He'll come running to us. He'll do whatever he can to win back our junket business."

"How can you be so sure?" Kate asked.

"Because his ego won't allow him to let us take our money elsewhere," Nick said. "That would be losing."

"If he's got such a big ego," Billy Dee said, "he's not going to humble himself by apologizing to you and groveling for your money."

"He won't see it that way," Nick said. "He'll see it as using his awesome powers of persuasion on us. And when we say 'Yes, we'll come back,' he'll love us for it. We'll be in solid. Having us around will reinforce his image of himself as absolutely irresistible. Look at it from his angle. Why else would we go into business with him again, and overlook the terrible things that he did to us, unless he was amazing? Best of all, because we walked away, our legitimacy never comes into question again."

"So he's conning himself and doing our work for us," Kate said.

"Wonderful, isn't it?" Nick said.

"It's a thing of beauty." Kate raised her glass to him. "If it works."

And if it doesn't, she thought, by her calculations they'd just given a crook $625,000 to keep up his good work.

16

Kate got out of bed the next morning, opened her drapes, and stared at the Wynn and MGM Grand across the street. To her right, on the tip of the peninsula, was the thousand-foot-high Macau Tower, a Chinese version of the Seattle Space Needle.

She was about to turn away when she saw someone dive off the Macau Tower to certain death. Her breath caught in her throat and she pressed her face against the glass, wincing into the glare, when she saw another person jump. It took her a moment to realize that both people were tethered to bungee cords and that leaping off the tower was some kind of tourist attraction. Even so, it was a startling way to start her day. But at least she could inform Billy Dee that it was still possible to cheat death in Macau.

. . .

She showered and dressed in a sleeveless black knit top, black jeans, and her trusty ballerina flats. Breakfast was being served down the hall, in the VIP gambling suite.

Nick, Boyd, and Billy Dee were already there. They were eating fresh fruit, pumpkin cakes, steamed milk pudding, and eggs that were scrambled with onions, vegetables, and minced *bacalhau*, fried Portuguese salted cod. They were being served their breakfast by Natasha Ling, who greeted Kate with a warm smile, as if she was genuinely pleased to see the woman who'd decked her.

"I hope you had a restful evening," Natasha said.

"Likewise," Kate said.

"What would you like for breakfast?"

Kate took a seat beside Nick. "I'll have whatever they're having."

"Very good. I'll be back in a moment."

Natasha went away to wherever the eighth-floor VIP kitchen was hidden, and Birgita came to the table with a silver tray that held a platter of donut holes and four large red paper cups with the Tim Hortons logo on them.

"Would anyone care for an extra-large Caramel Latte Supreme and fresh Honey Dip Timbits?" Birgita asked.

"I'll be damned," Boyd said. "Where did you get that?"

"There's a Tim Hortons in Dubai. We sent our private jet and one of our chefs there yesterday for you." She handed Boyd a cup. "Careful, it's very hot."

Boyd handled the cup gingerly, cracked open the white lid,

and sniffed the aroma with obvious pleasure. "Nice. Why did you send a chef?"

She used silver tongs to delicately place a few Timbits on his plate as if they were exquisite gourmet pastries instead of glazed donut holes. "It was his responsibility to keep the coffee and Timbits at the optimum temperature to retain their flavor, consistency, and freshness during the seven-hour flight. The jet landed in Macau just a few minutes ago."

"Now *that's* service," Boyd said. "You've all got to try this. Best coffee and donuts on the planet."

Birgita passed out the coffees and Timbits to each of them. Kate tried one of the Timbits and nodded in appreciation.

"It's donut hole perfection," she said.

Billy Dee sipped the coffee. "I must admit that it's a fine cup of joe."

"I agree," Evan Trace said, strolling into the room with a large Tim Hortons coffee cup in his hand. "Maybe I should talk to Horton about opening an outlet here in Côte d'Argent."

Trace probably could have built a Tim Hortons for what it cost him to make that coffee run to Dubai. But in the cosmic scheme of things, Kate knew, the gesture was inexpensive compared to the money he'd already earned from them and the profits he stood to lose if they took their business elsewhere.

"You do and I'll never gamble anywhere else," Boyd said.

"I'll hold you to that," Trace said with a smile. "Nick, Kate, could I please have a word with you in the living room? Bring your coffees with you if you'd like."

Kate and Nick got up and followed Trace into the living room. They were still within view of Boyd and Billy Dee but presumably out of earshot if they kept their voices low. Kate knew Trace did that to make them feel safe. Trace didn't know, of course, that Boyd and Billy Dee could hear every word on their earbuds.

"I understand that you stopped by the Grand Lisboa last night and had drinks with the manager of guest relations," Trace said.

Nick and Kate knew that Dumah had probably dutifully reported that to Trace last night.

"We were in the neighborhood," Nick said. "We didn't want to miss the opportunity to establish a personal relationship with the people we might be doing business with on our next junket."

"I don't blame you," Trace said, a somber expression on his face. "You had a very unpleasant experience here yesterday."

"That's an understatement," Kate said.

"Yes, it is. We've comped your rooms, of course. But that doesn't go nearly far enough. You and your guests lost six hundred and twenty-five thousand dollars at the baccarat table. I have wired that amount, along with the two million that you lost playing blackjack in Las Vegas, to your bank account in St. Kitts," Trace said. "You aren't out a dime to me and you're up six hundred and twenty-five thousand if you choose not to share the refund of yesterday's gambling losses with your guests. Whatever you decide, it will remain our secret. I just hope this small gesture demonstrates my remorse, the sincerity of my apology, and my fervent hope that we can begin a new relationship built on a foundation of mutual trust and respect."

Trace didn't wait for a response to his contrition speech. He bid them farewell with a slight nod and walked out of the suite. It was a classy exit.

Nick and Kate remained stony faced, although they were cheering inside. Natasha and Birgita were watching and would definitely report to the boss.

"He's hooked," Nick whispered.

"Yeah," Kate said. "We should have asked him to reimburse us for the jet."

"Better yet, I think we should let him know there are no hard feelings by bringing him a new whale. Preferably one from Hawaii with Yakuza money."

They went back to the table and finished their breakfast. An hour later the four of them were on a Côte d'Argent chopper headed to Hong Kong International Airport to begin their long journeys back home.

The day after Kate got back from China, she went to her sister Megan's home in Calabasas to relax in Megan's backyard. Megan and her family lived in a Spanish-Mediterranean McMansion on a hillside that overlooked the Calabasas Country Club and the San Fernando Valley. They had lots of comfy outdoor furniture, a pool, a Jacuzzi, and a barbecue island with a smoker, a bread warmer, and a refrigerator. Kate considered the place her own personal resort. So did her father, who lived on the property in a detached garage that had been converted into an apartment.

Kate and Megan were sunbathing on side-by-side chaise longues, drinking homemade sangrias and sharing Nacho Cheese Doritos from a huge bowl on the table between them. Kate was in a black bikini and Megan wore a floral "miracle-slimming" one-piece with a skirt that was supposed to hide her butt, though there was no one around to hide it from. Roger was at work, Jake was on the golf course, and the kids were at school.

"While you've been away, we've been terrorized by coyotes," Megan said. "They're killing pets and crapping all over everybody's yards. Dad wants to shoot them, but that's illegal. So he's come up with another approach."

"He's planting land mines on the hillside?"

"Even better. He and Roger go out at night and pee all around the yard."

"You're making that up."

"It's true. Roger read somewhere that human pee keeps the coyotes away."

"I bet a guy wrote the article just to give other guys an excuse to pee outdoors."

"Men are strange," Megan said, taking a sip of her sangria. "While we're on the subject, anyone new and exciting in your life?"

"Maybe," Kate said.

"I knew it." Megan sat up on the chaise longue. "Have you had sex with him yet?"

"There is no sex."

"But there's heat," Megan said.

"Scalding," Kate said.

It was the first time Kate had admitted to the attraction out loud, and she was surprised that she said *scalding*. *Scalding* was pretty heavy-duty in terms of attraction.

"So what's the problem?" Megan asked.

Kate sipped her sangria. "We're co-workers."

Megan dismissed the comment with a wave of her hand that ended with her scooping a bunch of Doritos from the bowl. "Nobody at the FBI has a life except at the FBI, so don't tell me everybody isn't sleeping with everybody. You'll have to do better than that. What's his name?"

"Bob," Kate said.

"Bob," Megan said, clearly not buying it. She ate a couple of chips and stared at Kate. It was an effective interrogation technique that Kate had used herself.

"I can't tell you his real name because he's an undercover agent. In fact, he's been undercover for so long that he's spent more time as a criminal than an FBI agent," Kate said. "I think he actually prefers being a criminal. He enjoys breaking rules, defying authority, and being unconventional. The thing is, that's what makes him so good at what he does."

"I can see how that would drive you crazy," Megan said.

"I believe the rules exist for a reason."

"I meant crazy horny," she said.

"Oh," Kate said. "There's some of that."

"There's a *lot* of that or we wouldn't be having this discussion," Megan said. "Bottom line, you want to sleep with Bob but you're not. So let's see if we can figure out what's really holding you back. What are his pros and cons? Pros first."

Kate began ticking them off on her fingers. "He's charming, funny, adventurous, romantic, daring, and hot."

"Cons?"

"He's dishonest, manipulative, egotistical, reckless, and hot."

"I noticed *hot* is in both columns. Your problem is that you live for the chase," Megan said. "It's like what happened with Nicolas Fox."

Kate froze for an instant. "What does Fox have to do with this?"

"I saw how happy you were when you were chasing him, and how miserable you were when you finally caught him, and how thrilled you were when he escaped so you could go back to chasing him. It's the Fox Complex all over again."

"You've given it a name?"

"We've talked about this a lot," Megan said.

"We?" Kate said. "Who is *we*?"

"Me, Roger, Dad, and the kids."

"The kids, too?"

"You're afraid if you catch this guy, you'll lose the excitement in your life and the goal-oriented sense of purpose that drives you."

"You've got me all wrong," Kate said, hearing the lack of conviction in her voice.

"So you're telling me that you won't be miserable if you catch Nicolas Fox."

"*When* I catch him, not *if*," Kate said. "It's going to happen."

"Okay, then, if the outcome is inevitable, what you should be thinking about isn't all the ways you can avoid getting what you want, but how to accept it once you have it."

"Are you talking now about me catching Fox or going to bed with Bob?"

Megan looked Kate in the eye. "It's the same thing."

Kate wondered if her sister really knew that it was, or if it was purely intuition or just a coincidence that she brought Nick into the discussion. Not that it mattered. Megan was right.

17

Kate showered, changed into a T-shirt and jeans, and walked into Megan's kitchen to find her sister cutting the crusts off sandwiches, leaving the crusts on the counter, and arranging the sandwiches on a plate.

"Wonder Bread, cold cuts, and Kraft cheese slices," Kate said. "Dad's favorite."

"He's always hungry when he comes back from the golf course," Megan said, sweeping the crusts off the countertop and into the trash masher. "You should have seen Dad when he got back from Hawaii. He was sunburned and covered in bug bites. I've never seen anyone so happy to be uncomfortable."

"That's what happens when you fall asleep on the beach."

"That's what happens when you sleep in the jungle," Megan

said, setting the plate of sandwiches on the center island in front of Kate.

"Why would Dad do that?" Kate asked, playing innocent.

"Nostalgia. Sometimes I worry that he's going a little crazy here."

"He's the same man he always was. He hasn't changed at all."

"I hope you're wrong. Because if that's true, and his pee stops scaring off the coyotes, he *will* start putting land mines on our hill," Megan said. "Where did all of your bruises come from?"

Kate helped herself to a salami and cheese sandwich. "What bruises?"

"The ones all over your body. Your bikini doesn't hide much."

"Kickboxing."

Megan raised an eyebrow, dubious. "Since when do you kickbox?"

"It's a great way to relieve tension."

"So is sex."

"Kickboxing is a lot less complicated."

"But you don't get the Big O."

"I can have all the Oreos I want. Kickboxing burns a lot of calories."

"That's not the 'O' I was talking about."

"You are oversexed."

"And proud of it. Look, Kate, I know a beating when I see one. Dad used to come back from his military missions with the same kind of bruises that I saw all over you. I know it's got to hurt, and I'm not just talking about the injuries that I can see. If you ever want to talk about it, I'm here."

"I know that." Kate gave her sister a hug. "But I can't."

"At least tell me the other guy looks worse."

"Other *guys*," she said. "And yes, they do."

Megan smiled. "That'll teach them to mess with my sister."

They heard the front door open and Jake came in, wearing a bright yellow Greg Norman golf polo shirt and white slacks.

"I thought you were a man who likes to blend in," Kate said. "I need sunglasses to look at you."

"It's a matter of survival. There are a lot of seniors with bad eyesight on the course on weekdays," Jake said. "You have to stand out or you could get hit by a golf ball."

Megan grabbed her car keys off the counter. Her huge key chain had six keys on it, a dozen charms that her kids had made, a tiny flashlight, and countless membership cards from various stores.

"I have to pick up the kids," Megan said.

"They don't get out of school for another hour," Jake said.

"If I don't park in front of Bay Laurel now, I'll get stuck for an hour in the pickup line and the kids will have to wait." Megan gave Kate a kiss. "It was great to see you. Let me know how it goes with Bob."

"You bet," Kate said.

Megan left the house and Jake selected a sandwich from the plate.

"Who is Bob?"

"Nobody you know. How are you?"

"Eager to hear how the con is going." He took a bite out of his sandwich.

"Things didn't quite go according to plan, but we think we've hooked Trace."

Kate told him all about what happened in Macau. By the time she was done with her story, Jake had eaten all of the sandwiches and finished a can of beer.

"Those men are lucky they're still alive," Jake said. "But what amazes me is that you got through all of that without sacrificing the con."

"It might even be stronger now."

"You and Nick are good together," Jake said. "Probably in more ways than you know."

"Let's not go there."

"You keep saying that to yourself, but maybe it's time for a rethink."

"Since when are you interested in my love life?"

"You don't have one. You're all about the job. With Bob, you can have both."

"You don't know anything about Bob."

"I know it's got to be Nick, because there isn't anybody else," Jake said. "Who could possibly compete?"

"Someone who isn't a criminal on the FBI's Most Wanted list for starters."

"How boring would that guy be? He couldn't match the excitement Nick brings to your life. For instance, what's up next in the scam?"

"A few weeks off," Kate said.

"Since when do you take a vacation in the middle of a scam?"

"We can't rush right back into business with Trace. Because if we do, it will seem suspicious after what he did to us. He's got to believe that it was a hard decision for us to go back to Côte d'Argent. Or he needs to come to us in the meantime. So now it's a waiting game."

"You're terrible at that game."

"I'm working on it," Kate said. "They say that patience is a virtue."

"That might be true," Jake said. "But in my experience, the virtuous are usually the first to die."

18

Kate spent the next few days in her cubicle at the Federal Building, catching up on paperwork. Not her favorite thing to do but part of her job. It was especially gruesome now that she was partnered with Nick, because the paperwork involved a secret expense account. She had to itemize and justify Nick's outrageous purchases, and she had to do it in code.

Purchased $1,200 size 5 designer bandage dress to disguise informant in sting operation, she typed as Special Agent Seth Ryerson came up behind her on his way to the coffee machine. He wasn't much older than her and was spending a lot of time cross-training and lifting weights to make up for his rapid hair loss. He was bulking up in direct proportion to how much his hair was thinning out. To cover his bald spots, he'd started using spray-on particles that resembled wet chocolate cake mix dumped on his head.

"I haven't seen you around much," Ryerson said.

"I'm not going to find Nicolas Fox or close my other cases by sitting at a desk," Kate said. "I do my best work in the field."

"The scuttlebutt is that one of those other cases involves high-stakes gambling."

"I can't talk about it," she said. "It's very hush-hush."

"I understand, but if you need help, I'd be glad to jump in. I know my way around a deck of cards."

"You don't strike me as a gambler. You break out in a flop sweat scratching a lottery ticket."

"You haven't seen me play bridge," he said. "Or canasta. I'm a warrior who doesn't take prisoners."

"You know those aren't big casino games, right?"

"Because they're too brutal," Ryerson said. "Anybody can play poker or blackjack. Those are for the timid. Tournament bridge is a blood sport. It's the cage fighting of card games, believe me. I've got the scars to prove it."

He showed her his hands, palms up.

Kate squinted at his hands. "What am I looking at?"

"This." He used his left hand to point at a barely perceptible line on the tip of his right index finger.

"It looks like a paper cut."

"It's a scar," Ryerson said. "It came from bridge. I've felt the sting. The point is, I've got the experience if you need someone to play any card games for you as part of your investigation."

Jessup walked past them toward his office. "Kate, could I see you for a moment?"

"Sure." She got up from her seat and edged past Ryerson. "Thanks for the offer. I'll keep you in mind."

Kate walked into Jessup's corner office and closed the door. He had an unobstructed view of the Sepulveda Pass to the north and could see clear to the Pacific to the west, but she was sure that he rarely ever noticed any of it. His desk was intentionally arranged so his back was to the window and he faced two walls.

"Ryerson just asked me about the gambling investigation I'm doing," Kate said. "You're the only one who could have put that news on the grapevine."

"I'm watching your back in case anyone sees you in Vegas, particularly at a buffet. There's so much illegal activity surrounding the gambling industry that the town is swarming with FBI, DEA, ATF, and IRS agents all investigating something."

"Why the special concern about buffets?"

"Because I've never met a federal agent or an ex-soldier who can resist all-you-can-eat, especially on an expense account."

"Good point," she said.

"How are things going with Evan Trace?"

"We've succeeded in firmly establishing ourselves in his money laundering operation and even got him to reimburse us for almost every dollar we've spent doing it," Kate said, hoping that reminding Jessup that she'd saved money would score her some points. "Now we're in position to set the trap that will take him down."

"That's good, because you're going to have to spring it right away," Jessup said. "The CIA has picked up some intel. A month from now an al-Qaeda representative is going to Côte d'Argent Macau on a junket to pass money to a terrorist cell planning an attack in Europe. We can't let that happen."

"The CIA could kidnap or kill the guy," Kate said.

"Of course the CIA will try, *if* they can ID him, but that would be a delaying tactic at best. Al-Qaeda will just find someone else to be their front man," Jessup said. "The best way to stop the money from changing hands is to destroy Côte d'Argent's money laundering operation."

"If we appear too eager to get back into business with Trace, it could rekindle his suspicions about us."

"That's a chance you'll have to take."

"Would you ever work with someone who'd dangled you over a pool of piranha?"

"Maybe I would if he gave me two million six hundred twenty-five thousand dollars and said he was very, very sorry," Jessup said. "Most criminals I know put money ahead of everything else. Rushing back into business with Trace might just prove to him how crooked you really are and bolster your covers."

"I hope you're right," Kate said.

"Me, too," Jessup said. "I've never had one of my agents devoured by fish before and I'd like to keep it that way."

.   .   .

Shortly after noon on the following day, Nick and Kate pulled into the red-dirt parking lot of Da Grinds & Da Shave Ice in Kahuku, Hawaii. Nick parked their blazing red Ferrari California convertible beside Lono Alika's brand-new Ford F-150 Raptor, which had a modified grill that resembled shark teeth. A big Hawaiian with his right leg in a cast sat in a folding beach chair in the truck bed, guarding Alika's ride from getting dinged by a tourist or blown up by any retired soldiers.

Nick and Kate got out and walked up to the restaurant's patio, where Alika held court. Kate wore a Versace black-and-violet leopard-print racer-back minidress with a pair of palazzo leather sandals. Nick was Gucci casual from head to toe in white-rimmed aviator sunglasses, a red cotton polo, white skinny jeans, and white canvas sneakers. They'd picked their ride and their designer clothes so that Alika would know they were young, rich, and lived the high life.

The monstrous Hawaiian was eating a multicolored shave ice with a plastic spoon that seemed ridiculously tiny in his massive paw. He was in his usual tank top and board shorts, showing off the Polynesian tattoos that covered his arms and legs. His eyes were hidden behind wraparound shades so dark, they might as well have been blindfolds.

A Hawaiian with a bandaged nose sat at the next table, and Neon Nikes stood nearby, with his right arm strapped to his midsection in a sling, stabilizing his wounded shoulder. Kate couldn't help smiling. Her father had left his mark on Alika's crew.

Neon Nikes glowered at her. "Watchu smilin' at?"

"You look like you were run over by a monster wave," Kate said.

"Why boddah you?" Neon Nikes said.

"Easy, brah, wassamattayou?" Alika said to Neon Nikes, and then he smiled at Kate. "Watchu want, sweet wahini? You likkah da shave ice, yeah?"

"Maybe later, Mr. Alika," Kate said, sitting down across from him. "I'm Kate Porter and this is Nick Sweet. We've come to Hawaii to offer you a deal."

"Wat kine deal you talkin'?"

Nick sat down beside Kate. "A VIP gambling junket to Côte d'Argent Casino in Macau."

"You travel agents, yeah?"

"Of sorts," Kate said.

"This would be more than a vacation," Nick said. "We know you've made a lot of money that you can't spend without attracting the attention of the authorities. Our junket offers you, and your associates in Japan, a way to move large amounts of cash to and from the islands."

"Dat sounds illegal," Alika said.

"For sure," Kate said.

"So, if I were you, I'd assume that we're both undercover feds," Nick said. "Don't say anything now that you wouldn't want to hear played back in a courtroom. All we're asking is that you let us make our pitch. If you like it, then you can check us out and we'll go from there."

Alika scratched one of his sleeveless intricately tattooed shoulders while he thought about Nick's proposition. "'Kay den, you have a shave ice an' talk story wit' me."

Alika told Bandage Nose to bring Nick and Kate each a shaved ice with a scoop of vanilla ice cream and another one for himself. While they ate, Nick explained how money laundering was done through junket gambling at Côte d'Argent Macau and how Alika, and his Yakuza partners, could benefit from it. When Nick was finished, Alika smiled at Kate.

"Wat you tink da shave ice?" Alika asked.

"Onolicious," she said.

Alika grinned and turned his bald, bullet-shaped head to Nick. "If you check out as fo' real, where you be?"

Nick passed a card to him with an address written on it and then stood up. "We'll be there for two days."

"I find out you no fo' real," Alika said. "I da kine come break your face fo' waste my time."

Nick took the threat in stride. He flipped Alika the *shaka*, the sign for "hang loose," his thumb and pinkie extended and his other fingers tucked against his palm, as he walked away with Kate.

Nick and Kate got into the Ferrari and headed south on Kamehameha Highway, the surf on their left, the mountains on their right, and the wind whipping their hair.

"That went well," Nick said.

"We won't know until he comes to us, either to make a deal or to smash our faces," Kate said. "But at least we got to try the best snow cones ever made."

"Where did you learn to understand pidgin?"

"The Navy. It's full of surfers. Where did you pick up what you know?"

"Hawaii Five-O," he said.

19

Evan Trace walked his Cotai Strip property. Right now it was just a ten-acre patch of dry earth and sand, dredged up from the bottom of the Pearl River Delta and moved around by a battalion of bulldozers, but Evan pictured a thirty-nine-story Côte d'Argent tower rising from a lake of fire. Flames would swirl atop the water and reflect off the black glass of the building.

The flaming water would be the signature image of his new resort and a radical departure from his *No freakin' gondolas* philosophy. But that was never based on a deeply held belief anyway. It was based on having *no freakin' money.* Now, in order to remain competitive and lure the international high rollers, he needed to think big, like everyone else around him.

Across the street was the massive Venetian Macao, the seventh largest building ever constructed by man and nearly twice the size of the Pentagon. To either side of the Venetian, Trace could see dozens of construction cranes, hurriedly building mega-casinos, a re-creation of New York's Broadway theater district, and a monorail system that would carry hundreds of thousands of tourists each year to the Cotai Strip. Trace would either become part of that explosive growth or he would be buried by it.

Natasha crossed over to him from one of the half dozen construction trailers on the edge of his property. She wore a white hard hat, which was a ridiculous safety requirement. Grading was the only thing being done now, and there was nothing that could possibly fall on her head. He wore a hard hat, too, but that was because his was gold-plated and identified him to everyone as the boss.

"Are you familiar with the Tiki Palace in Las Vegas?" she asked him.

"It's a cheap downtown casino that caters almost exclusively to Hawaiians, offering them cheap plane tickets, budget rooms, lots of nickel slots, and spam for breakfast," Trace said. "It's strictly small-time."

"Mr. Goodwell called me. He was asked by Sammy Mokuahi, who runs the Tiki, if Nick Sweet and Kate Porter are bona fide junket operators with us here."

There was no reason that Trace could think of for Nick and Kate to be interested in a dump like the Tiki. There wasn't any real money to be made there for junket operators in their league.

"Did Mokuahi say why he wanted to know about them?"

"He was asking as a favor for one of his good customers, a Hawaiian named Lono Alika," Natasha said. "So I checked out Alika. He's a big shot in the Hawaiian mob and runs the Yakuza's heroin, cocaine, and ecstasy sales on Oahu. He also exports Hawaiian-made meth back to Japan for distribution there. What should we tell Mr. Mokuahi?"

Now it all made sense to Trace. He could think of only one reason why Alika would ask somebody he trusts in the casino business about those two. Nick and Kate had invited Alika to Macau on a junket. "Tell him that Nick and Kate do big business with us and that Evan Trace personally and enthusiastically vouches for them."

She cocked an eyebrow. "May I ask why you'd do that?"

"Those two obviously have an amazing range of contacts. Canadian mobsters, Somali warlords, and now the Yakuza as well," Trace said. "Those are some major high rollers they're bringing us. So hell yes, I want their business, and I am going to get it."

Natasha did a slight bow. "Very well, sir."

Once again, Trace was amazed with himself. The $2.6 million that he'd given back to Nick and Kate was a daring gamble, and it was already paying off. It was gratifying to know that his instincts bordered on clairvoyant and that his powers of persuasion were nearly irresistible.

And he had to admit, he was looking forward to welcoming

Kate Porter back into his life and enticing her into his lair. He had romantic plans for her, and he was sure she'd find those plans to be *excruciatingly* pleasurable.

The turquoise water was eighty degrees and clear at Kailua Beach. The stretch of sand was lined with multimillion-dollar homes, widely spaced apart and set back among tall, slender palms, flowering plumerias, and colorful hibiscus hedges.

Nick had rented a plantation-style retreat with an ocean-facing veranda. He and Kate were hanging out on the porch, enjoying the view and sipping pomegranate iced tea. They were side by side on a thick-cushioned wicker chaise longue that was as big as a king-size bed.

"I'm feeling lucky today," Nick said, looking out at the surf. "Let's go swimming."

"How does 'lucky' equate to swimming?"

"You would put on a little bikini, and we'd go into the water together, and then I'd get even luckier."

"That's a fantasy."

"True, but I plan to make it a reality."

"Not gonna happen."

"It's inevitable. I always thought we'd eventually get together," Nick said.

"Well, so did I, but I imagined it would be in an interrogation room, a courtroom, or your jail cell."

"This is better."

"I suppose, but it was fun when I hit you with a bus."

"Yeah, and I enjoyed crashing into you with the armored car." He moved close and kissed her just below her ear. "Thinking about it gets me feeling romantic."

"Listen, mister, there's no romance."

"Okay," he said, "no romance. Just hot, sweaty sex."

"No!"

"Just a little."

"No."

"A kiss."

"Maybe a kiss."

His mouth found hers and some tongue got involved. It might have been Kate's tongue that started it. Or it might have been his. It was definitely Nick who started the groping. Then again, she wasn't far behind. His hand was under her shirt, cupped around a breast when a shadow fell over them.

Kate looked up to see if a cloud was blocking the sun, and gasped when she saw that it was Lono Alika standing over them.

"Mr. Alika," Kate said. "What a nice surprise."

"Dis a bad time fo' you?" Alika asked.

"No, not at all," Kate said, sitting up, rearranging her clothes. "We're glad to see you."

"Da bruddah don't look so happy."

"Maybe you could come back in an hour," Nick said.

"You tink it take dat long?" Alika asked.

"Nick's just kidding," Kate said. "What have you heard about us?"

"Good tings or yo' face be buss'up already, yeah?" Alika sat down on the edge of the chaise. The wicker crackled under his enormous weight, but it held. "I'm in for two mil. When do we go to Macau?"

"In two or three days," Nick said. "I'll make all of the arrangements and get in touch with you."

"One ting," Alika said and held up one of his huge hands. "You see dis?"

"That's a big hand," Nick said.

"Look closah. You see da lines here?" He pointed to faint white scratches that crisscrossed the dark skin on the back of his hands, between the knuckles. "You know wat dat from?"

"Breaking faces," Kate said.

"Dat's right. Back in da day, I used to hammer a lot o' faces, yeah? I'd get all kine o' teeth stuck in my skin. Dat my old life." Alika leaned close to them. "But I will do worse to you if I get screwed."

"We can't guarantee that you won't lose everything," Nick said. "That's up to you and your luck."

"I lose my money, dat's okay," Alika said. "*You* lose it, dat's death. Fo' you, fo' sure."

The threat didn't bother Kate. It reassured her that at least Alika would behave as they'd hoped and that maybe, barring any more bad luck, like Dumah showing up, Nick's ballsy con would go exactly the way they'd planned.

"Fine," Kate said. "We're in business."

· · ·

Nick and Kate spent the rest of the day and the next making all of the necessary financial and travel arrangements to get themselves, Lono Alika, Boyd Capwell, Billy Dee Snipes, and $15 million to Macau.

On the morning of their third day in Hawaii, Nick and Kate met Alika in front of their private jet on the tarmac at Honolulu International Airport. Alika was in his usual tank top, board shorts, and flip-flops, as if he were heading out for another day at the beach instead of to a casino in Macau.

"Ho, brah, dis is choice," Alika said, referring to the plane.

"The only way to fly," Nick said.

"I like yo' style." Alika climbed inside, grabbed two beers from the galley, and dropped himself into one of the big chairs. "I'm gonna chillax, dat okay witchu."

"Go for it," Kate said.

Once they were in the air, Alika washed down a pill with a bottle of beer. Kate assumed it was a sleeping pill, because thirty minutes and three beers later, he was out cold. Loudly snoring and farting his way across the Pacific.

Kate and Nick moved to the rear stateroom, settled onto one of the couches, and watched three of Nick's favorite movies: *The Sting* with Paul Newman and Robert Redford, *The Thomas Crown Affair* with Steve McQueen and Faye Dunaway, and the original *Ocean's 11* with Frank Sinatra and the Rat Pack.

"I'm sensing a theme here," Kate said when the movies were over.

"Just getting myself in the mood."

"For what?"

"For work."

The plane arrived in Macau in the late afternoon of the following day. Two Rolls-Royces, one for Lono Alika and his enormous girth and one for Nick and Kate, were waiting at the airport to transport them the seven miles to Côte d'Argent.

Natasha Ling greeted them in the lobby with the key cards to their eighth-floor rooms. Boyd and Billy Dee wouldn't be arriving until later, so the games in the VIP suite wouldn't be starting until the next day.

"Two questions, yeah?" Alika said. "Where da women an' where da buffet?"

"We're going to leave Mr. Alika in your very capable hands," Nick said to Natasha.

Natasha smiled politely and inclined her head. "Of course."

Kate couldn't blame the hostess for going pale under her makeup. If Kate had been tasked with keeping Alika happy she would have handed in her employee name tag and taken the first plane off the island.

Nick walked Kate to the elevator. "I'm going to the casino floor for some blackjack," he said. "Would you like to join me?"

Kate shook her head. "No. I'm going to my room to take a shower and do some paperwork."

"What paperwork?"

"Our expense account, for one thing. Helicopters, private jumbo jets—"

"It wasn't a jumbo."

"You order expensive wines and caviar. You rent sports cars."

"You should be happy I'm not stealing them."

"And you buy me designer dresses that are too small. How am I going to explain all this to Jessup?"

"They aren't too small. They fit you perfectly, and you look amazing in them."

"Thank you, but that's not the point."

"Of course it's the point. You're a distraction."

"Oh great. Oh joy." Kate flapped her arms. "Now my role is reduced to being a *distraction*. That's all I am in the grand scheme of our partnership."

"You're more than just a distraction," Nick said.

"Oh really? Like what?"

He pulled her flat against him and kissed her. Their tongues touched, and Kate got a rush that rivaled the time she parachuted out of a rust-bucket plane in the middle of the night over Mount Athos.

"This isn't the time or the place for me to go into detail about what you mean to me," Nick said. "So let's keep it simple. You're *everything*."

"Um, okay then," Kate said, inching back, adjusting her shoulder purse. "G-g-good to know."

The elevator doors opened, and Kate stepped inside and pushed the button for the eighth floor.

"Be careful what you put online or on paper," Nick said. "I'm sure the instant we leave our rooms someone combs through them for information."

"Roger that."

The doors closed and Kate slumped against the wall of the elevator. *Everything.* Holy cow. He liked her. Maybe he even loved her. She was pretty sure she'd never been *everything* to anybody before. Maybe her father. Everything was *big*. She wasn't sure if Nick was *everything* to her, but he was definitely *a lot*.

Good thing she was such a badass, dedicated FBI agent or she might still be back there kissing Nick. Or worse, she might have dragged him into the elevator and pressed the hold button between floors. She looked around. Undoubtedly there were cameras, so good thing she didn't have her way with Nick between floors. They would have ended up on YouTube. She'd never hear the end of that from Megan.

She let herself into her suite and found that her bags had already been delivered. Nick had chosen blackjack as a way to unwind from a long flight. Kate opted for a run. She changed into a tank top, shorts, and running shoes and headed out.

Dumah was still on protection assignment and was caught unprepared for her jog. He was forced to keep up with her in his Dolce & Gabbana suit and dress shoes. Kate didn't make it any easier for him by running through the narrow, winding streets of the old town and up the grand staircase to the ruins of St. Paul's Cathedral. A three-story sculpted stone façade was all that remained of the ancient cathedral and was the required selfie backdrop for every Macau tourist.

She paused on the cobblestone plaza to look down at the tangled warren of European-style streets, the Forever 21 and Starbucks at the base of the grand staircase, and Dumah struggling up the steps. She smiled to herself as she jogged west across the plaza and up the much steeper steps to Mount Fortress.

Kate ran alongside the ramparts that bordered the park, all that remained of the fortress that had protected Macau for centuries from invaders. Now the dormant cannons that lined the battlements were aimed south at the Grand Lisboa and the invading forces of greed, democracy, and Forever 21. She noticed that there wasn't a single cannon pointed north anymore toward mainland China.

She headed back down the steps as Dumah was coming up. He was out of breath, his fitted dress shirt drenched with sweat, his wrinkled jacket clinging to his damp back.

He held up a hand to her. "Could we rest up for a minute?"

"Sure." She stood in front of him, bouncing in place to keep her heart rate up.

"Thanks." He leaned his back against one of the stone walls that were on either side of the steps.

"You're out of shape, Dumah."

"I'm a security guard. All I need are muscles and attitude. My work doesn't usually involve chasing."

"I wasn't running from you, I was jogging," Kate said. "If I was running, I would have lost you long before we got to the grand staircase."

"I wish you had," he said. "That was a lot of stairs."

"So what do you do when someone runs away from you?"

"They don't. I hit them or shoot them before they get the chance. Mostly I just need to look menacing."

"I suppose that's enough to handle most people."

"But you're not most people," he said. "I'm still trying to figure out what you are."

"Catch up with me and maybe you'll find out." She started jogging down the stairs.

He took a deep breath.

"At least it's downhill from here," he said to himself and jogged after her.

20

There was a fruit basket and fresh flowers on the coffee table when Kate returned from her run. The handwritten note stuck into the flower arrangement was from Evan Trace, inviting her to his penthouse for dinner in an hour. No mention of an invitation for Nick.

Great. Just fanfreakingtastic. Dinner with the megalomaniacal pervert. She shoved her earbud transmitter into her ear and she could hear the din of the casino floor and people shouting in Chinese.

"Do we still have money left?" she asked Nick.

"I'm on a roll," Nick replied. "I'm up seventy-five thousand."

"That's a relief," she said. "I have flowers and a dinner invitation from Trace. What am I supposed to do?"

"Enjoy the meal," he said. "But don't take the seat next to the piranha pond."

Kate showered and left the bathroom to stare at the clothes in her suitcase. She didn't want to send the wrong message by looking too sexy. A dress was definitely off the table. She didn't want to give Evan Trace an opportunity to slide his hand up her skirt.

She pushed the earbud back into her ear and connected to Nick. "I don't know what to wear," she said to him.

"Wear whatever feels comfortable. Go with your instincts."

"My instincts tell me full body armor, but I didn't bring any."

"Definitely not the red dress," Nick said. "I have erotic dreams about you in the red dress."

"I figured that one out on my own. I'm going with jeans and a T-shirt. I wish you were invited, too."

"I'll be there," Nick said. "You'll just have to be my eyes, ears, and hot body."

"Are you referring to my attributes or yours?"

"Yours, but I can see how that comment might have been confusing if you think I have a hot body, too."

"Now you're blatantly fishing for compliments."

"More like testing the water."

Kate wriggled into the jeans. "Where are you?"

"In my room," he said. "I've got a platter and a bottle of wine coming up."

"Are Billy Dee and Boyd going to be listening in on my dinner when they arrive and power on their earbuds?"

"Nope. I brought my clicker with me," he said, referring to the remote control, disguised as a key fob, that he used to control their transmitters, muting some and keeping others live. "You don't want too many voices in your head when you're trying to think."

"I'm not sure I even want yours."

She pulled out a red blazer that was stuffed into the corner of her bag.

"It would be there anyway, answering you when you ask yourself 'What would Nick do in this situation?'"

"I'd never ask myself that."

"You should when you're conning someone," he said. "I'd ask myself what you'd do if I was ever investigating something."

"Like that'll ever happen."

She checked herself out in the mirror. Her blazer was slightly wrinkled, but that was how she liked it. The only way she could be more comfortable was if she had her Glock holstered on her belt.

"Are you going to iron that jacket?" Nick asked.

Kate narrowed her eyes. "Have you got a camera in here?"

"Of course not. You swept the room for bugs already or we wouldn't be having this conversation."

He was right. She had a nifty device built into her iPhone protective case that detected bugs, audio or video, and it vibrated if it picked up any signal besides the unique one emitted by her earbuds.

"I just know you, that's all," Nick said.

"Then you'd know that I don't own an iron and I've never used one, at least not for ironing."

"What have you used one for?"

"Hitting a guy. He was coming at me with a knife and it was the only weapon handy."

"Irons are also handy for removing wrinkles from clothes that you've rolled up instead of folding."

"That's how we pack for an op in the military."

"Honey, this isn't an op in the military," Nick said.

Kate blew out a sigh. "So sadly true."

She laced up a pair of running shoes and headed to the elevators.

"Going silent," she said. "Showtime."

The elevator doors opened, and she stepped inside, slid her key card into a slot, and pressed the button for the penthouse. When the elevator doors opened again, Evan Trace stood there to greet her.

"Thank you so much for coming, Kate," Trace said. "I was afraid you might not accept."

"Curiosity overwhelmed me."

"You and the cat." Trace led her into the circular foyer that was lined with marble and lit by an enormous dragon-shaped chandelier.

"I'm counting on ending up better than the cat did," she said.

"That's a safe bet," he said.

"Never believe a casino owner who tells you that," Nick said. It was like he was right there, hiding under Harry Potter's invisibility cloak and whispering in her ear. *"There's no such thing as a safe bet."*

The foyer opened onto a wide living room that, like in the penthouse in Las Vegas, opened onto a terrace with an amazing view and an infinity pool that seemed to spill out over the city. On a table in the center of the room was an intricately detailed architectural model.

"I wanted to show you this." Trace stepped up to the table and swept his hand over the model. "It's the Côte d'Argent project that I'm building on the Cotai Strip."

A tiny neon sign atop the hotel tower model glowed with the words "Monde d'Argent." Lights were lit up in many of the windows, and tiny cars moved on the streets to create an illusion of activity. What grabbed Kate's attention were the actual flames that flickered from the water, in front of the casino mock-up.

"What's with the fire?" she asked.

"I was looking for a striking, signature image for the resort so I hired some engineers to create a lake of fire, fed by hidden gas jets. Spectacular, isn't it?"

"Sure," she said. "But isn't it off-brand for you?"

"Brands evolve or they die. The attitude and décor inside the casino will still reflect a straightforward but elegant approach to gambling. But the fire is dramatic and it's going to be a big draw."

"Like the Mirage volcano, which you supposedly hate."

"The volcano is vulgar, crass, and over-the-top," Trace said. "This is a work of contemporary art that's striking, frightening, even sensual. That's a big difference. These flames represent sin in all of its myriad temptations."

"Clever," Kate said, trying not to look horrified. "Very impressive."

"I hope you'll be equally impressed with dinner," Trace said. "We're having a Matsuzaka steak, the best in the world, and also the most expensive. The meat comes from three-year-old virgin cows raised in the Mie prefecture of Japan. The cows are massaged each day, fed tofu and beer, and entertained with classical music. The result is perfectly marbled meat that literally melts in your mouth. I'm willing to pay the price because I appreciate the best of everything. That's why you're here, Kate."

Eek, Kate thought. She was getting massaged like a virgin cow.

"I appreciate the thought," she said, "but you don't know anything about me."

"I know that you're an exceptional con artist and a highly skilled killer."

"He must have read your dating profile on DesperateSingles.com," Nick whispered into Kate's ear.

Kate took a beat to clear Nick's voice from her head.

"What makes you think that I've killed anyone?" she asked Trace.

"I didn't say that you *have,* but it's obvious that you *could.* I believe that my men who fought with you are lucky they're still breathing."

"I had no reason to kill them."

"Did you come to Nick's rescue because you're lovers, or was it simply to protect your business interests?"

"What difference does it make to you?"

"I want to know how committed you are to him," Trace said.

"If you're asking if I'd ever betray Nick, or cheat him out of his share of a deal, the answer is no," she said. "But I'm a free agent."

"In all respects?"

"I don't belong to anyone."

The answer seemed to please Trace. "There's a reason why I wanted you to see the model of Monde d'Argent. It's a huge project, crucial to the future of my business, and it's going to come under attack from my competitors, criminal syndicates, and professional cardsharps. I need someone who can protect my interests from them and any other potential adversaries."

"You're offering me a job?"

"Head of security for Monde d'Argent," he said.

"Even though you think I'm a professional crook and a stone-cold killer."

"That's what makes you exceptionally well qualified for the job. I was a gambler, a swindler, and a cheat before I got into the management and ownership side of the casino business. A criminal background is an asset in this business. It gives you savvy."

"There's nothing like firsthand information," Kate said.

"Exactly. For instance, some of my management style comes from a mistake I made a long time ago. I got caught cheating by a casino, so they had one of their men smash my hands with a mallet."

"Like the man who works for you?"

"It's the same man. He did this to me." Trace held his mangled hand out for her to see.

"Horrible," Kate said. She'd noticed his hands at their first meeting and had tried not to stare, wondering if it was a birth deformity.

"Not at all," Trace said. "It was a learning experience."

Trace moved from the casino model in the middle of the room to a small table by the window. The table was set for two with candles and flowers and linen napkins. He selected a fork from one of the place settings, laid his hand flat to the table, and stabbed the fork hard into the back of his hand.

A wave of nausea rolled through Kate's stomach.

"So what did I learn from this?" Trace asked, clearly undisturbed by the fork stuck in his hand. "I learned that this is an excellent way to deter cheating. I learned that there are more monetarily rewarding ways to make a living than cheating. And I learned that I like extreme sensations." Trace pulled the fork out of his hand as if his hand were just a piece of meat. "My hands work fine, but I hardly feel a thing. Nerve damage."

Kate swallowed back her revulsion and put on her game face. This was a man who fed on fear and suffering. She didn't want to give him the satisfaction of seeing any of her real emotions. And she especially didn't want to show him anything he would interpret as weakness.

"Is stabbing yourself with a fork a regular part of your job interviews, or is that just your favorite parlor trick?" she asked him.

"Both," he said.

He set the fork on the table, and casually pressed one of the linen napkins to the bleeding wound. Natasha swooped in from the back of the room and reset the table with a clean fork and napkin.

"Are you interested in the job?" Trace asked Kate.

"I'll keep the offer in mind," Kate said. "It will be a year or more before Monde d'Argent is built. A lot could happen between now and then."

"I'm prepared to hire you now. You could run security here in the meantime. You've certainly proven that it needs to be beefed up."

"No, thanks," she said.

"We haven't even talked salary or perks."

"Maybe another time. I've had a long flight and I'm afraid the jet lag is catching up with me. I need to get some sleep before we host the junket tomorrow."

"Of course," he said. "You need to be at your best for your guests. Would you like me to send your meal to your room?"

"That would be appreciated."

"My pleasure," he said.

Trace walked Kate to the elevator. "We should do this again soon."

"I can't imagine how you'd top the fork," Kate said.

"Try," he said. "I'd like to hear any ideas you come up with."

She stepped inside the elevator, faced him, and slid her key card into the slot. "They could hurt."

"I hope so," he said, and then the elevator doors closed.

"I'm sorry I missed the hand stabbing," Nick said into Kate's ear. "Next time we'll have to strap a GoPro camera to your head so I get the video with the audio. This guy is freaking nuts."

"He stuck the fork into his hand, and I almost threw up. It was sick."

"Are you okay? Would you like me to come to your suite?"

"You want half of my steak, right?"

"No, sweet cakes, I want all of *you.*"

Kate took a beat to steady herself. "I need time."

"The ball's in your court."

21

Natasha was waiting at the door when Trace returned to the suite.

"Mr. Ould-Abdallah and Mr. Blackmore have arrived," Natasha told Trace. "We have eyes on them both. Mr. Ould-Abdallah is visiting an opium den near the harbor and Mr. Blackmore is in the casino playing pai gow."

"What's Alika doing?"

"He's entertaining three prostitutes in his room," Natasha said. "He just had six bottles of champagne sent up."

"Alika has big appetites," Trace said. "I can appreciate that."

"Earlier tonight, he gorged himself on four lobsters and had drinks at the bar with this man." Natasha showed Trace a security camera picture on her iPad of a wiry Japanese man in a tight black turtleneck and black slacks entering the casino. "The man is not staying with us, but our facial recognition system got an ID. He's Richard Nakamura, a sales representative for a Japanese auto parts company that's owned by a senior Yakuza member. He usually gambles at the Galaxy."

"So he came here specifically to meet Alika. That confirms your intel that Alika is a pipeline to Yakuza's money and therefore a man we should make very happy. Make sure he has all the lobsters, champagne, and hookers he desires."

Trace untied the napkin from his deformed hand and examined the puncture wounds. The bleeding had stopped, but the skin was beginning to bruise from the impact of the fork.

"Does it hurt?" Natasha asked, taking his hand in hers.

"I'm feeling no pain."

"Neither am I," she said, squeezing his hand hard, making the wounds bleed again.

"Let's change that," he said and led her toward the bedroom.

Kate walked into the eighth-floor VIP gambling suite in the morning to find an enormous breakfast spread that included an array of Chinese, Portuguese, and Hawaiian dishes. There was also an assortment of Tim Hortons donuts, kettles of his coffee, and stacks of his signature paper cups.

Nick, Boyd, Billy Dee, and Alika were already gambling at the baccarat table, and Luisa was once again dealing cards. Natasha stood behind the dealer and tracked the wagers on an iPad. Birgita stood at the bar, ready to serve the gamblers whatever refreshments they wanted.

Alika was in his usual attire, from the wraparound shades on his head to the sandals on his huge bare feet, and he was the player being dealt the cards. Billy Dee was at the far end of the table, looking groggy.

"Good morning, gentlemen," Kate said. "How is your luck running this morning?"

"I got lucky last night an' it's still wit' me t'day," Alika said, sharing a leer with Boyd that conveyed the kind of luck that he was talking about.

"That's a different kind of luck," Boyd said. "And you paid for that."

"Dey was on da house, but I still got da luck," Alika said, flipping over his cards to prove his point. He had a five and a four. "See? Try beatin' dat rippin' poundah."

It was the dealer's turn. She flipped over her cards. She had a three and a seven.

"Ho!" Alika pounded his fist on the table and rattled everyone's chips. "We pumpin', brahs!"

Boyd nudged Billy Dee. "Wake up, Sheik, you won."

"I'm not sleepy," Billy Dee said. "I'm carefully considering my next wager."

He was also stoned, Kate thought, and set a cup of coffee in front of him.

"There's nothing to consider," Boyd said. "It's all about seeing which way the winds of luck are blowing." Boyd licked his right index finger and stuck it in the air. "It's blowing toward the Big Kahuna."

"Ass right," Alika said. "I plenny lucky."

Kate helped herself to a donut and coffee and joined Birgita at the bar. "What are the chances of getting one of those Matsuzaka steaks with a couple of eggs, over easy?"

"It's no problem," Birgita said.

Nick looked over his shoulder at Kate. "It's one of the best steaks in the world. Why bother with the eggs?"

"That's what makes it breakfast," Kate said. "Plus egg yolk is nature's steak sauce."

"You're going to dip a Matsuzaka steak in egg yolk?" Nick shook his head. "Sacrilege."

"I like da way you eat," Alika said to Kate, then shifted his gaze to Birgita. "Make dat fo' two."

The gambling went smoothly the rest of the day. Billy Dee, Boyd, and Alika established a friendly rapport as they gambled and gorged on the constant supply of food and top-quality liquor. Nick and Kate took turns at the baccarat table, keeping the game moving.

Billy Dee and Boyd each started the day with $5 million, Nick and Kate with $3 million, and Alika with $2 million. By the end of their eight hours of gaming, Billy Dee's slow and thoughtful approach had paid off. He broke even, while Alika was down $175,000, Nick and Kate had lost $500,000, and Boyd was out $1 million. It was a winning day for everyone. The casino was happy to make money. Boyd and Billy Dee were happy to gamble with someone else's money. Alika was happy to launder his illegal profits for a reasonable transaction fee, taken as gambling losses, while indulging all of his desires. And Kate was happy that no one had been killed.

Alika rose from the table and clapped Nick hard on the back. "Dat was to da bomb, bruddah, to da max. Tanks, eh?"

"Glad you had a good time," Nick said.

"How do I cash out?"

"Any way you like," Nick said. "You can trade the chips in with us for cash in any currency or we can wire the money to any account, or to anyone, anywhere in the world."

"What if I want to give some chips to a friend here in Macau?" Alika asked. Kate noticed he'd dropped the pidgin act and wondered if he was even aware of it.

"These chips have no value outside of this room," Natasha replied. "But we'd be glad to exchange them for chips of equal value that can be played, or cashed, in the casino downstairs by your friend."

As if on cue, there was a knock at the door, and Birgita led a lithe Japanese man into the gaming room. He was dressed in all black, including a black onyx ring and a black-faced Rolex Cosmograph Daytona watch.

"My name is Nakamura," he said. "I'm here to see Alika."

Alika lifted the bottom of his tank top to create a pouch,

swept a little more than half of his chips off the table into his shirt, and carried the chips over to Nakamura.

"Dis fo' you," Alika said, stopping in front of Nakamura. Alika shook his shirt, making the chips rattle. "Unreal, yeah?"

The Japanese man stared at Alika as if the Hawaiian had asked him to reach into a latrine.

Natasha quickly brought a silver tray and held it at Alika's waist. "If you'll give me the chips, Mr. Alika, I'll escort your friend to the cashier's window downstairs and exchange these for new chips or for cash, whatever is Mr. Nakamura's preference."

"That would be much appreciated," Nakamura said.

" 'K'den, whatevah," Alika said, emptying the chips onto the tray.

Nick offered his hand to Nakamura and flashed his most winning smile. "I'm Nick Sweet. I organized this game. Perhaps you'd be interested in joining us next time."

"Perhaps," Nakamura said.

He declined the handshake and walked away with Natasha to the elevator.

Alika had just successfully laundered $2 million in cash, for himself and the Yakuza, Kate thought. The whole thing took less than two minutes. The FBI had not only let it happen, they'd enabled the unlawful transaction. Jessup wasn't going to like it. She wasn't thrilled about it, either. If the truth ever came out, it would be a huge scandal that would land them both in front of a Senate subcommittee and end with them in a federal prison.

Nick watched Nakamura walk away. "Friendly guy."

"You should see him when he isn't so relaxed," Alika said. "You can cash da rest of my chips an' wire da money to my Cayman Islands account."

"Will do," Nick said.

Alika leaned close to Nick. "Let's talk soon about doing dis ting again, brah."

"Anytime," Nick said. "Would you like to join me, Kate, and our other guests for dinner? I've got us a table at a five-star restaurant in Taipa that usually has a three-month wait."

"No, tanks, I'm going back to my crib an catch da next wave." Alika turned to Birgita, who stood nearby. "I'd like da same kine room service as last night, only one more of everyting."

"It will be our pleasure," Birgita said. "And with our compliments, of course."

Alika shot a grin at Boyd. "My lucky day."

22

Nick and Kate returned to Nick's suite after dinner. Nick switched off the transmission on their earbuds so they could hear Billy Dee and Boyd, but the two men couldn't hear them. Billy Dee was snoring and Boyd was singing in the shower.

"Things couldn't have gone better today if I'd scripted every moment," Nick said.

"The FBI laundered two million dollars in drug money for the Hawaiian mob and the Yakuza," Kate said.

"A key part of the con. We had to do it to draw in a real mobster and create a genuine threat."

"I know, but I still don't like it."

"I've corrupted my principles, too," Nick said.

"You have no principles."

"Not true. I was a criminal, running cons and stealing things for fun and profit. Now I'm doing it to put people like me in jail. I've betrayed the whole notion of honor among thieves," he said.

"Honor among thieves is a bunch of baloney."

"Maybe, but fear of reprisal is real. I'd be a dead man if the people I used to work with knew what I am doing now." He looked out the floor-to-ceiling window. In the distance, beyond the hills of Taipa, he could see the glow cast by the casinos on the Cotai Strip, lighting the sky. "You're still basically doing the same thing that you've always done, arresting people who break the law, only now you're being a bit of a crook to do it."

Kate nodded. She knew this to be true.

"At least we're having some success," Nick said. "Alika is already itching to come back and he hasn't even left yet. As a bonus, we've snagged a Yakuza soldier. After a shaky start, everything is going according to plan. A week from now, I'll run off with all of Alika's money, and the Yakuza will be screaming for blood. All you'll have to do is flash your badge at Trace and he'll run into your arms. Côte d'Argent will be finished, and so will Alika."

They went silent when through their earbuds they heard Boyd abruptly stop singing "Camelot" in mid-chorus. Someone was knocking on his door.

"Hold on, I'm coming," Boyd said. "Be right there."

Nick and Kate heard footsteps, and then a door opening.

"Evan," Boyd said. "What a surprise."

. . .

Trace had a bandage wrapped around his hand and held a bottle of Evan Williams Single Barrel whiskey by the neck.

"I hope I'm not disturbing you, Mr. Blackmore, but I wanted to have a private chat with you before you leave tomorrow. May I come in?"

"I'm always glad to see a man at my door with a bottle of fine whiskey." Boyd was in his Côte d'Argent terry cloth bathrobe, which was cinched tight, but he cinched it even tighter as he stepped aside and let Trace in.

A new performance had begun, this one pure improvisation, unless Nick and Kate started giving him direction in his ear, which Boyd hoped they wouldn't. He wanted to let his character guide his artistic choices, to live in the moment, to be a trapeze artist walking on a razor's edge.

Trace went to the bar, opened the bottle, and poured out two glasses. "It's a cheap whiskey, only about twenty bucks a bottle, but it's my favorite. Straight out of Louisville, Kentucky. I won't drink any whiskey that doesn't come from the bluegrass state."

He handed Boyd a glass. Boyd took a sip and smacked his lips with pleasure. "Goes down nice and smooth, like caramel with a kick. But you didn't come here to talk whiskey with a bootlegger."

"You're a bootlegger, too?" Trace said. "I didn't know that about you."

Boyd didn't know that about Shane Blackmore, either, until that moment. It was exciting, making it up as he went along.

"I'm sure you know everything about me, right down to the brand of deodorant I use." Boyd sat down on the couch and put one arm up on the backrest, owning the space and showing how relaxed he was. Body language was an important part of his performance.

Trace took the armchair across from him, set his whiskey on the armrest, and ran a fingertip contemplatively around the rim of the glass.

It was bad acting, Boyd thought. Trace wasn't contemplating anything. It was for dramatic effect and it was amateurish, straight out of community theater.

"I have a business proposition for you," Trace said. "I'd like to invite you to come back to Côte d'Argent in a week or two and lose millions of dollars gambling. A colossal loss of ten to fifteen million dollars would be nice."

Boyd laughed. "I can see how that might be good business for you, but how does that benefit me?"

"Because your losses will actually be an off-the-books investment in the Monde d'Argent project that I'm building on the Cotai Strip," Trace said. "Over the next ten years, I guarantee that you'll reap ten times or more whatever amount you invest with me."

"So I get to launder my cash as gambling losses," Boyd said. "And right into a secret moneymaking ownership stake in a Macau casino."

Trace smiled. "Sweet, isn't it?"

. . .

Nick stood ramrod straight and absolutely still, as he listened to the conversation over his earbud. Kate thought he looked like a man in a minefield. And from what she was hearing, he'd already stepped on one and was obliterated.

"We're finished," she said. "Our whole con was built on our gamblers losing all of their money and Alika going after Trace for it. Now he's *asking* them to lose everything as an investment in his new casino."

"It's a brilliant scam," Nick said.

"He's just destroyed our entire operation! This is no time to be impressed."

"Let's not overreact. I want to know more about Trace's scam," Nick said and used his key fob to activate the transmitter in his earbud. "Boyd, get us the details."

"If the profit potential is so great, why share the pie with a Canadian mobster?" Boyd asked. "Why do you need my measly investment?"

Trace shifted in his seat. He was in the difficult position of admitting weakness while trying to demonstrate strength. It was an acting challenge, and Boyd was curious to see how Trace would overcome it.

"I'm a small casino operator and my pockets aren't nearly as deep as my competitors'," Trace said. "Opening Monde d'Argent is my biggest gamble yet but also a necessary risk if I'm going to succeed. The new Chinese president has launched an anticorruption campaign as a publicity stunt. It won't last, but for now, it has made mainland China's high rollers, the titans of industry and leaders of government, reluctant to gamble and draw attention to their wealth. It has hit the bottom line of all the casinos in Macau very hard."

"How much has Macau's gambling revenue dropped?"

"Forty-nine percent from the same month last year," Trace said. Before that bad news had a chance to sink in, he leaned forward and rested his arms on his knees, with an excited smile on his face. "But you have to look at it from a global perspective, Mr. Blackmore. Macau's gambling revenue last month was three billion dollars, and while that's a big drop, that's still half of what all the casinos in Las Vegas combined generate in *an entire year*. We're sitting on a gold mine. I can't let a temporary slowdown in my cash flow stop me from building Monde d'Argent and reaping decades of enormous profits."

Boyd admired the way Trace used his own enthusiasm and body language to mask the dire position he was actually in. Perhaps Trace wasn't as much of an amateur at acting as he thought.

"So because of these temporary, troubled times, you're willing to explore alternative funding options," Boyd said.

Trace grinned, leaned back in his seat, and took a sip of his bourbon. "I like the way you said that."

"It does take the stink off of it," Boyd said, twirling his mustache. "It makes what you're proposing almost sound legitimate."

"I'm going to Billy Dee's room," Kate whispered to Nick. "If Trace is making this offer to one of our players, he's going to make it to all of them. I want to record his conversation with Billy Dee."

"What good is recording the offer going to do us?"

"It's a crime," Kate said. "He's asking them to participate in an illegal conspiracy."

"What *we're* doing is an illegal conspiracy. Whatever you record is worthless as evidence."

Kate was already at the door. "Don't care."

"We need you to buy us some time," Nick said to Boyd. "String him along."

"I'm intrigued," Boyd said to Trace. "It's an ingenious and yet simple scheme."

"Thank you," Trace said.

"But I have some questions."

Trace opened his arms in a welcoming gesture. "Ask whatever you like."

"How would I lose?" Boyd asked. "Are you going to rig the games?"

"I would never do that. I believe in an honest game because the odds are tipped in our favor anyway. Play long enough and you're bound to lose."

"And if I don't?"

Trace shrugged. "You'll come back and lose it tomorrow. When you go home with some of our money, we know you're only taking a high-interest loan because you'll eventually return with what you've won and more. Our biggest profits are from winners, not from losers."

"Where do Nick and Kate fit into all of this?"

"The same way they do now. I don't want to lose their business or their access to potential under-the-table investors like you," Trace said. "Come here next time without them just to gamble . . . and lose big."

"If I make this investment, what's to stop you from reneging on the deal?"

"You'll kill me," Trace said.

"You *do* know me."

Billy Dee answered his door on the second knock.

"Trace is coming over any minute now to make you an offer," Kate said, "and I want to get a video."

The suite consisted of a living room, a small kitchen, a large bedroom, and an opulent bathroom. She stood for a moment, looking around for a place to put her phone that would provide a good angle for filming the discussion, but not draw Trace's attention.

She spotted Billy Dee's phone charging on the kitchen counter. Go with the obvious, she thought, swapping out Billy Dee's phone for her own, tipping her phone in such a way that it faced the living room.

"After you invite Trace in, I want you to sit in one of the easy chairs," Kate said. "Trace will want to sit across from you, not beside you. If you take a chair, that will force him to take the couch. If he does, he'll be facing the kitchen."

Kate didn't have the slightest idea yet how they would be able to use the recordings. The recording would be worthless as evidence in a court, but it might give them an upper hand in other ways.

Nick spoke up in both of their ears. "Trace just left Boyd. You can't leave now, Kate. If he's heading to see Billy Dee or Alika, he'll spot you in the hall."

There was a knock on Billy Dee's door.

"I'll hide in the bedroom closet," Kate whispered.

Billy Dee waited a couple beats before opening his front door to Trace.

"Sorry to bother you at this late hour," Trace said. "But I'd really appreciate a word with you."

"It's your hotel," Billy Dee said. "So make yourself at home."

Trace made the same pitch to Billy Dee that he had made to Boyd, almost word for word. Kate heard it clearly in the closet, thanks to the earbud.

"I like the idea of having a stake in Monde d'Argent," Billy Dee said. "I'm getting too old to hijack ships, and I want to protect what I've earned. But I'm a pirate by nature. I take things. I measure my wealth by what I've got in my hands. What are you going to give me so I know I've got a piece of your casino?"

"For obvious reasons, I can't give you any paper that shows you've invested in Monde d'Argent. No offense, but you're a known criminal and that could cost me my gambling license in the United States," Trace said. "What I can do is sign over deeds to you for condos in the new tower, equal to the value of whatever funds you give me."

"A couple of condos are not going to be as valuable as a percentage of your business."

"No, they're not," Trace said. "But until you see a return, and are assured that you can trust me, having those deeds in your pocket will reassure you that you've actually left Macau with something to show for your money."

"Have you talked to Blackmore? What did that loudmouth Canadian want in return for his money?" Billy Dee asked.

"He took me at my word," Trace said.

"He's a bigger gambler than I thought. Are my hosts in on this, too?"

"No, and I'd appreciate it if you'd keep this between us."

"And Alika, too, I suppose," Billy Dee said.

"I'll be talking to him next. I'm seeking investors with a certain profile, and Nick Sweet doesn't match it. Mr. Alika does."

"So you're using Nick to find guys like me. He thinks he's playing you, but you're playing him."

"Nick is making money out of this, so everybody wins," Trace said. "When does that ever happen in a casino?"

"Never," Billy Dee said.

23

Nick and Kate's flight back to Los Angeles the next morning on their private jet was a somber affair. Alika had taken a commercial flight back to Hawaii, so at least they'd been spared the prospect of spending a dozen hours trapped in the air with a three-hundred-plus-pound reminder of their failure.

"It's so incredibly frustrating," Kate said. "Here Trace is, on video, admitting to a crime. If Billy Dee and Boyd were really big-time crooks, and if this was recorded as part of a legitimate FBI sting operation, then Trace would be finished."

Nick selected a tea sandwich from the buffet that had been set out for them on the plane's credenza. "There was no way to know that Trace would turn this into an opportunity to run a scam of his own."

"We underestimated him."

"True."

"You don't seem very upset by this. We were supposed to take Trace down. Instead, we spent weeks and over a million dollars bringing Trace, Alika, and the Yakuza together so they could all get richer and more powerful while we got *nothing*. This looks to me like a disaster. And the worst part is that the next time al-Qaeda pulls off some horrific terrorist attack on foreign soil that kills scores of people, we'll have to live with the possibility that it was financed with money laundered through Trace's casino and that we blew our chance to stop it."

"We didn't blow our chance. We just hit a speed bump. We need to come up with an even bigger and better con than the original."

"Okay, I like that thinking. At the very least we have incriminating evidence that he's using gambling losses from criminals to secretly finance the construction of his new Macau resort casino. If this video got out, it might not put Trace in jail, but it would certainly cost him his gambling license in Nevada, and that would shut him down in Macau, too."

"The recording is inadmissible in court," Nick said. "Even if it wasn't, you'd have to admit that you were running a con with the international fugitive that you're supposed to be chasing, a retired Somali pirate who did covert ops with your dad, and an actor whose last role was in a talking-potato version of *Great Expectations*. We'd end up in prison, and Trace would still be free."

"As an FBI agent I should be able to do *something* with that video. Organize some sort of sting."

Nick grinned. "I've got it. You're absolutely right. We use the video. The way to save the con is by revealing that it *is* one."

"We're going to reveal to Trace that our junket operation is a scam run by an FBI agent and a con man?"

"Of course not," Nick said. "We're going to reveal it to Lono Alika. We're also going to tell him that Trace is in on it, too. The video is the proof. Why else would there be an incriminating video?"

"But that's a death sentence. Alika will go crying to the Yakuza and they'll come gunning for all of us."

"Exactly, which basically puts us right back where we would have been in our previous scam, if Trace hadn't screwed things up."

"It's insane," Kate said. "But it might work."

They spent the rest of the flight honing the details of the con and by the time they landed at LAX Kate was sold on the scheme. To pull it off, they'd need to work very fast, recruit some old friends, commit grand theft, blow up an $80,000 car, and stage a violent shootout with automatic weapons.

"Those are all the ingredients of a great con," Nick said as they got off the plane.

"Or a disaster that ends with us all in prison or graves."

"At least then you wouldn't have to worry about adding the car to your expense account."

The next morning Kate found her father on the hillside between Megan's backyard and the golf course below. Jake was in the bushes, digging holes in the dirt with a hand shovel. Beside him was an open rucksack full of soda cans that had batteries, electrical wires, and what looked like dabs of clay stuck to them.

She stepped off the patio and noticed a row of freshly dug, and refilled, holes in the slope. "You aren't planting land mines, are you?"

"Of course not," Jake said.

"Then what are you doing?"

"I'm burying small, pressure-activated explosives in the dirt."

"That's a land mine."

"These hardly count. They are no more dangerous than a cap pistol. When weight is put on them, they make a loud pop that will startle the coyotes but won't injure them."

"I still don't think the humane society would approve."

"I've got no choice. Our pee isn't working as a deterrent."

"This is where you and Roger have been peeing?"

"And some of my golfing buddies, too. It's been a great excuse to sit outside and drink a case of beer," Jake said. "There's a severe drought going on but you wouldn't know it by how moist this hillside is."

Kate stepped back up onto the patio and scraped the dirt off her shoe on the rough edge. "I've got something better for you to do. We're ready to make our move on Trace and we could use your help."

"Would the humane society approve?"

"Probably. There are no animals involved in what we're doing."

"I once ran a stampede of cattle through a South American village to free CIA agents being held hostage by rebels," Jake said. "The cattle came out of it fine. Can't say the same for the rebels."

"Our con doesn't involve a stampede. But there are explosives."

"Count me in." Jake put his things back in the rucksack, slung it over his shoulder, and stood up. "The kids can finish up this project."

"You've taught them how to make land mines?"

"I wouldn't be much of a grandfather if I didn't."

"*Suspiria* was a classic," Ainsley Booker said. She was the rail-thin, stringy-haired, flat-chested, braless, twenty-something publicist for the horror flick *The Last Town on Earth*. She was admiring Nick's faded *Suspiria* T-shirt that featured a naked woman hanging over a pool of blood. "Dario Argento is the man."

Nick was posing as a writer for *Fangoria* magazine. To play the part, he wore the *Suspiria* movie poster T-shirt, hadn't washed his hair in the two days since he'd returned to L.A., and drove up to the movie's Closter City location in a 2006 Chevy Cobalt. Closter City was a small central California town that was abandoned in the mid-1980s after it was feared some of the population had developed cancer from pesticide-contaminated groundwater.

"We worship Argento at *Fangoria,*" Nick said. "They should carve his face on the Mount Rushmore of horror."

Ainsley gestured to Christian McVeety, the rotund eighty-two-year-old director who was standing in a jacket and tie behind the cameras in Closter City's weed-choked town square. McVeety watched intently as a gang of decomposing zombies with huge fangs chased two buxom screaming girls in halter tops and short-shorts past the cameras.

The movie took place after the human race had been decimated by a virus that turned most of the population into vampires. Now a handful of survivors were battling the last starving vampires, who wanted to breed humans like cattle. The humans were eager to breed, especially with buxom girls in halter tops and short-shorts. They just didn't want to be eaten, hence the conflict.

A production assistant stood directly behind McVeety with his hands palm out in a halting gesture. Nick was about to ask Ainsley what the PA was doing, but it became obvious when McVeety began to tip backward and the PA gently pushed him upright again.

"It's the PA's job to keep McVeety standing," Ainsley said, following Nick's gaze. "It's an honor. Film students line up for the opportunity."

"I'm sure they do. He's a legend."

"McVeety is old school, in the best sense. None of that post-production, green-screen, CGI crap for him. If it's not in front of the camera, it's not in the film. He's all about authenticity. That's why we're shooting in Closter City. You know, for the allegory."

"Allegory and gore," Nick said. "That's Christian McVeety's trademark. I'm going to ask him about that."

"You can interview him after his nap," Ainsley said.

"Cool. I'd like to talk to his special effects guy in the meantime."

"That'd be Chet Kershaw. Follow me." Ainsley led him toward a big tent where several zombie vampires in various stages of decomposition sat in folding chairs, killing time listening to music on their smartphones or reading books. One female zombie vampire nibbled on an Atkins bar, careful not to disturb her makeup.

"Chet's family has been doing monster makeup and on-set special effects since the days of silent films," Ainsley said. "What he does is a dying art."

"So it's ironic that he's using his talents on the walking dead. The same could be said of McVeety."

Ainsley smiled at Nick. "Sounds like you've already written your story."

"I never start anything without an angle," Nick said.

Chet had his back to Ainsley and Nick as they approached. He was a bear of a guy, big enough to be a boxer or a linebacker, but his size was belied by the delicacy he was using to apply latex pustules to the face of the zombie vampire sitting very still in the director's chair in front of him.

"Chet, do you have a minute to talk with *Fangoria*?" Ainsley asked.

"I'm a crew of one who has to make up thirty zombies and rig two exploding heads. I don't have time to pee and I've needed to for an hour." Chet turned around, holding a latex pustule daintily with two fingers. When he saw Nick, he broke into a big smile. "But peeing is overrated."

Ainsley saw the recognition on Chet's face. "You two know each other?"

"I've interviewed Chet before," Nick said. "I'm a big fan of his work."

Kate had drafted Chet for the Derek Griffin con. Chet believed that Nick and Kate worked for a private security firm that pushed the boundaries of legality to get the job done.

Chet stuck the fake pustule on Ainsley's cheek. "Hold on to this for me. We'll be right back."

Chet put his arm around Nick and took him to the far corner of the tent, where they could speak privately.

"It's so good to see you," Chet said. "Seems like just when I'm ready to slit my throat out of boredom and self-loathing, you or Kate show up to save me."

"Is working on this movie really that bad?"

"No, I'm thankful to be here. I've hardly worked since I did that last project for you," Chet said. "I got this gig because McVeety is computer illiterate and my grandfather worked on his first film in the 1950s."

"*Attack of the Flesh-Eating Martians*," Nick said.

"That's the one," Chet said. "He's been basically making the same movie for sixty years. But God bless him. Once he's gone, I may have to find a new line of work. I've been studying for a realtor's license."

"That would be a tragedy. Maybe I can save you from that, at least temporarily. We'll pay you a hundred thousand dollars to help us take down a bad guy who launders money for mobsters and terrorists."

"What do I have to do?"

"Kill me," Nick said.

Chet smiled. "I'd be glad to."

24

It was early evening when Kate walked into Tom Underhill's workshop in an industrial section of suburban Rancho Cucamonga. It was a cinder block building that had once been a mechanic's garage. The workshop walls were covered with pictures of the imaginative playhouses, tree houses, and dog houses that Underhill built for a living. She saw photos of kid-sized castles, hobbit dens, igloos, gingerbread houses, and even a flying saucer that seemed to have crashed into a tree. What she didn't see were any photos of the structures and vehicles Tom had built for their cons.

In the center of the workshop was a vintage Airstream trailer that had been gutted. Tom was inside the trailer, working on something with a blowtorch, his back to Kate.

"Knock knock," Kate said, raising her voice to be heard over the sound of the torch.

Tom peered out of the trailer and smiled when he saw her.

"Kate!" He dropped the blowtorch, lifted off the goggles, and stepped out of the trailer. "This is a first. It's always been Nick who stops by."

"I wanted to see where the magic happens," she said. "What are you building this time?"

"You know I have three kids, ages four, ten, and twelve," Tom said. "Well, my wife is pregnant again."

"Congratulations," Kate said.

"Thanks," he said. "We're thrilled, but it was a surprise. It means I either have to turn my office into a nursery or buy us a new house. So I'm giving her a nursery and building a man cave on wheels that I can park in my driveway. It's going to be a home theater, game room, and office all rolled into one."

"So you're finally creating a playhouse for yourself."

"I hadn't thought of it that way but, yeah, I guess I am," he said. "It was building that fake oceanographic survey ship and remote-controlled submersible for that con in Portugal that helped pay for this."

"We have another job for you, if you're interested."

"I've got to put four kids through college someday and I'd like to do it without having to sell my man cave on wheels or take a second mortgage on my house," Tom said. "So yes, I'm interested, especially if it pays as well as the last gig."

"A hundred thousand dollars," she said. "But I have to warn you, it comes with the same risks."

"And I hope the same adventure. These jobs make me feel great. My wife notices the change in me, too. She jumped my bones the minute I got back from Portugal. That's how she ended up pregnant again."

"Just a reminder," Kate said. "We're going after a major criminal, but we're using illegal means to get him."

"If he's even half as rotten as the last two guys I helped your detective agency take down, then so be it. There's something wrong with the law if it allows people like Griffin and Menendez to remain free."

"Maybe so, Tom, but if things go wrong, you could end up in prison or worse."

"You keep warning me about that."

"I couldn't live with myself if I didn't," Kate said. "You're a husband and a father. I'm torn every time we come to you. I want your help, but part of me always hopes that you'll turn us down."

"That's why I trust you," Tom said. "What am I building?"

"For starters, you're putting an escape hatch in the floor of an Audi A8."

"That's not much of a challenge," he said. "How about if I also add an ejector seat, machine guns behind the headlights, and a flamethrower in the exhaust pipe?"

"That won't be necessary," she said. "But those would be nice to have in my car."

"I'm sure we could work something out," Tom said. "Where are we going this time?"

"Las Vegas."

"No freakin' gondolas," he said.

"Funny you should say that."

The San Luis Obispo County courthouse looked like a large mausoleum and, perhaps fittingly, Sara Quirk, the twenty-something assistant district attorney, had the pallor of a corpse, the fashion sense of a mortician, and the warmth of a tombstone. She occupied a windowless office that felt as cramped and suffocating to Nick as a coffin buried under six feet of dirt.

"Mr. Petrocelli, your client is charged with grand theft auto, reckless endangerment, and fifty-six counts of kidnapping," she said, sitting across from Nick at a neatly organized gunmetal gray desk. "Your suggestion that we should simply release her with a stern warning is utterly absurd."

"I think it's the only way that your office, and the tour bus operator, can come out of this debacle without embarrassment and ridicule," Nick said, both of his hands flat on the briefcase resting on his lap. It was the day after his visit to Closter City. He wore the off-the-rack suit that he got for free from Jos. A. Bank for purchasing the suit that he wore for the State Department con. "The way I see it, we're doing you an enormous favor."

"You can't be serious, counselor. Yesterday morning, Wilma Owens stole a tour bus carrying fifty-six Japanese tourists from the parking lot of the Camarillo outlet mall and drove it a hundred and twenty-five miles before being apprehended in the parking lot of the Pismo Beach outlet mall by San Luis Obispo County Sheriff's deputies. That's a serious crime."

"Before arriving in Pismo Beach, Ms. Owens stopped the bus in Solvang, and stayed there for over an hour, did she not?"

The question seemed to bewilder Quirk. "Yes, but so what?"

"Well, then how can you say that my client kidnapped the tourists?" Nick said. "She let them all out in Solvang, where they wandered freely through the Danish village buying wooden clogs and eating *aebleskiver*, before happily returning to the bus with powdered sugar all over their faces for the drive up to Pismo Beach. That doesn't seem like the conduct of prisoners or people under duress to me."

Quirk shifted in her chair, making it creak. "Just because they were unaware that they'd been abducted doesn't make it any less of an abduction."

"Did any of the tourists lodge a complaint?"

"They don't speak English, and they were unaware of the jeopardy they were in."

"The only jeopardy they faced was maxing out their credit cards after visiting Solvang and two outlet malls in one day. The fact is, they were so delighted with the trip that they were posing for selfies with my client at the time the deputies arrested her."

"This is ridiculous! Wilma Owens was not the bus driver, nor the owner of the bus, nor does she possess a valid Class B commercial license," Quirk said, tapping the neat stack of papers in front of her with her index finger as she made each point. "She stole a tour bus and took it on a joyride up the California coast."

"'A joyride' is the perfect way to describe this. She brought pure joy to those fifty-six tourists, not to mention the merchants that they patronized in Solvang and Pismo Beach. The one who deserves your scorn is the bus driver who abandoned his vehicle in Camarillo to get high on pot. If anything, my client may have saved their lives. What would have happened if that impaired driver had taken the wheel of that bus? It's his negligence that is the crime here."

Her pale skin had flushed bright red during the course of Nick's argument. He was glad to see it. Because he was beginning to worry that she might be a vampire. She spoke slowly, trying to control her rage.

"There is no evidence that the driver was smoking pot or impaired in any way."

"There's no evidence that he wasn't," Nick said. "Did you give him a drug test?"

Quick bolted up from her seat, unable to contain her anger for another second. "Of course not! He didn't commit any crime."

"Can you prove it?"

"I don't have to prove it."

"You will by the time I'm done raising reasonable doubt with the jury, who will already have seen all of those pictures of smiling, sugary-faced Japanese tourists with their friendly, cheerful bus driver."

"She wasn't their bus driver!"

"She was driving the bus, wasn't she?" Nick said. "Or are you disputing that now, too?"

Quirk leaned forward on the desk, looming over Nick and jabbing her finger at his face. "Stop twisting my words."

Nick smiled and looked her in the eye. "You clearly have no case, Ms. Quirk. So unless you and the bus company crave embarrassment, which is what you'll surely get once I alert the media, share the photos, and present my compelling version of events, then I'd release my client and call it a day."

Forty minutes later, Nick was standing outside the San Luis Obispo County jail as Willie emerged, a spring in her step, as if she were leaving a party instead of a cell.

"Thank you for getting me out," Willie said. "I didn't know you were a lawyer."

"I didn't know you were a bus driver." Nick led her toward his rented Cadillac in the parking lot. "Why did you steal it?"

She fell into step beside him. "It wasn't something I set out to do. I went to the mall to buy some bras and there it was, a new four-hundred-twenty-five-horsepower, forty-six-foot-long motor coach, a big vehicle that I'd never driven before, with the door wide open and nobody at the wheel. It was an incredible opportunity. But before I could drive away, the Japanese started piling in."

"Where was the driver?"

"I don't know. Probably went to get a pretzel or something. Who cares? That fifty-four-thousand-pound monster has a three-hundred-and-fifteen-inch wheel base and a forty-foot turning radius. It's like driving a battleship. It was one of the vehicles on my bucket list."

"If you wanted to drive a bus, you didn't have to steal one. With what we've paid you, you're rich enough to charter a bus for yourself."

She waved off the suggestion. "That's too much trouble."

"Stealing one packed with Japanese tourists from the parking lot of an outlet mall is easier?"

"It was right there," she said. "I couldn't help myself."

"It's your ADD."

"Thirty-four double-D, to be exact. But you're right, it's really their fault." She gave her breasts a gentle heft. "I wouldn't have been at the mall if my bras didn't wear out so fast."

"I wasn't talking about your cup size, but your undiagnosed attention deficit disorder. You have no impulse control."

"You're beginning to sound like Kate."

"Well, occasionally she's got a point. Sometimes there are easier ways to do things than breaking the law."

"You just impersonated a lawyer."

"This wasn't one of those times."

"Because you were in a hurry to get me out to help you with a new scheme," she said. "What do you need me to do for you now?"

"Nothing much." They reached his car and he unlocked it with his remote key fob. "A drive-by shooting."

She laughed. "And you're giving me grief about stealing a bus?"

25

The crew gathered two days later in the sweltering heat of a barn in Ojai, California, to go over the plan. Scattered around them were a half dozen standing floor fans, their heads turning left to right like the audience at a tennis match, but their whirring blades barely moved the heavy, dry air.

Willie Owens, Chet Kershaw, Tom Underhill, Boyd Capwell, and Jake O'Hare sat on picnic table benches facing Nick and Kate, who stood in front of three dry-erase boards covered with blueprints, photographs, and maps. To their left, displayed like the big prize on a game show, was a new black Audi A8 with darkly tinted windows. To their right, like the booby prize, was a mannequin dressed in a blue polo shirt and tan slacks.

"We're here to create a big, violent action sequence worthy of a Hollywood movie," Nick said. "The purpose is to scare the bejeezus out of this man and make him go running to the FBI for protection."

Nick taped a photo of Evan Trace on the board behind him. There was also a photo of the Côte d'Argent tower, which had been cut out and stuck on a blowup of a Las Vegas street map.

"The FBI will throw Trace into prison and shut down his casino, or they'll let him remain free and keep his casino going as a front for a government sting operation," Kate said. "Either way, he's done financing terrorism and organized crime."

"Wasn't that the plan to start with?" Jake asked.

"It was, but how we're getting there has changed," Kate said. "The original endgame was to convince Lono Alika, the Yakuza's man in Hawaii, to join Boyd and Billy Dee and launder his stash of drug profits through another junket at Côte d'Argent. We were going to run off with the cash, crippling Alika's business and leaving Trace to face the Yakuza's wrath."

"And the relentless fury of the Canadian mafia," Boyd said. "We'd hunt Trace down like a moose."

"Is that really a thing in Canada?" Willie asked.

"Moose hunting?" Boyd said.

"The mafia," Willie said.

"Oh yeah, they're fearsome up there," Boyd said. "They say 'Revenge is a dish best served cold' and it's very, very cold in Canada."

"Unfortunately," Kate continued, "Trace ruined our plan by offering Boyd, Billy Dee, and Alika the chance to secretly invest in his casino empire by losing millions of dollars at his baccarat tables. It's a clever scheme that cut us entirely out of the picture."

"But the good news is that Kate has Trace making that offer to Billy Dee on video," Nick said and then pointed to Boyd. "You're going to show that surveillance footage to Lono Alika. You're going to tell him that Trace and I are part of an FBI sting to bring you both down."

"That's a death sentence," Jake said. "Alika will go crying to the Yakuza and they'll come gunning for you both."

"Not if Boyd kills me first," Nick said. "Right in front of Trace's eyes."

Boyd grinned at Willie. "I told you the Canadians were badasses."

"I'm going to meet with Trace in Las Vegas," Nick said. "As I'm leaving in my car, Willie is going to drive by in a van carrying Boyd and his shooters, Chet and Tom."

"They're going to open fire on Nick's car," Kate said, gesturing to the Audi. "He'll lose control, crash the car, and it will explode, blowing him to bits."

"If you're going to do all of that," Jake said, "why do you need to tell Alika about the video? Why take the risk of bringing the Yakuza into this?"

"As a convincer," Nick said. "To prove to Trace that the jeopardy is real."

"Trace will hear from his own trusted sources that the Yakuza wants him dead," Kate said. "After seeing Nick and Boyd brutally killed, that terrifying news will close the deal."

"I get killed, too?" Boyd said. "Who is killing me?"

"I am," Kate said.

"Do I get a death scene?"

Kate pulled a gun from behind her back and fired three times in quick succession at the mannequin, blood spurting out of its chest on impact, splattering the polo shirt.

She lowered the gun and reholstered it. "Whatever performance you can squeeze into those three shots before Chet and Tom pull your body into the van and Willie speeds off."

"Plenty of time to make my death resonate emotionally with the audience," Boyd said.

Willie was still looking at the mannequin. "How did you do that?"

"Kate was firing blanks," Chet said and held up a tiny remote the size of a key fob. "I used this to ignite a vest filled with red-colored corn syrup under the shirt. It's a common Hollywood trick. Or at least it was until CGI came along."

"How are you blowing up the car?" Jake asked.

"I knew you'd have a special interest in that," Nick said.

"Do I get to use my rocket launcher?"

Chet stared at Jake. "You have a rocket launcher?"

"Doesn't everybody?" Jake replied.

"No, you don't get to use your rocket launcher," Kate said. "Or your hand grenades."

Chet looked at Jake again. "You have hand grenades?"

"The bullet hits to the car will be a special effect," Nick said. "The car will be rigged with explosives. But before Chet triggers the blast, I'll escape through a trapdoor constructed in the floor."

"I guess that's what I'm building," Tom said. "Where are you escaping to?"

"The sewer," Nick said. "I'll be crashing the car right above a manhole that will be rigged with a fake cover that you'll design to open when I drop on it. We'll replace it with a real, pre-scorched manhole cover from below immediately after the explosion."

Boyd applauded. "Magnificent. A grand finale."

"I see three problems," Jake said. "The first is that I don't get to use my rocket launcher. The second is Trace's security team. How are you going to stop them from shooting at the van?"

"Nick and I will handle that," Kate said.

"Okay, but that leaves the third, and the biggest problem," Jake said. "The fire department, the police, and the crime scene techs are going to come and they have to find Nick's charred corpse in the car."

"They will," Nick said.

"I'm sure Trace has contacts in the police department," Jake said. "He'll know immediately if it's not a real corpse."

"It will be," Kate said.

"Where are you going to get a body?"

"We have plenty of volunteers already lined up," Nick said.

Boyd arrived in Honolulu the next morning dressed for the part of a Canadian mobster in paradise. He walked off the plane in a wide-brimmed Panama straw hat, yellow bowling shirt, Bermuda shorts, and flip-flops, rented a Cadillac Escalade, and headed for the North Shore.

He'd been to Hawaii once before to host an infomercial for the Smootherizer, a blender that was specially designed to make tropical fruit smoothies. The Smootherizer infomercial aired nationwide, night after night, and Boyd had expected some big residual checks. That was before some Smootherizers that were left plugged in and unattended in kitchens spontaneously combusted and burned several houses to the ground. The infomercial was yanked, a class-action lawsuit was filed, and the manufacturer fled the country. Boyd never saw a dime. Thinking about the betrayal and the injustice of it all put him in the right mindset for the scene he was about to play with Lono Alika.

He parked in front of Da Grinds & Da Shave Ice as if he owned the place and got out of the car. Alika was sitting in his usual spot on the patio.

"Aloha, Lono!" Boyd called out.

Alika set aside the huge slice of lilikoi cream pie that he'd been eating. He wiped the whipped cream off his lips with the back of his tattooed arm, and stood up to greet his friend with a bear hug.

"Brah, dis a big surprise. Si'down, have a lilikoi pie. Make like dis home," Alika said and snapped his fingers at Neon Nikes, who immediately got up from his seat to get another slice of pie from the server at the window. "Watchu doin' here?"

"I came to see you." Boyd sat down across from Alika at the picnic table. "So this is your Bada Bing."

"Bada what?"

"Tony Soprano's strip club. His domain. Mine is a truck stop outside of Vancouver. I got a booth in the back where I do all of my business. Come up sometime and I'll treat you to poutine and some flapper pie."

Neon Nikes set down a paper plate with a slice of lilikoi pie and a plastic fork in front of Boyd and retreated to his seat at the back of the patio.

"You didn't come all dis way fo' talk TV an' eat da grinds," Alika said.

"Don't take this as an insult, but I don't get half of what you say. You're going to have to drop the Hawaiian gibberish and speak plain English, because it's important that we both understand each other." Boyd leaned forward on the table and lowered his voice. "I came to see you face-to-face because I don't trust phones, and we're both in deep trouble."

"What kind of trouble?"

"We've been set up." Boyd pushed aside the plate of pie, took out his cellphone, and held up the screen to Alika. "Take a look at this."

Boyd played a few seconds of the video of Evan Trace making his pitch to Billy Dee.

"*You won't really be losing your money,*" Trace said. "*Whatever you lose gambling will become your off-the-books investment in Monde d'Argent.*"

"I thought laundering my money playing baccarat was a good deal," Billy Dee said. *"But this sounds even better."*

"It is," Trace said. *"Instead of washing your illegal profits, you can make them work for you in the gambling capital of the world."*

Boyd fast-forwarded to another section of the video.

"What did that loudmouth Canadian want in return for his money?" Billy Dee asked.

"He took me at my word," Trace said.

"He's a bigger gambler than I thought. Are my hosts in on this, too?"

"No, and I'd appreciate it if you'd keep this between us."

"And Alika, too, I suppose," Billy Dee said.

"I'll be talking to him next. I'm seeking investors with a certain profile, and Nick Sweet doesn't match it. Mr. Alika does."

Boyd stopped the video and put the phone back in his pocket. "Evan Trace and Nick Sweet are informants for the FBI. They have us on video, too. They're setting us up in return for leniency on whatever charges the feds already have against them."

Alika's face had gone as rigid as stone. He spoke very slowly. "How did you get this?"

"I've been banging Kate," Boyd said.

"Fo' real?" Alika said.

Boyd had startled himself when he said it. He was supposed to say he had an informant in the FBI, but "banging Kate" came out instead. That's what happened when he was totally into character. His instincts took over. He was committed to it now.

"Nobody was more surprised than me. Maybe it started as customer service or maybe I'm irresistible or maybe she's never had a Canadian before. What do I care? Ass is ass."

"Dat's true."

"When Kate got back to L.A., she stumbled on texts between Nick and his FBI handler. It totally freaked her out. So she called me for help. Who else was she gonna call? She's terrified that she'll go down with us."

"We aren't going down. Dey are. Dey gonna die dead."

"Die dead," Boyd repeated. "Is that a Hawaiian thing?"

"Worse kine of dead. Da woman, too."

"Seems like a rotten thing to do to her after she tipped us off."

"If she'd bang you, she'd bang da feds. No disrespect, bruddah. But if dare's no witnesses to testify, dare's no case."

Boyd sighed. "It's such a waste, but you're right. Better safe than sorry. I'll kill Nick and Kate, and I'll go for Trace, too. Problem is, if I miss my shot at Trace, and he hops on a plane to Macau, I can't touch him. My reach doesn't extend that far. How about your business associates in Japan?"

"Nobody can hide from dem," Alika said. "They'd find you if you jumped in a time machine to da future, took a spaceship to a-nudder planet, an hid in a-nudder dimension. An den dey would cut out yo guts, string you up wit' dem, an' set you on fire."

"I'd like to see that," Boyd said.

"Trace will die dead, bruddah," Alika said. "Guaranteed."

26

There's always a surgical conference going on somewhere in Las Vegas and usually it's at one of the major casino resorts. The conferences are sponsored by medical device manufacturers in order to train doctors in the use of their latest high-priced surgical tools and implants. The hope is that those surgeons will then want to use those products, which would force hospitals to buy them. So there's a constant demand on the Strip for cadavers.

One of the companies that served the cadaver need was CorpsSource Services, Inc., which was located in a nondescript building in an office park near McCarran International Airport. Nick drove up to the front door in his 2006 Chevy Cobalt at 11 P.M., two days after Boyd's meeting with Alika. The only other vehicles in the lot were the two refrigerated trucks that CorpsSource used for hauling bodies.

"It looks dead to me. There isn't a living soul in sight," Nick said to Kate and Willie, who were also in the Chevy. The three of them wore white CorpsSource-logo jumpsuits. Willie's jumpsuit was too tight and unzipped to show off her cleavage, purely out of habit, not necessity.

"That's not funny," Willie said. "This whole thing creeps me out."

"All you have to do is hot-wire the truck," Nick said. "If you stay in the cab, you'll never see the body. Kate and I will do the rest."

"At least we're not in a cemetery," Willie said.

"That would be grave robbing, and I wouldn't do that," Nick said. "It would be desecration."

"How's this any different?" Willie asked.

"These people willed their bodies to science," Nick said.

"This isn't science," Kate said.

"It's criminal science," Nick said, and got out of the car.

The women got out, too.

"I'm sure that wasn't the science they had in mind when they made out their wills," Kate said, walking with Nick to the front door while Willie headed for the trucks.

"I'm thinking they no longer care," Nick said.

"Doesn't matter," Kate said. "We're all going straight to hell."

Nick took out a pair of lock picks and opened the door as easily as if he had the key. They stepped into the lobby, and Nick typed a code into the security keypad by the door, deactivating the alarm.

"How did you get the code?" Kate asked.

"I showed up yesterday, posing as a rep for a medical device company, at the same time the office manager arrived here to open up," Nick said. "I saw her punch in the code, and she was even kind enough to give me a complete tour."

Kate went around the receptionist's counter and opened cupboards until she found the DVR unit for the security cameras. She gave it a quick examination. "We're in luck. It doesn't back up to the Web."

"I've seen cookie jars with better security," Nick said.

Kate unplugged the cables going into the DVR, took it out of the cabinet, and lugged it away under one arm. The two of them walked through the front office and down a corridor to the cold storage room. They opened the heavy steel door, pushed aside the clear vinyl strip curtain flaps, and stepped inside what was essentially a very large walk-in freezer. Dozens of cadavers in black body bags were stacked on four long aisles of shelving units that looked like bunk beds. Nick grabbed one of the gurneys that lined the far wall and wheeled it down the first aisle, as if he were shopping at Costco. Kate put the DVR on another gurney and followed him.

Each body bag had a card in a clear plastic sleeve that listed the sex, age, and cause of death of its cadaver. There was also a bar code and some serial numbers. Nick and Kate each took one side of the aisle, checking out the cards on the body bags.

Female, 87, congenital heart disease. Male, 66, amyotrophic lateral sclerosis. Male, 83, lung cancer. Female, 72, kidney failure.

"There are a lot of old people here," Kate said.

"That's the nature of the business, especially in a retirement community like Las Vegas. Here's a possibility. Male, forty-two, massive body trauma." Nick unzipped the bag and immediately reared back. "Holy crap. He's flattened. That won't work."

"Why do they have a body like that here? Don't they prefer them in relatively good shape?"

"Most of the time," Nick said, zipping up the bag. "But they also need bodies for trauma surgery training."

They continued down the aisle and on to the next one, going from body to body. Kate found another contender.

"Male, thirty-eight, heart attack," she said.

Kate unzipped the bag and Nick came over to take a look. The dead man was about five foot five and 250 pounds.

"He won't work," Nick said.

They needed someone Nick's size. Kate zipped it back up and moved to the next bag. And then the one after that. And several more. They were down to the last row of the last aisle before Nick found another possible selection.

"This sounds promising. Male, thirty-eight, cerebral hemorrhage."

He unzipped the bag. The dead man was Hispanic, but roughly Nick's height and weight.

"What do you think?" Nick asked.

She gave the cadaver a quick appraisal. "He'll do."

Nick zipped up the bag and together they picked up the body, set it on the gurney, and strapped it in place. Kate put the DVR on top of the body and they wheeled the gurney out of the storage room, closed the door, and hurried to the loading dock. They lifted the slide-up garage door to find the refrigerated truck already backed up to the loading dock with the engine running.

Kate opened the heavy door to the truck's freezer-like cargo area and pushed aside the plastic strip curtains that kept the cold air inside. Nick wheeled in the gurney. The truck's interior was lined with shelves and belts to secure the body bags to them. Kate set the DVR on the truck's floor, then she and Nick lifted the body bag onto one of the shelves and strapped it in. Nick collapsed the gurney so it was flat on the floor and slid it into place under a shelf.

"This is the first time I've ever stolen a body," Nick said.

"That's not true. You stole a mummy from a museum in London."

"I stole a sarcophagus that had a mummy inside."

"So now you're stealing a body bag that has a cadaver inside," Kate said. "I don't see the difference."

"The difference is the thirty million dollars in jewel-encrusted antiquities that were in the sarcophagus with the mummy."

"Do you still have the antiquities?"

"I didn't keep any of it. The sarcophagus had been looted from an ancient burial site," Nick said. "I returned it to the rightful owner, the Egyptian government, for a handsome retrieval fee. Besides, the antiquities would have clashed with my Rembrandts."

"I hate when that happens," she said.

They got out and closed the door. Kate joined Willie in the truck's cab and Nick dashed across the parking lot to the Chevy Cobalt. Nick drove off first, and then Willie pulled out and followed Nick toward the glow of the Vegas strip.

"I really hope the slogan is true," Willie said.

"*'No freakin' gondolas'?*"

"What happens in Vegas stays in Vegas."

It was almost midnight when Willie, Nick, and Kate pulled into a warehouse in an industrial pocket of buildings on the south side of the Côte d'Argent casino. It was close enough to the resort to fall under the black tower's shadow for several hours each day. Willie drove the refrigerator truck into the warehouse, and Nick quickly closed the door behind her. She parked the truck but kept the refrigeration unit running.

Willie and Kate got out of the truck and went to check on the rest of the crew, who were finishing up last-minute details of the con.

Chet Kershaw was applying touch-up paint to the exterior of the black Audi A8 to hide traces of some of his special effects handiwork. Kate leaned in close to the car and examined the finish.

"They're nearly invisible," she said. "It looks like you've just touched up some parking lot dings."

"When these little charges blow, they'll leave M16 impact marks and gunpowder residue behind. Even the crime scene techs will be fooled," Chet said.

"That's above and beyond," Kate said.

"Not the way I look at it," Chet said. "The CSI guys are part of the audience, too. They're just coming late to the show."

Kate moved along to Tom, who was also busy painting, putting the final touches on a Styrofoam replica of a sidewalk manhole cover. He had a genuine manhole cover on the table, next to the fake, that he was using for reference.

"They look identical," Kate said, glancing between the two covers. "I can't tell the difference."

"You'd know right away if you tried to drop through that one," Tom knocked his knuckle against the real cover. "You'd break your feet."

She turned to Boyd, who stood nearby, trying on a vest made up of pouches filled with red-dyed corn syrup. Each pouch had a wire taped to the outside that ran down to a battery pack on his hip.

"This brings back memories," he said, adjusting the Velcro straps on the vest. "I wore one of these in my starring role in *Taken 3*."

"I don't remember seeing you in that movie," Tom said. "Who did you play?"

"Thug number twenty-seven," Boyd said. "I was shot five times by Liam Neeson, but most of my performance was lost due to the director's terrible staging."

"In other words," Kate said, "the camera was on Neeson instead of you."

"The man is a camera hog," Boyd said. "Everybody in the business knows that. He robbed the audience of my indelible performance."

"That won't be an issue tomorrow," Kate said. "I guarantee you'll have everyone's attention."

"But it won't be on camera," Boyd said. "From my professional prospective it's unfortunate that we have to come at the casino from angles that will obscure our faces from security cameras."

"Not unless you'd like to be doing dinner theater in a prison cafeteria for the next five to ten years."

"The long run and captive audience is appealing to me," Boyd said. "But the venue leaves a lot to be desired."

Kate moved on to Jake, who was cleaning an M16, one of a half dozen rifles laid out on a table in front of him.

"That's more weapons than we're going to need," Kate said.

"You can never have too many weapons," Jake said.

"Does that mean you brought your rocket launcher?"

"It's in the trunk of my car in case of a roadside emergency."

"What kind of roadside emergency would require a rocket launcher?" she asked.

"You don't want to find out and not have one handy," Jake

said. "It's also why you should always have a paper clip in your pocket. You can do just about anything with a paper clip."

She gave her dad a kiss on the cheek. "Don't ever change."

"That's a given," Jake said.

Willie popped the hood on a beige panel van parked behind them and examined the engine. Kate joined Willie at the front of the van.

"What are you looking for?" Kate asked.

"I'm checking the belts, fluids, and plugs one more time. I'd hate to have this barge crap out on me when we need to make our fast getaway. I don't see why we couldn't use a Mercedes G500 AMG or a 7 Series BMW 760Li M Sport instead."

"Because we wanted a vehicle that would blend in," Kate said. "Not stand out."

"When Boyd, Chet, and Jake start shooting from the van with M16s, we're going to stand out anyway," Willie said. "We might as well be cradled in soft, Veneto Beige Nappa leather with a raging V-12 twin turbo under the hood when we do the drive-by."

"Look at the upside," Kate said. "You get to drive recklessly at blazing speed through gunfire and flames."

"That *is* my favorite kind of driving," she said. "But it goes much better with a sexy ride."

"You can't have it all," Kate said.

"At least I won't be the one driving with a corpse," Willie said.

Everyone looked at Nick, who stood facing three

whiteboards on easels. The boards were covered with photos of the VIP entrance at the back of the Côte d'Argent casino and street maps of the surrounding area.

Kate walked up beside him. "Going over the choreography in your mind one more time?"

"Trace put the VIP entrance to Côte d'Argent behind the building to provide some privacy for high rollers and celebrities. It's on the southwest side of the building facing this industrial park. There's almost no vehicle or pedestrian traffic on the two side streets that intersect at that corner. He also built an eight-foot-high wall of black marble and cascading water that curves along the corner for additional privacy. All of that gives me confidence that we can control the situation."

As he spoke, he pointed on the map to South Merton Street, which ran along the west end of the Côte d'Argent property and continued down through the industrial area where they were now. South Merton Street intersected with West Norbert, which ended in a cul-de-sac a block east of Côte d'Argent.

Nick tapped the cul-de-sac. "That's where the van will be waiting." He pointed to the southwest corner of the intersection, where he'd taped a photograph to the map. The picture showed the storm drain at the corner, and the low cinder block wall that bordered a parking lot. "And that's where the action ends."

"For you," Kate said. "I've still got to talk Trace into turning himself in to the FBI. I wish you and I could switch roles."

"You make a much more convincing FBI agent than I do."

"That might be true, but smooth talking people is your specialty, not mine."

"You're not smooth talking him," Nick said. "You're tough talking him. That won't be too hard after what he's going to see."

"What if he still doesn't fold?"

"He will as soon as he hears that the Yakuza is coming for him. Worst-case scenario, it takes another day or two for him to run to the FBI for protection."

"If the Yakuza doesn't kill him first," Kate said.

Nick shrugged. "At least he won't be in business anymore."

27

Trace had been back in Las Vegas for almost a week. During that time, he'd often studied the four puncture marks on the back of his hand and thought about Kate Porter. She was smart, beautiful, cunning, devious, and violent. She could take a beating and inflict one with gusto. He'd found women who possessed some of those qualities before, but never one who embodied them all so spectacularly. Thinking about her had him practically bursting out of his Calvins.

So as he sat at his million-dollar desk in his high-rise office that morning, he thought about stabbing his hand with his letter opener. He thought a fresh wound might be just the thing to match the ache in his privates.

That's when he saw Kate's face appear in one of the dozens of live security camera images that flitted across his touch-screen tabletop. It was as if she'd been conjured up by his desire.

Trace immediately expanded her image with his fingertips so it filled half the desk. Kate had just entered the high-limit room, where a few Japanese gamblers were bleeding yen at poker. He zoomed in on her. She wore a long charcoal-colored linen blazer, a loose-fitting white blouse, skinny blue jeans, and leather lace-up combat boots. It was a good look for her that projected sensuality, professionalism, and just a hint of aggression.

Trace watched Niles Goodwell waddle up to Kate to greet her. Trace tapped the "Goodwell" icon on his tabletop and Goodwell immediately reached inside his coat pocket to answer his vibrating cellphone. Before Goodwell could say a word, Trace told him to send her up . . . alone.

"Right away, sir," Goodwell replied.

Goodwell pocketed his phone and led Kate toward the door to Trace's private dining room. Inside was a private elevator that would take her up to his office.

Kate glanced at the security camera as they passed under it and she gave it a sly smile. Trace felt an instant buzz of erotic anticipation. Amazing things were about to happen, he was sure of that. She hadn't traveled to Las Vegas to reject him.

He got up and went to the elevator, timing his arrival so he got to the doors as they slid open.

"Kate," he said. "This is a surprise."

"I hope I'm not disturbing you."

"You've disturbed me ever since you pointed a gun in my face," he said.

"But you like it."

"I do," he said.

Kate walked past him into the vast office, her eyes roaming over the sunken conversation area, the long bar, and the two walls of floor-to-ceiling windows behind his high-tech desk. Trace thought she was like a soldier identifying potential threats and escape routes. Spring-coiled for violence. And for Trace, that was a mating call.

"You're accepting my offer?" he asked.

"I came to discuss it. You didn't mention salary or benefits."

"Name your price."

"I won't negotiate with myself. Hold out your hand."

She drew a lighter from her pocket, flicked it on, and held the flame about an inch below his palm.

"This stays lit until we agree on a price," she said. "And benefits."

"I'd think the benefits would be obvious."

"If you want to play it that way your hand is going to get cooked. If you move your hand away from the flame before we have a deal, I'm gone."

He smiled. The flame was like Viagra. "Half a million dollars a year, an apartment in Macau, and a car allowance."

"That isn't even minimum wage for me. Try harder."

He couldn't get any harder.

"One million dollars, the apartment, the car, free use of the private jet."

Dear Lord, she wished he would negotiate faster. If this went on much longer, she'd throw up.

"I don't want to be just an employee," she said, holding the flame steady and looking right into his eyes. "I want to share in the success of the enterprise."

A blister was forming on his palm, but the only sensations he was feeling were in his pants.

"I'll throw in a hundred-thousand-dollar bonus for each percentage point increase in Monde d'Argent's annual revenue. Plus full medical coverage, with no deductible, and an annual contribution of eight and a half percent of your salary, including bonuses, to your pension plan."

She flicked off the lighter. "You have a deal."

Trace wanted her more in that moment than he'd ever wanted any woman in his life. The only reason he didn't grab her was that he was afraid she'd break his jaw out of reflex.

"Don't you want to hear about the benefits?" he asked.

"I thought you already outlined the benefits."

"I left the big one out," he said.

Before he could demonstrate, a buzzer went off on his desk. It wasn't a sound he could ignore. It was the red alert. Even his desk was blinking red, indicating the severity of the situation. Trace hurried over and touched the tabletop, deactivating the sound and light and simultaneously answering a call on the speaker from the VIP lobby.

It was Tara, the red-haired VIP desk hostess. "Nick Sweet is down here, sir," she said, her voice quavering with fear and from the effort of trying not to show it.

"Damn," Kate said, coming up beside Trace. "He's smarter than I thought."

"He's quite agitated," Tara said. "He's disarmed Guido, the doorman, and he's threatening to shoot the ice sculpture unless you and Ms. Porter come down here."

Trace tapped a button on his table, bringing up the security camera feed from the VIP lobby. Kate leaned over his shoulder as Nick came up onscreen, aiming Guido's Smith & Wesson .38 at the ice sculpture of a hawk grabbing a rabbit in its talons. With his free hand, Nick helped himself to a cheesy canapé from the tray beside the sculpture.

Nick's behavior made no sense to Trace. "Doesn't he know the sculpture is going to melt anyway?"

"It's a stunt, Evan. He wants our attention. Don't send any security men down there, it will just escalate the situation. I'll handle it. Besides, it's my job now."

"I can't tell you how much it pleases me to hear you say that."

Great, Kate thought. And it would please *me* if he didn't have such an obvious boner.

"Good grief," she said, losing the fight not to glare at it.

Trace was glad she'd noticed.

. . .

Kate was relieved that Nick had successfully disarmed the doorman. As far as they knew, Guido was the only person packing a gun in the VIP lobby. If another weapon was stashed somewhere in the lobby, Kate could deal with it.

She and Trace rode the small private elevator down to his dining room. As the two of them hurried out of the dining room, through the high-roller salon, and past the Japanese poker players, Jake gave Kate an update on her earbud. He was outside monitoring the police band from the van.

"No one has reported any trouble at Côte d'Argent to the police. Somebody has stolen a Las Vegas tour chopper, there's a car accident on the Strip, and there's a liquor store robbery in progress downtown, so the police have their hands full anyway," Jake said. "We're in position and ready to go. Good luck, everyone."

Kate and Trace crossed the casino floor and paused for a moment at the door leading to the VIP lobby. It was all riding on her now.

"Keep it casual and friendly," Kate told Trace. "Pretend the gun isn't there."

Trace strolled in first, trying hard to appear completely relaxed. The truth was his sphincters were so tight, he feared it might take the Jaws of Life to open them again.

Tara, Guido, the bellman, and two other hostesses stood to his right with their backs against the wall. Their eyes were on Nick, who stood in the center of the lobby with his right arm outstretched, holding the gun on the sculpture. There was a tray on the floor and several broken crystal flutes in a puddle of spilled champagne.

"Hello, Nick," Trace said as jovially as he could. Kate stepped up beside Trace.

"Oh, for God's sake," she said.

"I'm disappointed in you, Kate," Nick said. "I didn't think you'd jump ship like this. I couldn't believe it when I got your note saying you were coming here to hook up with this jerk."

"It's not a hook-up," Trace said. "I've offered her a position with my company."

"That doesn't make it any better," Nick said.

"C'mon, Nick," Trace said. "We've had much worse misunderstandings than this and moved past them."

"Do you really want to remind me of that while I have a gun in my hand?" Nick asked.

Yes, he did. Trace wanted to show Nick that he could be forgiving, too, though the truth was that he wasn't forgiving *at all*. Very soon, Mr. Garver would be taking a mallet to Nick's hands for this insult. Trace might even invite Kate to watch. Maybe he'd even encourage Garver to take the mallet to a second, even more sensitive body part. That would be strictly for Kate's watching pleasure. And, of course, it would keep Nick permanently out of the bedroom competition.

"Evan is right, it's nothing personal," Kate said. "I saw a career opportunity and I took it."

"You betrayed me," Nick said.

"I'm tired of living like a gypsy," Kate said. "I wanted something steady and lucrative. That wasn't ever going to happen with you."

"I know you're upset," Trace said to Nick. "But nothing has really changed in the grand scheme of things. Your junket business is still welcome here. You'll still work closely with Kate. The only difference is that you won't have to split your take with a partner anymore."

"You haven't just taken my partner," Nick said.

I've taken your lover, Trace thought. Trace tried not to smirk. Yes, he definitely would have Garver take a mallet to Nick's nuts. He might even do it himself.

Nick took a step closer to him, so they were almost nose to nose. "You've also taken the money that Shane Blackmore, Lou Ould-Abdallah, and Lono Alika would have run through my junket and convinced them instead to secretly invest in Monde d'Argent with their gambling losses."

If Trace had a smirk, it was gone now. It was as if Nick had slapped it right off his face.

"How do you know about that?"

"You'll find out soon enough." Nick flipped open the cylinder of the .38, emptied the bullets out on the floor, and set the gun beside the sculpture. "I'd wish you two a happy life together, but I know that it's not in the cards."

Nick smiled, helped himself to another canapé, and walked outside to a black Audi A8 that was parked at the door.

Nick's words were ringing in Trace's ears. Who had talked? Surely, not all three of them. Why would they do that?

Kate followed Nick outside and Trace followed Kate, watching as Nick got into his car and drove around the motor court toward the street. A beige panel van screeched out in front of the driveway. The van's side door slid open and three men with M16s began shooting. One of the men was Shane Blackmore . . . and he was aiming his M16 at Trace.

Kate shoved Trace to the ground just as a spray of bullets raked Nick's car. The Audi was positioned between them and the street. If it hadn't been, Trace knew he would have been killed. Kate had saved his life, instantly earning her pay for the year.

Nick sped out of the driveway and into the intersection, fishtailing in front of the van, bullets riddling his car, shattering his windows, and blowing out one of his tires. He lost control of the Audi, jumped the next curb, and slammed into a low cinder block wall, the trunk of the car popping open on impact.

To Trace's astonishment, Kate reached under her jacket, whipped out a Glock, and began firing at the speeding van. The three shooters continued to pummel the disabled Audi with bullets.

Her steady fire drew Blackmore's attention. The enraged mobster whirled around to spray her with his M16 and Kate shot him three times in the chest. They were great shots, a perfect center mass cluster, and Trace saw the disbelief on

Blackmore's face. The mobster tumbled backward into the fleeing van just as the Audi exploded in a massive fireball.

The force of the blast shattered the lobby windows behind Trace and knocked Kate off her feet. She kept on shooting as she fell, holding her aim steady on the van, which screeched past Nick's car and disappeared behind a veil of smoke and flames.

28

All of the gunshots that were fired during the shootout were blanks. The bullets striking the Audi, the van, and Boyd were illusions, created by tiny charges that Chet ignited by remote control from his seat in the van. It was like another day at work for Chet, only without the cameras, the lights, or the catering.

Nick had opened the trunk on the Audi after the crash to block the rear window so that he could slip out through the escape hatch in the floor, and on through the breakaway manhole cover below, without being seen. He was safely in the sewer when Chet blew up the car with the cadaver inside. The blast was calculated to be strong enough to mangle the car and any evidence of a trapdoor.

After the blast, Nick lifted the real manhole cover into place and scrambled along thirty yards of dry sewer pipe that led to another manhole outside the warehouse they'd used as their base. He climbed out and ran inside the warehouse, where Chet, Ted, and Willie were busy peeling the beige skin off the van to reveal blue paint beneath. Boyd had taken off his shirt, which was soaked with red-dyed corn syrup, and was undoing the Velcro straps on his vest of exploded blood packs.

"Excellent work everyone," Nick said and headed straight for Jake, who sat in the van's passenger seat, monitoring the police band. "Where do we stand?"

"The police are dispatching units," Jake said. "The nearest patrol car is three minutes out. The fire department is on the way."

"Do you copy that, Kate?" Nick asked.

"Gotcha," Kate said as she dashed across the motor court to Trace, who'd risen to his knees and appeared to be shell-shocked. Kate holstered her gun when she reached him.

Car alarms were going off everywhere. Bits of broken glass from the hotel tower were falling on the lobby's broad portico.

"What just happened?" Trace asked. "Why did Blackmore kill Nick? Why did he try to kill me?"

Kate grabbed Trace roughly by the arm, jerked him to his feet, and practically dragged him alongside her into the VIP lobby. Glass shards crunched under their feet. Tara, Guido, and the others were stunned but physically unharmed.

"The police will be here soon," Kate said to Tara and Guido. "Give them your full cooperation."

Tara nodded and Guido stood slack jawed and glassy eyed.

"We need to go somewhere private and talk," Kate said to Trace, pulling him toward the casino's door.

"Why?" he asked. "What?"

Kate opened the door and they stepped into sheer pandemonium. People were screaming and running through the casino toward the main lobby exit. Dealers were hiding under their tables. Pit bosses and security people were watching over the chips.

Kate hustled Trace as fast as she could across the tide of escaping people to the high-roller salon. Goodwell was nowhere to be seen, but the Japanese gamblers were still in their seats at the poker table.

When they reached the door to Trace's private dining room he swiped his key card over the scanner. Kate glanced back at the three Japanese gamblers. Something wasn't right. Why weren't they running for an exit like everyone else? Her gaze locked on one of the men. It was Nakamura, the man from Macau. Out of the corner of her eye, she spotted a pair of shoes. They were on the feet of Niles Goodwell, who lay crumpled on the floor behind the blackjack table.

"Crap," Kate murmured.

She pushed Trace into his private dining room, kicked the door closed behind her, and drew her gun as they crossed the bridge.

"Now what?" Trace asked, noticing her gun.

"Three Yakuza assassins have Goodwell's key card, and they

are coming to kill us," Kate said, more for Nick listening in than for Trace.

Jake also heard the message about the Yakuza and jumped out of the parked van.

"We need to help her," Jake said.

"Not necessary," Nick said. "The police will be there in two minutes."

"And it'll be another five minutes before they can get to Trace's dining room," Jake said.

"You're not going to get there any faster," Nick said. "She can take care of herself, and she has a gun."

"Her gun is loaded with blanks."

"The assassins don't know that," Nick said.

Good point, Kate thought. The bad guys wouldn't know she was firing blanks.

She flipped over the dining table and pulled Trace down behind it. The door to the high-roller room flew open and the Yakuza came in, guns drawn.

She waited until one of them was midway over the bridge, and then she popped up and fired. Two of the Yakuza dropped to the floor. The man on the bridge dropped into the pond. Big mistake. Instantly the water surged with piranha and the man screamed and thrashed around as he was devoured.

One of the Yakuza sat up, staring in horror at the roiling

water. Kate threw her gun at him, fast and hard, catching him between the eyes, knocking him out cold.

Nakamura, the remaining Yakuza, fired two shots at Kate in quick succession. Kate ducked behind the overturned tabletop. Trace crawled as fast as he could toward the elevator. Kate stood and flung a chair at Nakamura. Nakamura dodged the chair and Kate tackled him, knocking the gun from his hand.

Kate and Nakamura went to the floor, and Kate used the momentum of the fall to her advantage. She flipped Nakamura over her and rolled into a crouch, coming face-to-face with him as he rose up.

At that instant, a spinning mallet slammed into the side of Nakamura's head, and split it open like a ripe melon. Kate turned and saw Garver standing in a doorway across the room.

"The police are coming," Garver said.

Trace got to his feet and swiped his key card over the call pad for the elevator. "Stall them, Garver. Kate and I need a few minutes to talk."

Garver picked up his beloved mallet and glanced at the crimson pond, which had begun to calm. Bits of cloth from the consumed man's clothing floated on the surface. Garver gestured with his mallet at the two unconscious men.

"What do I do about these two?"

"What you do best," Trace said. "Make sure they tell no tales."

Nick didn't want his crew hearing Kate reveal her genuine FBI background. Using the key fob remote in his pocket, he cut off the transmission from Kate's earbud to everyone but himself and Jake. "It's a wrap," Nick announced. "Let's get out of here."

Chet, Tom, and Willie piled into the blue van for the drive back to Los Angeles. Jake walked outside with Nick to his Buick. On his way out of town, Jake would drop Nick off in Henderson, where a private jet was waiting for him. Kate would remain in Las Vegas for a few days to tie up the case.

"I can't believe the Yakuza picked today to make their hit on Trace," Jake said. "He's lucky Kate was there to save him."

That was exactly the point Kate intended to make to Trace when they emerged from the elevator into his office.

"Surprise," she said, flashing her badge.

"You're an FBI agent," Trace said. "Could today possibly get any worse?"

"Yeah, you could be dead," Kate said. "But I was here, so you're not."

"You didn't come here to save me."

"I've been working undercover to nail Nick Sweet. But then he came to you, and my mission objectives changed. I can arrest you right now for money laundering."

"No, you can't," Trace said. "The alleged crime happened in Macau, where you have no jurisdiction, and it was done through Nick's junket. My hands are clean. That's the beauty of junkets. The only person you might have a case against was just blown to bits. So we're done."

Trace turned his back to her and went over to the

floor-to-ceiling window behind his desk. He looked forty-five stories down at the police cars and fire trucks converging on the burning Audi and at the hundreds of Côte d'Argent guests streaming out of the main lobby to the parking lot.

Kate stepped up beside him. She noticed a Las Vegas tour chopper heading their way. Côte d'Argent wasn't usually on the sky tour itinerary, but perhaps the explosion changed that.

Trace glanced at her. "You're still here?" he said.

"Aren't you curious why Blackmore and the Yakuza want you dead?"

"Maybe it was you they're after and I just got caught in the crossfire," he said.

"Nick bugged his guests in Macau and recorded your pitch. I got hold of the recordings and passed them on to Quantico to an agent that we suspect is dirty," Kate said. "Now we know that we were right about him. He alerted Shane Blackmore, Lou Ould-Abdallah, and Lono Alika that you and Nick are FBI informants."

"But I'm not one."

"You will be if you want to live. Blackmore is off the field, but the Yakuza will keep coming after you until you're dead." Kate's gaze kept drifting to the chopper. "Wouldn't surprise me if some Somali pirates came after you, too."

"I'll take my chances."

"What happened today is just the beginning. You've been branded as an informant. The killers will keep coming. They will be relentless and unforgiving. You'll need an army to protect you. Fortunately for you, we have one," Kate said. "We can put you on an Army base until you've finished testifying against every mobster and terrorist group you've worked with. Then we'll put you into the witness protection program."

"I'd rather be dead."

His comment made her think about the attempt on his life. The *real* one. The three Yakuza assassins didn't know they'd have the distraction of a drive-by shooting and an explosion to cover their hit. What was their exit strategy after killing Trace?

Once again, her gaze was drawn to the approaching helicopter. In a few seconds, it would be close enough for them to wave at the tourists. Then she remembered the report over the police band about a chopper being stolen from a tour company and she knew the answer to her question. The three assassins had planned to escape off the roof.

"Crap," she said.

She grabbed Trace, turned him around, and ran toward the sunken conversation pit. Behind them, the side door of the chopper slid open and two gunmen with AK-47s started shooting.

Jake and Nick had driven only a block south when they heard Kate say "crap" and knew that she was in trouble. Jake made a sharp U-turn in time to see the tour chopper hovering outside the penthouse and the rapid flashes of gunfire going into the building. Through their earbuds, they heard the hundreds of rounds shattering the windows and obliterating everything in Trace's office.

Kate stood, took the two steps out of the conversation pit, and surveyed the damage. The windows were shattered and wind blew through the office. The storm of bullets had passed over their heads. The million-dollar desk was decimated. The walls and the bar were riddled with hundreds of holes. The control panel for the elevator was destroyed. The only way out was the stairwell, where they were sure to be mowed down by Yakuza assassins.

The sprinkler system burst on. The gunfire must have automatically triggered the sensors in the deluge fire suppression system. The sudden, drenching downpour gave Kate an idea.

She turned to Trace and yelled over the sound of wind and rain. "I'll be back. Stay right there."

Screw her, Trace thought. He wouldn't just sit there while she hid and left him to be executed. There was a gun hidden behind the bar. At least that would give him a slim but fighting chance against the assassins. He scrambled to his feet and immediately tripped on the rain-slicked floor, slamming his knee hard into one of the steps leading out of the pit.

The pain was a shock and a humiliation, and it pissed him off. He tried to stand up again and there they were, the two

Yakuza assassins, charging out of the stairwell into the office, their AK-47s pointed at him. In that instant, Trace regretted telling Kate that he'd rather die, because now that it was about to happen he realized he'd do anything to live.

A thick jet of water came out of nowhere and slammed into the side of the lead assassin like a battering ram, knocking him off his feet and sending him sliding across the glass-strewn floor. Before the second man could fire, the blast of water sent him sprawling, too.

Trace turned to see Kate, wielding the standpipe fire hose.

The first assassin sat upright and fired where Kate had been standing, but she'd moved to one side and pummeled him with 250 gallons per minute at a force of one hundred pounds per square inch. It propelled the assassin across the floor and out the window. He fell forty-five stories without screaming because his nose and mouth were full of water.

The second assassin dove for his fallen assault rifle and grabbed it. When he stood to fire, Kate hit him in the gut with the water, smashing him against a wall like a bug hitting a windshield. He slid to the floor, his head hanging at an unnatural angle. He wouldn't be getting up ever again.

Kate switched off the nozzle and dropped the hose. Trace rose shakily to his feet, one leg unable to sustain his weight, and looked at her. He knew with sickening certainty what he had to do. There was no other option.

"Colt Ramsey," he said.

"Excuse me?" she asked.

"It's the name I'd like to have when you put me into the witness protection program."

It was close to midnight when Kate let herself into her budget room in the budget motel off the Strip. She'd chosen the motel not so much for the price as for the location. She'd wanted something that wasn't in the shadow of Cote D'Argent. And she'd wanted something that was *her* normal and not Nick's. Not that she didn't love the thousand-thread-count sheets and the complimentary champagne and fruit baskets that she enjoyed when she traveled with him. It was more that she needed to re-center herself to a more grounded reality. It had been an exhausting day. Successful but emotionally draining. Everyone on her team had come through unscathed. Thank heaven for that. They'd been paid off and sent on their way, Nick included. She was never sure where he landed after their assignments were done. He could be in Los Angeles or Tibet or Rome or his house in the south of France.

She closed and locked the motel room door, flipped the light switch, and kicked her shoes off. She shed her clothes and headed for the shower, needing to wash the day's grime off her body and soul. She glanced over at the bed and saw it. The Toblerone bar. It was on the pillow.

"Hot damn," Kate said, with a sigh and a smile.

She heard movement in the bathroom, and before she could get to her gun, Nick appeared in the bathroom doorway.

"It's a tradition," he said. "You always get a Toblerone at the end of a mission."

He looked relaxed and fresh from a shower, wearing only a towel wrapped low on his hips.

"This is embarrassing," Kate said. "I didn't expect you to be here. I'm sort of naked."

"Yeah, me, too," Nick said. And he dropped the towel.

29

The parking lot was full, and cars were parked along the shoulder of the Kamehameha Highway for the grand opening of Harlan's Rib Shack, which was now located in the building that only a few weeks before had been Da Grinds & Da Shave Ice.

Many of the customers wore blue surgical scrubs, because they were either coming or going from the Kahuku Medical Center. The crowd also included quite a few other locals, among them Lieutenant Gregg Steadman, who sat with Kate and Jake at the patio table that had once been Alika's iron throne.

"I don't know how you did it," Steadman said.

"I didn't do anything," Kate said. "It was Lono Alika's own decision to walk into the FBI field office in Honolulu and confess to his crimes."

"He did it because he was afraid for his life," Steadman said. "He thought the Yakuza would kill him for getting them involved with Evan Trace."

"He was right," Jake said.

Trace had agreed to fully cooperate with the FBI in exchange for immunity from prosecution and entry into the witness protection program. Based on his testimony, law enforcement agencies in fourteen countries had arrested 230 people, all of them mobsters, terrorists, or corrupt government officials who'd used the casinos to launder money. The arrests and the closure of the Côte d'Argent casinos had a chilling effect on money laundering throughout the global gambling industry.

"What I don't understand," Steadman said, "is how Harlan ended up with Da Grinds & Da Shave Ice."

"The FBI discovered that Alika was using the restaurant as a front to launder his drug profits," Kate said. "So they forced him to forfeit the property to the U.S. government, who made it available for rent pending an eventual auction. Harlan was the only applicant for the space."

"Well, that's no surprise," Steadman said. "There aren't any locals who'd dare move into Alika's place. They'd be too afraid of what he'll do to them when he comes back."

"He's gone for good," Kate said. "After Alika testifies against the Yakuza, the witness protection program will relocate him as far away from here as possible."

"He'll be living in an igloo in the North Pole," Jake said.

"That'd be Alika's version of hell," Steadman said. "He's

spent his life in Hawaii. He's never experienced an outdoor temperature colder than sixty degrees."

Harlan Appleton and Cassie Walner came up to their table. He wore an apron splattered with barbecue sauce and carried a platter piled high with spareribs. She was in her nurse's scrubs and carried their drinks.

"Dig in," Harlan said and set the platter in the center of the table. "For you, it's all-you-can-eat and no charge."

Jake inhaled the smoky smell of the ribs. "I may never leave."

"Great," Cassie said as she passed around the drinks. "Then you can start waiting tables for Harlan instead of me."

"You're working for Harlan now?" Kate asked.

"Part-time," Cassie said. "I want to be sure that he makes enough money to pay his share of my rent."

"You're living together?" Jake asked.

"In separate rooms," Cassie said.

"Most of the time," Harlan said.

"And only until his house is fixed up and habitable again," she said.

Harlan whispered to Jake, "Which may be never."

Cassie went off to see to another order. Jake watched her go and shook his head with disbelief.

"She's got to be twenty years younger than you and two hundred pounds lighter," Jake said. "How'd you win her over?"

"My ribs are an aphrodisiac," Harlan said.

"I'm bringing my wife here," Steadman said.

The talk of romance prompted Kate to check her watch.

She'd expected to hear from Nick by now. His private plane had landed in Honolulu at 4 P.M., and he was supposed to text her after he'd settled in at the beach house. But that was nearly three hours ago and there was still no word.

She hadn't seen Nick since Las Vegas, but they'd stayed in touch by text while she'd led the dismantling of Trace's operation for the FBI. This trip to Hawaii was their first chance to properly celebrate the success of their mission beyond the one unforgettable, sleepless night they'd had together, and they were both looking forward to it. So why had he suddenly gone silent?

Kate sent him a text: *Do you want me to bring you some ribs?*

Over the next twenty minutes, she ate some more ribs, had a Diet Coke, and checked her phone again about a dozen times. But still no reply.

Kate looked up from her phone and saw her father regarding her with concern. She tilted her head toward the parking lot. The two of them got up, said their goodbyes to the others, and met at her rented Jeep.

"What's wrong?" he asked.

"I'm supposed to get together with Nick tonight at a house on Kailua Beach. But I should have heard from him hours ago. I'm going over there now, and I could use some backup."

"I think you can fend off Nick's advances on your own," Jake said.

"That's not the trouble I'm worried about."

"Did you pack an extra gun?"

"Of course," she said. "You can never have too many weapons."

Jake smiled. "I raised you right."

Kate and Jake parked two blocks away from the house and approached it from the beach so they wouldn't be seen in case Nick was being watched by a law enforcement agency or by one of his many enemies.

They stayed close to the ocean-side property lines of the homes, which were spaced widely apart from their neighbors and separated from the beach by patios, pools, and lush landscaping. The shadows cast by the trees and hedges were the only cover that Kate and Jake had on the otherwise open moonlit beach.

It was a perfect tropical night. A warm breeze with a rich, floral scent rustled the tall, slender palms and seemed to move in time with the gentle surf. But it wasn't relaxing Kate. Her heart was racing, jacked up with a shot of pre-combat adrenaline. Her instincts were warning her. She glanced at her father to see if he was feeling it, too, but all she sensed from his posture was reluctance.

"Are you sure you need me?" Jake said. "Maybe Nick just wants to surprise you."

"I've got a bad feeling," Kate said. "Keep your eyes open."

She led the way. Tiki torches illuminated the path from the beach to the backyard, where dozens of candles framed the lap pool, the water covered with flower petals. The house was dark and the shutters were closed on the windows. A gas-fed fire was burning in a lava-stone campfire pit, casting flickering light on a wide-pillowed hammock that was strung between two palms.

"It looks like Nick has a romantic evening planned," Jake said, and started back down the path. "You two have fun."

"Wait," Kate said. She spotted a bottle of champagne sitting in an ice bucket within arm's reach of the hammock. She glanced in the bucket and immediately drew her Glock.

"Your sister's right," Jake said. "You really are afraid of intimacy."

"That's a five-hundred-dollar bottle of champagne sitting in a bucket of tepid water and the candles around the pool are melted," Kate said. "What does that tell you?"

Jake pulled his gun out from under his untucked shirt. "That the evening was supposed to get started hours ago but something got in Nick's way."

Kate moved quick and low to the dark house, her father close behind her, and they flanked the French doors. She reached out with one hand, gripped the door handle, and tested it. The door was unlocked. Jake moved a few steps away from the wall, took a firing stance at a slight angle from Kate, and nodded to her that he was ready.

She opened the door and crept inside in a crouch, ready to shoot at anything that moved in the darkness. Nothing did. But she'd heard shards of glass crunch under her feet and a couch was overturned in front of her. That worried her. So she took the risk of standing up, hitting the light switch on the wall, and making herself a target.

What she saw almost brought her to her knees again. The glass coffee table was shattered and the jagged shards on the bleached-wood floor were splattered with blood. A body had hit the glass. From there, her eyes were drawn to a wide smear of blood that ran from the wrought-iron legs of the coffee table all the way to the front door. There'd been a fight and a body had been dragged outside. Was it Nick? Had he been hurt? Or was he dead?

Jake hurried in behind her and went into the kitchen, methodically moving through the room.

"Clear," he yelled when he got to the other side.

That snapped her out of it. She went across the living room to the entry hall, then into a bedroom, peering under the bed, in the closets, and the adjoining bathroom.

"Clear," she yelled.

Together, Kate and Jake swept the entire house, room by room, until they were sure that there was nobody else there. They ended up in the master bedroom, where Nick's clothes were hanging in the closet above his empty suitcase.

"We know he made it here alive," Kate said.

"There is no reason to think he didn't leave here alive, too."

"You saw the living room," she said. "You saw the blood. A body was dragged out."

"That doesn't mean it was his," Jake said.

She holstered her gun, went back to the entry hall, and cracked open the shutters to look out the front window. Nick's rented Ferrari was parked in the driveway.

"Who did this?" Jake asked. "How did they know he was here?"

"We stayed here before," Kate said. "Maybe he was spotted by one of Alika's gang or by the Yakuza."

"There are no signs of forced entry," Jake said. "His attacker could have been someone he knew."

"Or Nick left the doors unlocked for me so whoever it was just walked right in." Kate surveyed the damage in the living room. "I think Nick was outside, setting things up, and when he came back in, they attacked him . . . and he was either seriously wounded or killed."

"Or he fought back, escaped, and whoever his adversaries were dragged away their casualties."

"Nick's car is still outside."

"All that means is that he didn't have his keys and had to flee on foot."

"If Nick escaped, he would have contacted me already."

"Unless he's still running, or he's unconscious in the bushes or on the beach somewhere, or he's in an ambulance right now, on his way to the hospital," Jake said. "It's too early to tell what happened or where he is."

"Or if he's still alive."

"You can't assume the worst. You've got to assume that he's alive and that he needs you."

"I need him." Kate turned away from her father so he wouldn't see the tears welling in her eyes.

"I know you do."

"I will find Nick, wherever he is, alive or dead and make whoever did this pay. Nothing will stop me."

"Us." Jake put his arm around her.

"Us," she said.

ABOUT THE AUTHORS

JANET EVANOVICH is the #1 *New York Times* bestselling author of the Stephanie Plum series, the Fox and O'Hare series, the Lizzy and Diesel series, the Alexandra Barnaby novels and Troublemaker graphic novel, and *How I Write: Secrets of a Bestselling Author.*

evanovich.com

Facebook.com/JanetEvanovich

@JanetEvanovich

LEE GOLDBERG is a screenwriter, TV producer, and the author of several books, including *King City, The Walk,* and the bestselling Monk series of mysteries. He has earned two Edgar Award nominations and was the 2012 recipient of the Poirot Award for Malice Domestic.

leegoldberg.com

Facebook.com/AuthorLeeGoldberg

@LeeGoldberg

ABOUT THE TYPE

This book was set in Minion, a 1990 Adobe Originals typeface by Robert Slimbach (b. 1956). Minion is inspired by classical, old-style typefaces of the late Renaissance, a period of elegant, beautiful, and highly readable type designs. Created primarily for text setting, Minion combines the aesthetic and functional qualities that make text type highly readable with the versatility of digital technology.

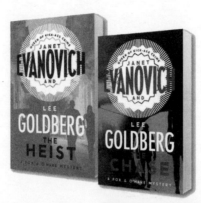

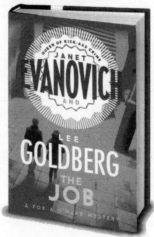

STEPHANIE PLUM
is back in
TRICKY TWENTY-TWO

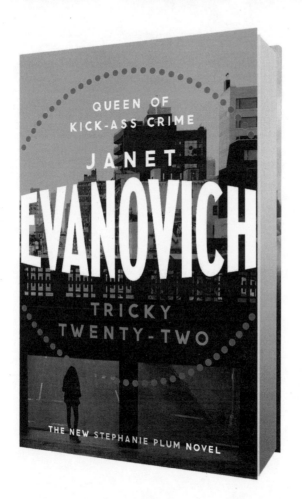

QUEEN OF
KICK-ASS CRIME

JANET

EVANOVICH

TRICKY
TWENTY-TWO

THE NEW STEPHANIE PLUM NOVEL

AVAILABLE FROM 17.11.2015

Connect with **JANET EVANOVICH**
on social media!

Facebook.com/JanetEvanovich

@janetevanovich

Pinterest.com/JanetEvanovich

Google+JanetEvanovichOfficial

instagram.com/janetevanovich

janetevanovich.fancorps.com

Visit **Evanovich.com**
and sign up for Janet's eNewsletter!